UNTIL MY LAST BREATH

TIFFANY PATTERSON

CHAPTER 1

Then ... Spring 1974
Deborah

"This *has* to be a mistake," I mumbled to myself as I stared at the paper in front of me. Written in blue ink was the name Robert Townsend. My new, semester-long partner for this World Mythologies elective I'd decided to take my final semester. *This isn't going to work.*

My left hand shot into the air. "Excuse me, Professor James," I called, my voice reaching the professor's ear as he moved to the front of the large lecture hall.

"Yes, Ms ..." He paused as he peered down at this clipboard running his index finger down the row of seats he'd meticulously assigned us to.

Seriously, what type of professor gave his students assigned seats? In a class of over a hundred students no less?

"Ms. Tate, how can I help you?"

"There has to be some sort of mistake. I think I received the wrong partner assignment."

His bushy, greying eyebrows scrunched together and brown eyes narrowed behind the thick-rimmed glasses he wore. He lowered his head to look down at the clipboard again, this time flipping the page.

"Let's see … it says here you're partnered with Mr. Robert Townsend, is that correct?" He raised his stare to me.

"Yes, but—"

"Then it's correct."

"Right, but I'm sure there's been a mix up. Is it possible to be reassigned?" I briefly caught a few students looking back at me, likely wondering what the big deal was.

"I'm sorry, Ms. Tate," Professor James responded in a voice that made it clear he wasn't actually sorry. "Partner assignments are final. Now …" he began to continue on with the rest of the lecture.

I slammed my back against the wooden, foldable chair, tossing the paper on the wraparound desk in front of me. This was ridiculous. I waited years to take this elective. For four years I'd pushed myself to power through my grueling course load including trigonometry, applied mathematics, and statistics courses to get my degree in mathematics. I'd opted to take the World Mythologies class in my last semester, thinking it'd be a breeze in my final semester here at Stanford, and yet—

"Don't fret, princess. I don't bite … well, only on the rare occasion."

I stiffened, my eyes moving before I slowly pivoted my neck to the right, twisting around to find myself staring into the dark brown eyes of none other than Robert Townsend. In typical fashion, his lips were parted, half smirking, but his eyes were dark, contradicting the smirk. Those freckles that lined his upper cheeks prominent as he grinned.

I narrowed my gaze but didn't respond to his words. Silently, he stared at me for another second before I turned to face the professor who was lecturing about some Greek god I'd probably heard of already.

Just great.

"We need to discuss this project," I stated, impatiently, as students hurriedly exited the lecture hall. I'd stopped Robert just outside of the door, needing to get this over with. This might be a low level class, taken by mostly freshman and sophomores, but I wasn't going to let it mess up my nearly 4.0 GPA.

"What's there to discuss, princess?" he asked, a dark eyebrow raised.

I huffed, hating that stupid moniker he'd used with me ever since our first encounter freshman year. I rolled my eyes at that particular memory.

"My name's Deborah. D-e-b-o-r-a-h. Got it?"

Another smirk. "I think so."

"Freakin' trust fund babies …"

"What was that?"

"Nothing. Listen, you might have been okay with skating your way through these last four years and—"

"Is that what I've done?" He folded his arms across his chest, voice deepening.

Shaking off the silly shiver that moved down my spine, I straightened my back, lifted my chin, and looked up … and up, until my eyes caught his. He stood tall, towering over my five-foot-six frame by at least eight inches. I opted not to stare directly into his eyes for too long, for reasons I couldn't quite put my finger on, at that moment.

"Look, I don't care what you've done these last four years. It's our last semester and I'm not going to let you mess up my nearly perfect GPA. We need to develop a plan for this final project. I've written out a schedule to track our progress—"

"Really? Already? Today was the first day of class."

I blinked and tilted my head. "And?"

He didn't respond, not directly, anyway. He chuckled.

Swallowing, I had to avert my eyes as anger and something unfamiliar bubbled up in my chest at the sound.

"Don't worry, princess. I wouldn't dream of destroying your precious grade point average. But I have another class to get to. We'll have to meet some other time." He tilted his head, winked at me, and then sauntered off, leaving me fuming.

Why I was so angry, I didn't know, nor did I care to actually explore. I had another class to get to as well, and it was halfway across campus. I was grateful to have a reason not to just stand there and watch Robert as he walked away. Despite my gratitude, however, I couldn't help my eyes from staring at his back as he strutted off as if he owned the entire campus. Loathe as I was to admit, I'd observed him from afar over the past four years, although I'd done everything to avoid Robert Townsend and the snooty group he socialized with.

All I needed to do was get through the next sixteen weeks of the semester and I'd never have to see, speak of, or think about Robert Townsend again.

"Good riddance," I murmured as I turned and headed in the direction of my next class.

* * *

Present

I inhaled his signature scent prior to feeling his embrace, just before those thick arms of his wrapped themselves around my waist from behind. I didn't bother to look over my shoulder, preferring to continue staring out the window viewing the construction of the playground on the property we were in, as I leaned back against my husband's hard chest.

"You know, I hated you at first."

I grinned as my eyes fluttered shut when Robert lowered, the small hairs of the short beard he'd recently let grow out brushing against the sensitive skin of my neck, as he pressed a kiss there. I sighed, again becoming enveloped by the smell of lavender and nutmeg from his L'Occitane Eau De Toilette cologne. The only fragrance he'd worn since I first bought it for him as a Christmas present years ago.

"You didn't hate me." He pressed another kiss to my neck, causing me to shiver. Even after all of these years he still had that effect on me. He braced my shoulders with his large hands, turning me to face him.

I stared up into his dark eyes.

"You couldn't stand how I made you *feel*."

And because, naturally, he was correct, I angled my head, lifting my chin. He lowered his head, our lips meeting in the middle. I was expecting a short, sweet kiss, but nothing was short or simple with Robert Townsend. His lips parted as he used his tongue to separate my lips, deepening the kiss. Luckily, before we got too carried away, I pulled back.

"You thought you knew me," I stated, returning to our original dialogue.

His pink lips parted on a smirk. The same cocky grin he'd given me after that World Mythologies class, decades earlier.

"I did know you, maybe not every detail, but from the first moment you parted those sleek thighs and let me slip inside of you, you've been mine. Every. Single. Part. Of. You."

"Aw, c'mon! We don't need to hear that shit!"

I laughed as Robert's eyes narrowed and he spun around to face our third youngest son, Joshua. I giggled even harder seeing the disgusted expression on Joshua's face as his green eyes shifted between his father and I.

"Leave them alone, Josh. It's so adorable how in love they still are after all of these years."

That was one of my daughters-in-law, Kayla, Joshua's wife.

I watched as Joshua shifted his gaze from us, down to his wife at his side, and his eyes softened. My heart shifted in my chest. Just like his father, Joshua wore his love for his wife on his sleeve. All of my boys did.

"Destiny's on the phone finding out the delivery time for the computers," Carter, our oldest son, chimed in, pushing his way past Joshua, as he entered the conference room we'd been standing in.

The room was mostly empty, save for a few office chairs and lots of empty cardboard boxes.

My stomach grumbled as soon as the scent of the pizzas Carter carried hit my nose.

"Lunch is served," he stated, setting the three boxes of pizza on the one desk in the room.

One by one, the rest of our children began piling in.

"What was Josh so pissed about?" Carter asked at the same time as he handed his wife, Michelle, a paper plate with a slice of pizza on it, before holding out a chair for her to sit.

I smiled at how chivalrous all of my boys were.

"Your brother was upset because I was about to remind him of how sexy your father still is."

In unison all four of our sons—Carter, Aaron, Joshua, and Tyler—groaned in horror. Each of their faces were a display of disgust, as their wives giggled.

Tyler, our youngest, who happened to be holding one of his own children, covered his daughter, Annalise's, ears. "There are children around!" he stated, with narrowed eyes looking between Robert and I.

"You nor your child would be here if it weren't for us, so can it," I admonished, just before Robert moved past me to pluck our granddaughter out of Tyler's arms. Anna, as I called her, giggled when Robert tickled her little belly.

A second later, Tyler's wife, Destiny, entered the conference room, hanging up the phone. "Computers will be delivered in an hour, and cable and internet company will be out first thing tomorrow morning to get us all connected," she stated, excitedly.

"Good news," I responded, handing Destiny, who reminded me of a younger version of the actress, Nia Long, a slice of pizza.

"Thank you," she gushed. "I haven't eaten all day."

At that, Tyler frowned. "Why the hell not?" he questioned, his voice darkening from the lighthearted tone he'd expressed just a minute earlier.

Destiny rolled her eyes, before looking up at her football player husband. "Because we have three children under the age of one, I run my own company, *and* my sisters and mother-in-law have been working our butts off to open this new women's shelter. In other words, I've been a little busy."

"We have a damn chef just to make sure this doesn't happen."

"Lay off her, Ty," I interjected, knowing how possessive and controlling my sons could be. They learned it from their father.

"He's right, princess."

I rolled my own eyes at Robert's words. I knew he'd take Tyler's side.

"All of you ladies have been busy working your asses off to get this project off the ground, but you need to take care of yourselves first."

"Thank you, Father," Tyler agreed.

"Robert—"

"Don't *Robert* me. Did you have breakfast this morning before you left the house?"

I looked to Tyler. "See what you started?"

"See," Destiny chimed in, "now you're causing a rift between your parents. Happy with yourself now?"

"He's right," our second oldest son, Aaron, added, causing, his wife, Patience, to roll her eyes.

"Let it go, Destiny, you're not going to win this argument with these four. Aaron practically force feeds me if it's past ten in the morning and I haven't eaten."

Aaron, with his ever present scowl, simply glared down at his wife and shrugged because what else could he say? Everyone in the room new Patience was telling the truth.

A frowning Destiny finally decided to drop it and continue eating.

"Deb, did you know Robert was the one when you first met?" Michelle asked once we were about halfway through eating our lunch.

Robert turned to me, giving me the same smoldering stare he'd been giving me for forty years, and nodded.

"Of course."

"Psh, don't believe him," I responded, glancing between our children and two of our now ten grandchildren. The rest were back at our home with three nannies and two babysitters between the eight of them.

"No, princess didn't realize I was the one. But I knew early on."

"Oh, we all know the story," Carter added, causing us all to glance his way. "You both met in college, fell in love, and the rest is history."

Robert and I looked at each other with raised eyebrows.

"History, huh?" Robert questioned.

"You've told us the story, Father," Aaron added.

"You got the *abridged* version, son. Maybe it's time we tell them the full story," Robert stated, staring at me.

Lifting my eyebrows, I shrugged. I looked at our children whose faces had shifted to ones of curiosity instead of impatience. "I don't see why not."

CHAPTER 2

hen

Deborah

I crouched down low behind the bar, pulling my notecards from my shoulder bag to study for the next twenty minutes before my shift began. The loud music, constant chatter, and strobe lights that were gaining so much popularity in clubs like this, didn't make for the easiest of studying locations, but I fit my studying in wherever I could. Thus, as uncomfortable as I was, I snuggled into the far corner behind the bar where patrons couldn't see me, and where I was out of the way of Pia, the bartender for the night's, way, and went about memorizing the notes I'd taken earlier in my Theory of Probabilities class.

"Hey, you're studying already? Wasn't this, like, your first week of the semester?"

Startled, I looked up to find Pia's two long, blonde pigtails hanging low as she tilted her head downward, staring at me.

I nodded. "Yeah, but our professor gives us a quiz each week. Just trying to stay prepared," I muttered the last part before turning back to my notes to continue studying.

"You've got another ten minutes. And don't let Mike catch you back here doing that."

I nodded, not bothering to look up. I knew Pia would alert me if he came out from his back office. I'd gotten used to the absurdity that studying while not even on my shift could be a thing to hide. Mike, the owner, wasn't looking for girls who wanted to study to make it out of this place.

"Trinity's on tonight and it's a Friday. You know what that means," Pia continued as she wiped down the bar.

Again, I nodded, but kept my eyes on my notecards. I really wanted to start the semester off well. As a math major, I loved numbers and working analysis by running numbers, as we did in statistics. However, when it came to theory courses that required the understanding of historical explanations, as well as written papers to explain said theories, that was a weakness of mine. I needed to focus on doing well from the very beginning.

After what felt like only a few minutes, I looked at the watch on my wrist and saw that I only had another two minutes before my shift.

"Time flies when you're having fun," I mumbled to myself, before inserting my notecards into my leather, over the shoulder backpack, and pushing it all of the way behind the boxes of unopened liquor bottles under the bar.

"Time to get to work," Pia noted as I stood up and smoothed down the edges of the red, checkered mini-skirt I wore.

"It's that time," I responded, using my hands to adjust my boobs so they sat up in the midriff, white T-shirt I wore. I pulled up the suspender straps holding my skirt in place. The knee-high white socks and platform heels I wore completed the supposed school girl outfit the owner of *Richie's* was going for. After three and a half years of working there, I no longer thought about the ridiculousness of the outfit. The pay was decent, but the tips more than made up for it, and while my academic scholarship paid for my school and living expenses on campus, I worked to save so I'd have money to move once I finished school.

"How do I look?" I held out my arms, asking Pia.

Her pink lips spread into a wide grin. "Damn good. Now go make that money." She smacked me on the ass as I walked past her.

I pushed her arm away, used to her teasing by now. As soon as I stepped from behind the bar, the main lights darkened and the strobe lights turned up. I looked up as the music started playing. I immediately recognized The Rolling Stones' "Brown Sugar". Trinity had a thing for anything by the Rolling Stones. Her long, thin frame made its way from behind the red velvet curtain to the stage.

"Hey!"

I turned toward the bar to Pia.

"Mike says we've got a big crowd coming in. Potential big spenders or something. Look alive."

I stood up straight.

"Poke your tits out. Come on, you know the drill!" she yelled back.

Rolling my eyes skyward, I stood up straight, shoulders back so that my boobs stood at attention, and pulled my long, brunette locks, over my shoulder.

"That's it. Now work those baby blues of yours!"

I blinked rapidly, emphasizing my eyes.

"Go get 'em," she called just before moving farther down the bar to make a drink for a patron that'd just entered.

Spinning around, I grabbed one of the circular trays I carried the drinks and plates of food on, when ordered, ignoring the growing voices of the men catcalling Trinity as she danced on stage. I could tell at what point of her set she was on by how loud the cheers were.

Soon enough the door opened and a group of about ten guys pushed through, moving past the bouncers. Inhaling deeply, I braced myself before heading over, but I stopped short when I recognized the leader of the group.

"Shit!" I cursed, wishing at that moment, I wasn't the only cocktail waitress on shift tonight. But unfortunately, MaryAnne, the other waitress, had called out sick.

Pushing those thoughts aside, I took a deep breath and made my way over to the four tables the guys had chosen, right in the center of the club. The stage was front and center from their view, but my back was to the woman on stage as I greeted the men, many of whom I recognized.

"Good evening, gentlemen. What can I get started for you?" I questioned, pulling my notepad and pencil from my hip where I'd tucked them earlier.

"Deborah?"

My heart sank a little, at the almost gleeful tone I heard in Jack Lassiter's voice.

I turned. "Jack. How nice to see you here. What can I get for you?"

"I decided to treat the guys to a night out to celebrate my twenty-first birthday. Fucking California and its legal drinking age bullshit."

I had to fight hard not to roll my eyes. I didn't care why Jack or his friends were out that night. But, of course, he continued.

"Damn liberals are destroying the country with their nonsense. Look at all of the protests and upheaval they've caused—"

"It sucks, but I assume you're all here to have a good time tonight, right? So what can I get started for you all?" For some reason my gaze shifted from Jack to the guys he'd come in with. I relaxed slightly when I didn't see one in particular. Although, truth be told, I would've known immediately if Robert Townsend was with them. He didn't blend in like the rest of these guys. And even if he wasn't making a loud showing of himself, like Jack obviously needed to, his presence was still felt.

Why the hell I was thinking about Robert, or why I was grateful he wasn't with them that night, I didn't know.

"I'll have the best beer you have on tap," Jack finally answered. "And get these guys whatever they want." He pulled out a wad of money.

Again, I had to force myself not to show what I was thinking. Instead, I scribbled down in my notepad the orders from the guys who'd come in with Jack before departing as quickly as possible.

First, I brought the food orders to the back, giving them to the head chef so he could get started, then I took the drink orders behind the bar. I worked alongside Pia to prepare the drinks. Technically, I wasn't a bartender, but after a few years in that place, I could make drinks almost as well as Pia or any of the other bartenders. And since we were short staffed that night, she was thankful for the help.

"I can't stand that guy," I finally said out loud.

"Who?"

I gestured with my chin toward Jack. "He goes to Stanford. They all do. I've seen them on campus. Anyway, he's a real ass."

"Yeah, but he's a paying ass tonight. Just keep 'em liquored up. Drunk customers give the best tips." Pia winked at me as she added the final drink onto my drink.

I laughed. She was right. I didn't take this job to make friends. I took it for the money.

"Whoa!" one of the men shouted as he backed up, nearly knocking me over in his excitement. A new dancer had come to the stage and she was entertaining the hell out of the crowd.

"Sorry."

"Don't worry about it." I began placing the drinks in front of the different men who'd ordered them, thankful for my sharp memory. "Your food will be out shortly, guys," I stated, ready to depart, but my wrist was caught in someone's grip, causing me to turn back to the group.

I came chest to chest with Jack Lassiter.

Without thought, I yanked my wrist free and was ready to tell him to keep his damn hands to himself. But then I remembered I was at work. He wasn't the first customer to get a little too touchy feely.

"When is it your turn to get on stage?" he questioned, inching closer.

I glanced at the woman on stage who had just removed the tiny top she wore, displaying the flashy, neon pink pasties she wore.

"Never," I responded, returning my attention to Jack. "I'm not a dancer."

He moved closer. "What a waste of a body," he stated, eyeing me up and down.

In that moment, I loathed the skimpy outfit I wore, but didn't react.

"Your food will be out shortly. Enjoy the show." I turned and started to walk away when a smack to my ass caused me to jump, startled.

Furious, I turned back to face a smirking Jack.

"An ass like that definitely belongs on stage." A few of the dumb-asses with him laughed as if he'd told the funniest joke in the world.

"Hey, what's going on here?"

I relaxed slightly when I heard Pia's voice behind me.

"We were just talking with one of our classmates," a guy from the back replied.

I didn't know his name but I recognized him. We'd shared a class freshman or sophomore year.

"Yeah, well, classmate or not, we're only here for looking, not touching. Hands to yourselves," Pia added, before taking me by the arm to pull me away from the group.

"That's a shame," another douchebag added.

"How much to touch?" Jack questioned, waving his cash in the air.

I made a disgusted face. "You couldn't afford it!" I seethed while being pulled away by Pia.

"Hey, calm down," she encouraged, as I continued to stare at the men whose eyes were now trained on the dance on stage.

"What's got you so upset? You never let customers get to you like that," Pia noted.

Sighing, I slumped my shoulders. "I know. It's that I took a job forty minutes away from campus to avoid this type of thing. I can't stand guys like them."

"Like what?"

"Them." I gestured with my hand to the group of guys. "Stuck up, snooty—"

"Rich?"

"Yes!" I answered, adamantly.

I loved Stanford. Greatly appreciated the opportunity I had to not only attend the prestigious university but to do so on a scholarship, which was amazing for a woman who grew up like I did. Stanford was dubbed the Ivy League of the West Coast, and the professors worked diligently to live up to the hype. However, with the big name came big money. Most of the students on campus came from wealth I never even realized existed. While I'd made some great relationships on campus, not everyone was particularly welcoming of those who didn't come from their social circles or class levels. For the most part, I'd gotten used to it, and tried my utmost not to let it bother me, sometimes it did.

"Well, you've only got a few more months and then you're off to Williamsport to start that big fancy job," Pia stated, a hint of melancholy in her voice.

Looking over at her, I saw the shimmer of sadness in her hazel eyes.

"You're going to miss me?" I lifted an eyebrow.

"Hell yeah."

I giggled, my mood lightening. The idea of leaving Pia did make me sad. However, I couldn't help but feel a little bit giddy at the thought of starting my new job after graduation. The previous summer, I'd gotten an opportunity to intern in the finance department of a fashion company. And while I hadn't landed a position at that company, it had led to my interviewing with a few others, including one of the largest cosmetic companies in the world. I had interviewed over winter break, and just heard back a few weeks ago. I'd gotten the job as a financial analyst. I would be moving to Williamsport two weeks after graduation to start my new career.

"You're gonna be great!" Pia exclaimed.

"You'll come visit me, right?" I asked. Pia and I had grown close over the past three years of working together. She often covered for me when I took an extra long break to study, and I returned the favor, covering for her at the bar when one of her boyfriends came in and she needed to step away to argue with him. On the outside, it may not have seemed like Pia and I had anything in common aside from the place we worked at, but I often felt like I could relate to her more than most of the girls I shared classes and dorm rooms with.

"Of course. Anyway, we need to get back to work. There're tips to be made."

Groaning, I glanced over at the group of guys from Stanford. Their attention was on the new dances who'd come out to give them lap dances.

"At least now their hands are occupied and they won't be trying to grope you," Pia stated.

"Let's hope. For their sakes," I responded, and then headed back to the kitchen to retrieve the food they'd ordered.

* * *

THEN

Robert

"Princess!" I called for the third time to no avail. My voice was deep and loud. I knew she'd heard me, which only meant one thing—Deborah Tate was intentionally ignoring me.

I narrowed my gaze on her retreating back. There was no way in hell that would fly.

I jogged a little to catch up to her just as she exited the building we'd just had our World Mythologies course in. It was a sunny day in Palo Alto, but when Deborah spun around, glaring at me, snatching her arm away from my hold, it felt like the entire sky had darkened.

She was *pissed*.

Swallowing, I shifted, lowering the books I held in my hand in front of my crotch because I'd be damned if her attitude didn't turn me the hell on. It felt like all of the blood rushed from my brain to my groin. She had no fucking clue what she was doing, either.

"What?" she nearly shrieked.

In my peripheral, I noted a few heads turn our way, but I ignored them. They didn't matter.

"You're pissed," I said, stating the obvious.

"You think?"

I angled my head. She really had no idea what she was doing with those laser sharp, cerulean-blue eyes of hers. Her cheeks were tinted red, evidence of her anger, and her brunette brows were turned downward.

I decided to prod. "What for?"

Her eyes widened. "What for? It's been two weeks since you've been to class."

A smile touched my lips. "I didn't know you cared so much, princess."

A scowl this time around. "I don't. Trust me, I don't. But as I told you the first week of this class, I am *not* going to allow you to mess up my GPA. We have a major assignment at the end of the semester due, and smaller assignments along the way. You haven't even been around for us to decide a topic!" she seethed.

Not one to let anyone speak to me like this, I was almost stunned into silence. But not quite.

I knew she'd be angered at us not having picked our topic yet. Our first assignment for the semester was due the following week. And while I wouldn't explain what had kept me from class the past two weeks, I would let her know that I wasn't the rich slacker she assumed I was.

"I realize this, princess. Which is why I've been doing some research." Shifting to remove the backpack hanging on my shoulder, I placed the notebooks I'd been holding inside, then removed two books on Middle Eastern and North African mythologies before handing them to her.

Her angry gaze shifted from me to the books I held. Her face registered surprise when she noted the titles of the books.

I smirked, cockily.

"How'd you know?"

"I may have peeked over your shoulder the first day of class." She had jotted down some notes as to what mythologies she'd wanted to research for our project. "I looked through both of them. I think studying the Berber mythologies of Northern Africa seems pretty interesting, but I'll let you decide since I've been MIA the past few weeks. It won't happen again," I stated firmly.

Her head popped up, the corners of her eyes wrinkling as she scowled. "It better not."

Again, I was used to very few people speaking to me like that, and by very few, I meant only one. And that fucker was responsible for giving me life, among other things.

"Skim thru the books and then meet me in the library at five today. We can go over the topic you chose."

She remained silent.

"I'll see you at five, princess." I turned to head to my next class.

To my back, I heard her say, "Don't call me princess!"

I glanced over my shoulder and simply grinned. I wasn't giving up the nickname. She might as well get the hell used to it.

CHAPTER 3

Robert

I sighed as I inserted the key into the doorknob, not knowing what to expect on the other side once I entered. It'd been a long two weeks, and because of it, I was behind on my classes. Thankfully, it was still early enough in the semester that I hadn't missed too much between family bullshit and business bullshit.

Stepping over the threshold of my apartment that was just off campus, I glanced around. The brown leather couch to the left, in the living room, remained undisturbed. *It's dark*, I noted as I flicked on the lights. *And it's quiet. Too quiet.*

I shook my head and grunted, placing my books and school supplies on the floor next to the wooden coatrack, and moved down the long hallway. Entering the guest bedroom, I found my brother, Jason, a lump in the middle of the waterbed.

Angrily, I turned on the lights in the room and charged over to the bed, shaking it. The mattress rippled and waved due to the pressure. Jason grunted and attempted to turn over on his side.

"Wake up!" I growled.

"Wh-what?" he questioned, groggily, his eyes opening to slits. "Why's it so fucking bright in here?"

"Maybe because it's one o'clock in the fucking afternoon." And just to drive my point home, I pulled open the long, dark curtains my mother had begged me to don the windows with so Jason could sleep more comfortably. I snorted at the way she coddled her youngest son.

"Wake up!" I demanded.

"Ah, come on, Rob. Can't I get a little sleep?"

"Sleep is all you've been doing since we arrived in California last night. I only brought you back with me to keep you out of trouble. I missed two weeks worth of classes for you—"

"No, that wasn't for me," Jason retorted, finally sitting up. "You did it for Father."

"I did it for both of you." Two weeks ago I'd gotten a call from Jason, who had been taken to the police station after his ex-girlfriend called them, fearing for her safety. They were out at a nightclub, Jason had been drinking, per usual, and he wasn't a nice drunk. Add to that, Townsend Industries was going through some difficult times due to the ongoing energy crisis, and I was needed back home. Being the oldest, I was used to cleaning up Jason's messes. I was also expected to take the reins at Townsend Industries at some point, which meant that my father expected me to be heavily involved in the business, no matter what was going on in my life.

"You need to head down and register for classes."

"No fucking way I'm going to Stanford," Jason insisted, pointing a shaky finger at me.

I frowned as he tossed his legs over the side of the bed and tried to stand, but plopped back down onto the bed. He was either still drunk from the night before or severely hungover. Which one, I couldn't tell.

"You need to get your shit together. We discussed this three days ago in Father's office. There's no way Stanford would take you right now. There's a local community college we've registered you at. Even though their semester started, Father bought your way in. You take a few classes, get high enough grades, and maybe another school will accept you as a transfer." That was the plan, though it was likely a long shot.

"I ain't going to school," Jason defiantly protested, finally rising to his feet on his third try. He was younger than me by two years and only an inch shorter than my six-foot-three frame, but his descent into excessive drinking was already taking its toll. His normally lean frame was growing a potbelly while his limbs were wiry.

"That's the fucking deal. There is no way you're going to be living with me and sleeping all day and drinking all night. Get your fucking clothes on, drink a cup of coffee to sober up, and then go down to the admissions office to the community college to register for classes, or so help me—"

"So help you what? You gonna kick my ass, Rob?"

"Don't fucking tempt me," I growled.

"What if I don't want to take classes?"

"No one gives a shit what you *want* to do. You haven't made good choices up until this point. Getting yourself arrested over a woman."

"She was disrespecting me!" Jason yelled.

"How? By moving on with her fucking life? You two broke up months ago, didn't you? And you throw a temper tantrum in a nightclub over your ex going on a date. Grow the hell up."

"I'm not like you. I don't hop from woman to woman in a matter of weeks. I actually have feelings."

I grunted, rolling my eyes. "Yeah, the type of feelings that led you to trying to beat a woman up. Jesus Christ, Jason. Our father may be a piece of shit to our mother but he never hit her."

"Yeah, he just beat the crap out of us instead."

Frowning, I looked way, mostly because Jason was right, though I was loathe to admit it. "Well, he doesn't anymore, right? Just get your shit together," I grunted.

And because I really didn't want to knock my brother out, in spite of my temper, I took a step backward, gave him one last glare, and stormed out the door. I headed up the hall to grab my own books and book bag. Like I said, I didn't have time to bullshit around with my brother. I had shit in my own life I needed to take care of.

* * *

Deborah

"He better not stand me up," I mumbled, peering down at the watch on my wrist. I ran my hand along the beat-up leather band. It was only a minute after five, but I hated tardiness. If he insisted I meet him at the library the least he could do—

"Waiting on me?"

I abruptly turned, ignoring the chill that ran through me upon hearing his deep voice. I glanced up into those dark brown eyes of his, swallowing.

"You're late."

He frowned just before staring up at something behind me.

I turned to see what he was looking at to find a clock mounted on the wall above the library's entrance.

"And you're a stickler for time."

"If you tell someone you're going to meet them, the courteous thing to do is be on time. I—"

"You're right. It won't happen again," he stated, shocking me.

Did he really say I was right? My mouth parted, but no words came out. I quickly clamped my mouth shut but it was too late. He'd noticed, which was apparent by the cocky smile that touched his lips.

"Let's take one of the quiet rooms upstairs. I already reserved it for us."

Again, I was surprised at his preparedness. So surprised, in fact, that I didn't even notice when he'd taken me by the elbow, leading me toward the staircase where the library's quiet rooms were located.

"Did you have a chance to read over the books I gave you?" Robert questioned as he shut the door of the quiet room.

In spite of the fact that the room had windows on three of the four sides, and I could see out—as well as others being able to see in—being in such a small room, with the door closed, alone with him felt … overwhelming.

"Uh, what?" I questioned.

"The books? Did you pick a topic?" he questioned coolly from his position leaned against the door, arms folded over his chest, legs crossed at the ankles.

"Yes. The Berber religion as you said earlier. It appears to be interesting."

He nodded, his thick brown hair, which was only an inch or so away from touching his shoulders, swayed with the movement of his head. Not for the first time, I noticed the freckles that lined his cheeks and bridge of his nose. There was something distinctive about them.

"Agreed. Now that we've chosen a topic, let's discuss the ongoing research we'll need to do for this project." Pushing away from the door, he moved to the table and sat on a chair.

I swallowed and retrieved my notebook from my bag, ready to get down to business so that I could get out of there as soon as possible.

"I have to go," I stated, hurriedly glancing at my watch. It was a little after six, and if I was going to have time to eat dinner and then make it to work for my shift, I needed to leave right then.

As I stuffed my notebook back into my bag, I felt Robert's eyes on me. I paused, looking up to find his full concentration focused on me.

"Are you in a rush?"

Despite the past hour of getting along, my snarky attitude reared its ugly head. "Unlike some people, I'm on a schedule."

"I was two minutes late," he reminded me as he stood, placing his belongings back into his bag.

I didn't say anything as I passed through the door that he held open. I moved past him, and within a half a second I felt his presence at my backside. I carried myself down the steps and out the library's main doorway before he spoke another word.

"You want to grab something to eat?"

Pausing, I turned in his direction so quickly that he nearly walked into me. I took a step back.

"I can't," I responded.

"Why not?" His eyes narrowed and I had half a mind to tell him I didn't owe him an explanation but something told me that wouldn't go over too well. So I opted for the truth. "I have to get to work."

I waited to see what type of reaction that would garner.

His eyebrows lifted. "Work?"

"Yes, like a job. Something real people do to earn money."

"Real people? What the hell's that supposed to mean?"

"Everyday, normal individuals. As in those of us not born with the silver spoon in our mouths." For some reason I wanted to piss him off.

However, I only pissed myself off when instead of reacting angrily, he chuckled. A deep sound that came up from the pit of his stomach. The hairs on my arms rose. I took another step back, hating how I wanted to move closer instead.

"You really don't like people with money."

I rolled my eyes. "Maybe I just don't like you."

"Princess, we both know that's not true."

I grunted, frustrated. "And what is with the princess thing? My name is Deborah. Do I need to spell it out for you again?"

"That won't be necessary. I've got it memorized … princess."

Frustrated, I stomped my foot. He obviously wasn't listening. "I need to go."

"Do you need a ride?"

I stopped again. "What?"

"You said you needed to get to work. Do you need a ride?"

I shook my head. "I have a car." It was beat-up and old but it worked.

He nodded, and his lips parted to say something else, but he was stopped by someone calling his name behind him.

We both pivoted in the direction of the male voice. At first I thought it was one of Robert's friends. But as the young guy moved closer, I couldn't place him. I also realized two things; this guy was drunk or at least on his way to being drunk as evidenced by his wobbly stride, and two, he had to be related to Robert. He had the same dark hair and eyes, tall stature, and as he moved closer the freckles that Robert had on his cheeks, this guy did as well.

"Jason, what the hell are you doing here?" Robert's voice was low, agitated.

The new guy, Jason, glanced at me and smiled, looking between the two of us. "Am I interrupting something?"

"No."

"What the fuck do you want?"

Robert and I responded at the same time.

"I did as you said and I thought I'd come find you. I didn't know you would be occupied with a lady friend." Jason's eyes returned to me, smirking again.

"Jason, if you don't—"

"I need to get going. I'll see you in class," I told Robert. I gave the two one last look before turning and starting in the direction of my dorm room.

"That one's got a nice ass. I'm a—"

I gasped and turned around, stunned at the words that'd come out of Jason's mouth, but my eyes widened even more when I saw that Robert had literally wrapped his large hand around Jason's throat, choking off whatever he'd been about to say.

"I haven't laid a hand on you since we were children, but if you ever talk about her like that again, I will beat the shit out of you. Understood?" he growled.

I wasn't sure if he was intentionally talking loud enough for me to hear or not, but at that moment, as I stared at a livid Robert Townsend, I had no doubt that he meant every word he'd just spoken. I clutched the strap of my bag tightly in my right hand.

"Fucker," Robert grunted as he shoved Jason away.

I blinked and noticed Robert's gaze returned to me. A chill ran through me at the darkness I saw in his eyes. But with one blink it was gone. Wordlessly, I pivoted on my heels and moved quickly in the direction of my dorm room. I dared not to even think of the butterflies that floated in my belly at the dangerous gleam in his eyes.

Maybe I didn't have Robert Townsend all figured out.

CHAPTER 4

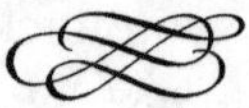

*P*resent

Deborah

"You didn't know me at all. But you were about to find out," my husband cockily stated as I turned in his direction. I laughed, shaking my head all while admiring the age lines in his forehead and around his eyes. He looked better today than he had all of those years ago. And he was a sight for sore eyes back then.

His eyes narrowed ever so slightly and a lascivious grin touched the corners of his lips. It was the grin that was solely reserved for me.

"So that's where it all started. You were partnered on a class project together and the rest is history."

"Not quite," Robert added, striding over to me, wrapping an arm around my waist, facing our progeny.

"There's a lot more to our story than that."

"But you'll have to wait to hear the rest. The computers are being delivered and I need you all to help us set it up," Robert told the boys.

I aided Michelle, Patience, and Kayla throwing out the now empty pizza boxes, while Destiny fed Annalise who'd gotten a little fussy.

"Hang on. I wanted to catch Aaron before they all left," I told my daughters-in-law. I moved out of the conference room and down the hall to the classroom area where the guys were helping the technicians setup the computers. Truthfully, they all were mostly standing, watching over to ensure the technicians did their job. All of my boys, including my husband, were overly protective. Security had been the first thing that had been set up in what would become our non-profit women's shelter. This place was wired directly to the police station as well as Townsend's security offices.

"Hey," I stated, tapping Aaron on his arm as I moved beside him. My second eldest peered down on me, the ever-present scowl on his face but his eyes were soft. While outsiders may not be able to see it, he'd softened over the past two years. His wife and now four children had filled the hole in his heart I was certain even he didn't recognize had been there for years.

"Is something wrong? Patience—"

"Your wife is fine," I responded, cutting him off. He'd begun looking as if he was about to bolt out the door to find his wife to make sure she was okay.

My words had put him at ease.

"I wanted to check on you to make sure you were okay. After hearing us talk about Jason." I lifted an eyebrow, watching him curiously for a reaction. Jason, Robert's younger brother, was a lousy son of a bitch who'd done a lot of harm in his life. He was also Aaron's biological father.

But while Jason may've been Aaron's father through DNA, he was my son, mine and Robert's.

My heart lightened when an actual smile, or something akin to it— Aaron didn't particularly smile—appeared on his face and he leaned down, pressing a kiss to my cheek.

"I'm fine, Mother. He's dead and I'm not. He can't hurt me anymore."

I blinked, taking his hand in both of mine and squeezing it. I'd said those same words to Aaron not long before he'd gotten out of the hospital following the car accident that killed his parents, and we brought him home to raise as our own.

"Out of my four boys, you are always the one to make me tear up the most," I told him, patting my eyes with the silk handkerchief I'd pulled from the back pocket of the jeans I wore. "I need to get back to the girls."

I gave Aaron one last look and then glanced over at my handsome husband. His eyes were already on me. Those same butterflies started flapping in my belly when he winked at me. For another moment, I stood there admiring how his dark brown locks were now much shorter than they'd been in the spring of 1974, and instead of brown they were grey. But he still had a head full of beautiful tresses, the wrinkle lines around his eyes more apparent, but I much preferred the distinguished look they gave him over the boyish, youthful appeal of our younger years. Truth be told, I'd enjoyed every stage of life with this man.

"When are you going to tell us the rest of your story?" Destiny questioned as soon as I entered the conference room with the rest of the women.

Grinning, I took Annalise from Destiny's arms, admiring her wheat-colored skin against the red curls of her hair and brown eyes. She got her hair color from her father, Tyler. I pressed a kiss to Annalise's nose, causing her to pull back and give me a funny look. I laughed at her expression, so much like her mother, before turning back to the rest of the women.

"Later." I glanced around. "I'm so proud to be finally building this place," I sighed out loud.

"We're even more proud to be building it with you," Patience added. "I can't wait to start with the literacy classes here. We've already got around fifty books donated. I expect we'll have much more by the time we open. As our resident librarian, literacy teacher, and grant writer, I am ecstatic for those doors to finally open," Patience stated excitedly.

It thrilled me to hear her excitement. I'd spent years wanting to open a location like this. A place to aid women, young and older, who were down on their luck, lost, and had nowhere to turn. After years of planning it finally came about, and thanks to the dynamic, intelligent, and competent women each one of my sons had married, I now had a team to help me bring it all together. This would be a family affair. The Williamsport Women's Shelter was the name we were going with for now.

"We really could've used a place like this on the mountain," I stated out loud.

"The mountain?" Michelle questioned, curious.

I smiled, still bouncing a giggling Annalise on my hip. "It's how I refer to home."

Michelle nodded. "Appalachia, right?"

I tilted my head. "More specifically, eastern Kentucky, Beattyville."

"Do you ever miss it?" Destiny asked.

Twisting my lips, I considered the question. "Honestly? Sometimes. Not often, but at times. Despite all of its problems, and trust me, there are many problems, there is a certain beauty about Appalachia. The natural rivers, streams, mountaintop views. Unfortunately, all that gets lost in the crushing poverty. We had our problems when I was a kid, but now with the opioid epidemic ... I wouldn't wish that life on my worst enemy."

I hadn't been back to the town I grew up in well over two decades but I'd heard a few cousins of mine had either overdosed or ended up in jail for some horrific crimes committed while trying to get their next fix.

"I left Beattyville just before my senior year of high school, to complete my high school education in a different town, and never looked back, mainly because my mother had told me if I ever did come back she would kick my ass."

"Seriously?" Michelle blurted out.

I looked her in the eyes and nodded. "She wasn't kidding either. My mother worked her fingers to the bone to make a better life for me. Both of my parents had but only she'd lived to see it through."

I sighed, my heart aching as it always did when I thought about my parents. Looking down into the big, bright eyes of my youngest granddaughter had me realizing, not for the first time, that their sacrifices had been worth it.

I didn't have time to get too lost in my thoughts when the guys piled back in to inform us that the computers were all set up. The ladies and I would be staying around for another couple of hours to get things like scheduling and administrative tasks figured out, but the men were headed home to the kids.

"You're thinking about home," Robert's deep vocal chords drowned out my thoughts.

I turned to him, smiling. "Now, I'm thinking about you," I responded as he wrapped his arms around my waist, pulling me into him.

"Kiss me."

I raised my lips to meet his and he didn't disappoint.

"I'm proud as hell of you. You know that, right?"

I did but it still felt great to hear him say it.

I lifted my arms to his shoulders. "When I get home, I'll show you precisely what your words mean to me," I purred just before pulling him in for another kiss.

"Here they go again," I heard Carter say.

"I'm going to kick his ass," Robert growled.

I giggled. He was always threatening one of our boys' lives.

"Leave him alone. Besides ..." I jutted my head in Carter's direction. Our eldest had already lost interest in us as he whispered something in Michelle's ear, making her blush.

"Chip off the old block," Robert stated proudly.

Once the men left, the ladies and I had our planning session. Patience and I would be the close to full-timers while Kayla, Destiny, and Michelle would put in a few hours at the shelter given they still had full-time jobs, in addition to their very full homelives.

"This all looks great, ladies," I stated, standing up from my chair and stretching. "I think I need to get to my yoga class in the morning."

"I'll join you, if you don't mind," Kayla inserted.

"I'd love that."

It wasn't unusual to attend a yoga or some other workout class with one or more of my daughters-in-law.

I glanced at the watch on my wrist before looking up and noticing Patience cover her mouth as she yawned.

"Boys still keeping you up at night?" I questioned.

She smiled. "They're doing better," she responded. In addition to seven-year-old twins, Aaron and Patience had a set of nearly one-year old twins. "I'll be right back," Patience stated, before standing and exiting.

I lifted an eyebrow but didn't say anything. Instead, I went over and worked with Destiny as she decided on what type of financial literacy courses she wanted to conduct in the five to ten hours she'd spend at the center throughout the week.

But I wasn't oblivious when I saw Michelle get up and follow Patience out toward the restroom. I smiled to myself.

CHAPTER 5

ichelle

I headed to the space where the soda and snack machine had been set up already. Thankfully, the soda machine did have ginger ale as an option, but the snack machine didn't have the saltine crackers I was hoping for, so I got the next best thing.

After grabbing the snacks, I exited the cafeteria area and headed farther down the hall toward the restroom. Just as I pushed the door of the multi-stall bathroom open, a toilet flushed and Patience exited one of the stalls wiping her mouth. She paused when she saw me enter.

I held out the contents in my hand.

"Animal crackers?" Grinning, she took the soda and crackers from me.

"The snack machine didn't have saltines. We should work on that."

She nodded. "I'll make a note of it."

I watched as she opened the can of ginger ale, taking a sip. "I would ask if it's that obvious, but ..." She held up the snacks I'd given her.

I giggled. "You two don't quit, do you?"

It was meant to be a joke but Patience's smile dimmed, becoming replaced by a forlorn expression.

"Hey, what's that about?" I questioned, moving closer.

She shook her head, her long sisterlocks falling over her shoulders, semi-covering her face. Pushing her hair back, she lifted her head.

"Aaron's going to be pissed." She sighed, placing the hand that held the unopened animal crackers to her belly.

I frowned. "Why would he—" I stopped myself, remembering. "Oh."

"Yeah, *oh.*" Shaking her head, she moved to the counter that held a row of white sinks. She placed the soda and crackers on the counter. "After what happened when Andreas and Thiers were born, he was adamant about not having anymore children. At least, not me birthing anymore."

I bit the inside of my cheek, feeling sorry for Patience.

"I almost died after having my babies."

I nodded, remembering that awful day, hours after she'd given birth. We'd received the call from Deborah after a distraught Aaron had called them, explaining what was happening. The entire family rushed back to the hospital. Thankfully, by then the excessive bleeding Patience had experienced was under control.

"But you didn't," I reminded her.

"Thank God."

"Thank God," I agreed. "And thankfully, you know now what to be on the lookout for. No two birthing experiences are alike. I'm sure this one will be so much better."

Patience gave me a humorless laugh. "I appreciate the words, Michelle. But trust me, I've already given myself every pep talk imaginable. Truth is, I'm not as frightened as I thought I'd be. I know this baby is meant to be." She cupped her abdomen again. "I'm just …"

"Terrified of Aaron's reaction."

She frowned. "Terrified is a strong word. Let's just say if I had the option of telling him versus just being able to have this baby and bring it home happy and healthy without having to tell him, I'd go with door number two." She smirked.

I grinned, understanding completely. Aaron didn't play when it came to his wife's safety and well-being. Hell, none of the Townsends did.

"I'm sure it'll be fine," I stated, rubbing her shoulder.

Her hand lifted to mine. "Thanks. And thanks for these." She held up the can of soda and animal crackers.

"Just returning the favor. You finish up in here and discard the evidence so the others won't see."

She nodded.

I'm sure eating in the bathroom was the last thing she wanted, but if she hadn't told Aaron about the baby yet, I doubted she wanted the other women to know about it. Not until she was ready.

As I exited the bathroom, a smile tugged at the corners of my lips at the thought that we'd have a new little niece or nephew in the family soon. In fact, it had me extremely excited to get home to my own husband that night.

* * *

"Hɪ, Mᴀᴍᴀ!" my oldest son, Diego, greeted as I entered the front door. He came from the direction of the kitchen, likely alerted by the dinging of the alarm we have whenever the door is opened. Not far behind him was his best friend, Monique.

"Hi, Mrs. Townsend," she added in her sweet voice.

My heartstrings pulled in my chest. Being a mom to two little boys was fantastic. Add a loving and adoring husband and I spent my days on cloud nine, but I'd be lying if I didn't say that I also wanted a little girl.

"Hi, baby. Hi, Monique," I replied to the pair, pressing a kiss to Diego's cheek and giving Monique a hug. "What are you two up to?"

"We're working on our volcano project," Monique responded excitedly.

I smiled. Diego and Monique were now in the same class, given that once her mother, Sandra, and Joshua's best friend, Damon, got married, they'd transferred Monique to Excelor Academy where my son also went. The school had an outstanding academic reputation, and all four of the Townsend brothers had attended. Diego had been in the school since he was in kindergarten. He loved it, but enjoyed it even more now that his best friend shared his third grade class with him.

"And how's that going?" I questioned, as I fully entered the living room area, my heels clicking against the hardwood floor.

"It was going well until someone added the vinegar a little too soon."

I glanced up and into the sparkling blue eyes of the love of my life. I grinned when I noticed the frowning expression on his face.

"Dad's just upset that he didn't get to pour in the vinegar," Diego added.

I giggled, covering my mouth. I didn't know who was more excited about this volcano project—the kids or Carter.

"Yeah, when you two get an A-plus on this thing, I want my props," Carter retorted, pointing at the kids. "Now go wash up for dinner."

Diego and Monique went scampering off, down the hall to do as instructed.

"Hey," he stated, pulling me in, his voice deepening. His lips captured mine before I even had time to respond.

I parted my lips because my body's reaction was no longer under my control when I was wrapped up in his arms. Carter deepened the kiss, pulling me in closer to his waist. I moaned into his mouth but forced myself to pull back before getting too carried away. I didn't need two ten-year old's running in and seeing us, although truth be told, Diego was probably used to such open displays of affection between us by now. My husband wasn't one to shy away from affection toward me or our children. One of the many things I loved about him.

I lifted my hand to cup his chiseled cheek. "I love you."

"Love you, too, sugar," he responded just before pressing another quick kiss to my lips.

I swallowed, staring him in the eyes. "I'd be devastated if something happened to you," I blurted out. Talking with Patience earlier had me thinking of losing my own spouse.

Raising a blond eyebrow, Carter moved my hand from his cheek to his lips before lowering it. "What brought that about?"

I shrugged. "Just thinking," I responded, not wanting to give away the conversation Patience and I had. "Your job is already so scary, and given everything that happened—"

"It's over now."

I pushed out a heavy breath. "I know, but that was a frightening time for all of us." I parted my mouth again but didn't want to say my next thoughts. My husband's job as a firefighter was terrifying enough even without some homicidal pyromaniac stalking his entire station. Regardless, with that last part out of the way, the reality was, he still ran into fires to save lives. I loved him for it. Hell, we met and eventually fell in love *because* he'd saved me from a terrible car accident and near explosion. And as much as I wanted to, I wouldn't ask him to give it up. His job, his need to be in the mix helping others was what made him who he was.

"You know I'm invincible, right?"

I giggled. He'd begun telling me that to reassure me.

"I'm sure you are, Lieutenant," I agreed, wrapping my arms around his neck, reminding him of his newly minted status at the station.

His smile was wide. "Speaking of …"

I lifted an eyebrow.

"I spoke with the captain the other day. Wanted to wait until it was final. I got the word today, the brass has asked me to split my time between Rescue Four and new recruits."

I wrinkled my forehead. "What does that mean?"

"It means I'll be half time at the station and the other half at the Academy, helping to shape the next generation of Williamsport firefighters. It also means less time I'll have to spend running into fires."

My eyes widened. "Really?"

He nodded. "Really, sugar." He kissed my forehead.

I frowned. "Wait. You didn't just do this because it's what you thought I'd want, did you?"

"You know I'd give you anything you wanted."

"I know, which is why I'm asking."

"Firstly, I didn't request this at all, but with my promotion and experience, my name was thrown in the pot for new instructors and I agreed. I'll still be with Rescue Four doing what I love, but I'll also be able to shape how recruits are instructed to graduate better prepared firefighters for the entire city."

I felt relieved at the excitement I heard in his voice at this new opportunity. And I was satisfied knowing that he would be spending less time in actual fires. Call me selfish, but I liked the idea of knowing my man was in less danger every time he went to work.

"With you as their instructor, Williamsport is going to have the best firefighters in the world," I gushed, pressing kisses all over his face.

He chuckled. "Any other wishes I can grant for you today?"

"Yes, I want another baby."

He went completely still, his breathing increasing.

I bit the inside of my cheek to keep from grinning.

"You're still on the pill—"

"I threw them out this morning." I'd started taking birth control after our youngest, Sam was born, and when things started getting crazy at Carter's job. The thought of bringing another child into this world while also fearing for my husband's life was too much to bear.

"We're getting started on that assignment tonight!" Carter yelled, causing me to laugh out loud.

"What assignment? Another volcano?" Diego asked as he and Monique re-entered the living room.

I parted my mouth to respond when the baby monitor that Carter had carried into the living room alerted all of us that our youngest, Sam, had awaken from his nap.

"No. Your mama and I have a special project of our own we're working on," I heard Carter say as I started for the stairs to retrieve Sam.

Covering my mouth to keep the laugh from escaping, I looked

back down to see Carter's glinting eyes firmly planted on my backside. He grinned, licking his lips when he saw me watching him.

I wouldn't bother to tell him that it would likely take at least a few days for the birth control to work its way out of my system. Heck, I was ready to started practicing as soon as possible.

* * *

Robert

"Fore!" Joshua yelled as Aaron took a swing at the ball with his golf club.

I squinted at the sun shining brightly, high in the sky, as I tried to follow the ball's trajectory. I lost it somewhere in the distance, not finding it again until it landed only a few inches away from the hole Aaron had been aiming for.

"Excellent," I grunted.

"You know, this is an eerily normal way for the five of us to be spending time together."

Frowning, I turned to my youngest, the shit starter that he was. "I almost told your mother to abort you," I responded.

Tyler, not taking me seriously, merely bent over, laughing. "Could you imagine this family without *me?*"

No. No, I couldn't. The problem was he knew it, too.

"Little shit he might be, but he does have a point, Father." That was Joshua, my more level headed, even-keeled child, except for rare occasions.

"We spend quality time together," I finally responded while pulling one of my sleek, new stainless steel clubs from the bag that held it.

"Yup, usually spent in basements of abandoned homes ..." Joshua stated.

"Or out in the woods," Carter added.

"And the hidden office in Townsend Industries," Aaron tacked on.

I made a sound, something between a grunt and a laugh. These little fuckers were right. We did have a particularly odd way of spending family time together. But that was because ... "A threat to one of us, is a threat to *all* of us. Someone messes with one of you, and the rest of you don't step up, you'll have to deal with *me*." I'd never hit my boys while they were growing up. Never even thought of it. I didn't want to raise them the way I'd been raised.

But I sure as hell taught them how to strike at someone who posed a threat to them or their family.

"Same lesson I expect you to pass on to all of your sons. I only learned the importance of protecting my family when I first fell for your mother."

"Are you going to tell us more of the story?" Tyler questioned.

I watched as all four of my sons moved in closer. They obviously wanted to hear more.

Acquiescing, I shoved the golf club back into my bag and leaned against one of the carts we'd rented for the day.

"Sure."

CHAPTER 6

hen

Robert

How in the hell does a woman make studying World Mythologies fucking sexy? That was the question that'd been dominating my thoughts over the last thirty minutes. We were in the library again, using one of the silent study rooms to work on our class assignment.

"Did you get the bo— What? Do I have something in my hair?" Deborah questioned when she looked up and saw me staring. She began running her hand through her long, dark brown tresses as if trying to remove whatever she thought was in it.

I grinned, a move I rarely ever did but came naturally when around her.

"Do you remember the first time we met?"

She frowned, forehead wrinkling. "Uh, yeah," she answered, confused. "You were …" Her words drifted off as she bit the tip of the eraser to the pencil she held in her hand.

Is she blushing?

"Fucking your roommate," I supplied.

Yup, she was definitely blushing.

Her eyes also ballooned at my words.

I shrugged.

"I walked in on you two." Her nose pinched angrily.

"Not my fault you don't know how to knock."

"It was *my* room!"

Another shrug. "It was Tracey's room, too."

Deborah groaned. "Don't remind me."

"You've avoided me since then."

I was glad when she didn't try to deny that fact. Four years we'd spent on the same campus, we even had some friends in common, but since that day freshman year she hadn't said more than two words to me.

"It's been a busy four years," she responded. "I didn't have time to mess around."

"I've noticed."

She peered at me, those blue eyes narrowing. "And I didn't like that since that first day you've called me princess."

"I call you princess because you acted like one."

Her mouth dropped.

"It's true. You walked in on your roommate and I fucking and freaked out as if you'd never heard of or seen two people having sex before."

"It's not a common occurrence to walk in on people having sex!"

"We're in college. You live in the dorms. I know that wasn't your last time walking in on your roommate fucking or vice versa."

"Do you have to keep using that word?"

"What? Fucking? See? Princess."

She rolled her eyes and I sat back in my chair, just staring. She was gorgeous with her hypnotizing eyes, long, dark hair, aquiline nose, and her slightly bronzed skin from the California sun.

"That's none of your business."

I sat forward, her words propelling me. Her thinking her sex life wasn't my business sparked something in me. What, I didn't know, being completely unfamiliar with the feeling.

"Besides, freshman year was my first and only time having a roommate. I learned my lesson early on. You weren't the only guy Tracey had in and out of our room that year."

I snorted. I was well aware of that. Tracey had been a one-time thing. I moved on almost as soon as I'd pulled out of her, but I didn't need to tell Deborah all of that.

"Where are you from?"

Deborah looked at me, again taken aback by my line of question. But I wouldn't take it back. I wanted to know more about her and I needed her to tell me.

"Why?"

"Because I want to know."

"Where are you from?"

"Williamsport."

Her eyebrows lifted. "Oh."

"You've heard of it, I'm assuming."

"Of course."

"Great. Now your turn."

She hesitated, then rested her chin in the palm of her hand as her elbow leaned on the wooden desk. She stared at me for a few silent moments, contemplating. She tried to appear confident, nonchalant, but her eyes gave her away. I was certain she didn't even realize it but her eyes revealed embarrassment.

"Beattyville, Kentucky."

I squinted. "Never heard of it."

She snorted. "You wouldn't have. It's a tiny town in eastern Kentucky, in the heart of Appalachia. Nothing like the big city of Williamsport, though we do have a little claim to fame."

"Oh yeah? What's that?"

"Ten years ago, President Johnson visited our town on one of his many stops to gain support for his War on Poverty."

I lifted my eyebrows remembering that particular tour. "That's where you're from?"

She swallowed. "That's where I'm from. One of, if not *the* poorest region in the country. But heck, I got to shake the president's hand when I was eleven so there's that."

I'd also shaken President Johnson's hand, once, but under very different circumstances. It was actually at a gala event that my father hosted at our home, Townsend Manor, but that information didn't need to be a part of this conversation.

"We come from two very different worlds," Deborah stated.

I'd known as much since the first time I met her. It may have been what drew me to her in the first place. Again, I kept that thought to myself. Instead, I glanced around the interior of the room we sat in and then let my gaze fall back to her, saying, "But we're in the same world right now."

The room fell silent as we gazed at one another. No words were needed as the air crackled around us.

I leaned in, as did Deborah, our lips closing in on one another's … but just before they touch the goddamned door of the room burst open.

"Robert, man, I've been looking for you."

"What the hell do you want?" I exploded on Jack Lassiter. He was something of a friend to me; however, he'd just interrupted the most important first kiss I was about to have. I felt that even before our lips touched.

Jack's brown eyes widened in fear. "Sorry, man, but this is important."

I scowled at him. "What is important?"

Jack's stare shifted from me to Deborah, his eyes narrowing.

"Look at me," I stated, my voice low. "What is important?"

"Oh, uh, the ski trip. The one for spring break. We need your money to register."

My frown deepened as I dug into my bag, searching for my wallet. Between classwork, family bullshit, and my growing preoccupation with the woman beside me, I'd forgotten all about giving my money for the annual ski trip.

"Here," I stated, practically throwing the money at Jack.

"Thanks, man, this trip is going to be epic."

As I started to turn away from Jack, I noticed Deborah beginning to pack up her books.

"Jack hang on. Princess, are you going on the ski trip?"

She looked at me, stunned. "What?"

"The trip? Have you signed up for it?"

"No."

"Why not? It's your last chance to go."

She shook her head. "I can't it's—"

"It's on a week where there are no classes, so you won't have to study. Can't use that as an excuse." I turned to Jack, pulling more money out of my wallet. "Here. Sign her up, too. Make sure she's registered. Deborah Tate."

Jack paused, staring at me as if he didn't understand what the hell I was saying.

"Is there a problem?"

He shook his head. "No. I'll get it done."

I nodded and watched as he gave one final look between Deborah and I and left.

"Why did you do that?" Deborah questioned as soon as Jack shut the door.

"Because I wanted to."

"And you think you can just do whatever you want?"

"*Think?* I know."

She rolled her eyes, sighing as she slammed her bag closed, standing to leave.

As she brushed past me, I grabbed her arm—not tightly, but enough to stop her from exiting. "I'll see you on the slopes."

"I might have to work."

"Take the week off. You have a month before the trip, that's more than enough time to find someone to cover you, or just speak with your manager."

She sighed. "It doesn't work like that."

"Make it work like that."

Her shoulders slumped. "Is that how you live? Just bend the world to your will as you see fit?"

I looked her directly in the eye. "Yes. Especially when it's this important."

"It's a spring break trip. What's so important about it?"

"It's not the damn trip." Walking forward, until our bodies nearly touched, I moved the hand that had been holding her arm up her body to cup the left side of her cheek. And without so much as a final thought, I lowered my lips to hers, completing what we'd started before Jack interrupted.

Our lips melded together and Deborah's lips opened up, welcoming me as I knew they would. The connection sucked me in completely. The more we kissed the more I wanted to kiss, something that'd never happened to me before. With every other woman I'd been with, this part had been just a prelude to the next step. With Deborah, I could keep kissing her until both of our lips were swollen, mouths dry, and lungs bursting from deprivation of oxygen. And even then I didn't believe it would be enough. Especially, if she was going to keep moaning the way she was.

Just when it began to feel like the earth shifted beneath my feet, Deborah pulled back.

"I have to go." Her voice was just above a whisper and it sounded like the very last thing she wanted to do was leave. "To work … I have to go to work."

Nodding, I stepped back, releasing her. I watched as she turned, and with a shaky hand reached for the doorknob. I quickly reached around her, pulled the door, and held it open for her. She gave me a small smile over her shoulder before exiting.

I watched her walk away, the tightness in my chest growing with each step she took.

* * *

Deborah

What am I doing here? I questioned as I exited one of the buses that carried more than fifty of us seniors from Palo Alto to Yosemite National Park.

As I stepped down from the bus, I began looking around at the snow-capped mountains.

"Oh shi—"

"Careful," a deep voice rang out from beside me.

A strong hand caught my arm, preventing me from falling on the icy snow. I didn't need to look up to know who the voice belonged to. Even if my ears hadn't given it away, the shiver that ran through my body when he made contact already told me who it was beside me.

"I knew you'd come." He was so damn cocksure I almost wanted to turn right around, get back on the bus, and return to Palo Alto just to prove him wrong.

"That bus isn't leaving until we do, princess," he stated as if reading my mind.

I finally looked up into Robert's smirking eyes. "You don't know what I'm thinking."

"Oh, I'm sure you don't have a problem letting me know what you're thinking. How was the drive over?"

Robert hadn't been on the same bus as me. He and a few of his friends, including Jackass, or *Jack,* as was his real name, had come over a day earlier.

"It was fine. I mostly read."

He nodded. "Good. So you got all your studying out of the way. The next week you won't be thinking about anything school related."

I frowned. "You can't tell me what to do." I knew I sounded ridiculous but I felt like I needed to prove he wasn't the one in charge here.

Robert just laughed.

"Hey, Rick," he called to someone behind me. "Make sure you get all of the stuff and bring it up to the rooms. Let's get inside. Are you hungry?"

I glanced over my shoulder to see a couple of guys unloading the equipment we'd brought.

"Are they your servants? They just do whatever you tell them to?"

Robert didn't even seem perturbed by the question. He shrugged. "Not quite, but they're freshman. Only allowed on this trip with us because they'll be doing the grunt work while he have fun."

"That's not right," I stated, still looking back at the guys while being led into the large registration cabin by Robert.

"Life's not fair, princess."

I made a sound deep in my throat. "Don't I know that."

"I'm rooming with Kimmy," I stated, glancing down at the room assignment along with the key I'd been given. I didn't know Kimmy all that well but from our handful of interactions over the past fours years she seemed nice enough.

"Room 338. You're one floor below me."

Oddly, that brought me a modicum of relief. Why, I wasn't quite sure, however.

"Did you bring your own skis or do you need to rent a pair?" Robert asked after we'd all settled into our rooms and then had a hearty lunch in the resort's huge dining area.

I grunted. "I'm not skiing," I insisted.

"How can you come on a ski trip and not ski?"

"You practically forced me into this trip."

Robert gave me a look. "You and I both know I didn't *force* you to do anything you didn't want to do. If you didn't want to be here you wouldn't."

I lifted my chin, folded my arms across my chest, and stated, "I would've felt bad for wasting your money."

To my surprise, Robert bent over, laughing. The deep sound moved something in me and I found myself giggling as well.

"You don't give a shit about wasting my money."

I lowered my head, continuing to laugh. "Whatever. Yeah, so, I wanted to come. Happy now?"

"Not quite, but we're getting there."

I didn't have time to ask him what he meant before he was dragging me out the door, and over to the cabin to rent a pair of skis for the week.

"I've never done this before," I stated nervously, as he helped me into my skis.

"Really? I couldn't tell," he responded sarcastically.

"Asshole."

He chuckled. "I've been called far worse, princess."

"I'm sure you have."

"We can do the bunny slopes a few times until you get used to the feel of these."

"Isn't skiing dangerous? Like, haven't people been killed skiing into trees?" I glanced around at the steep mountains, biting my lower lip.

"I won't let anything happen to you," Robert said.

I was taken aback by the sharpness of his tone, and when I looked into his eyes I could tell that he meant it. And God only knows why, but I believed him. Like Robert Townsend could move a planted tree on sheer will and desire alone if he needed to, just to keep me safe.

I lowered my head, choosing to stare at the white snow as the sun shone off of it. The natural scenery around us, gorgeous as it was, actually felt less hypnotizing than the gleam in Robert's eyes.

"Let's get started," he urged after a few heartbeats of silence.

And so began my first ski lesson.

CHAPTER 7

hen
Robert

"What the hell happened?" I growled at the two idiots who'd rushed into the resort's dining room to inform me Deborah had had an accident. The one fucking time I let her out of my sight in the five days we'd been there something goes wrong. I knew I shouldn't have let her ski with Kimmy and the other girls.

"We don't know."

"What the hell do you mean you don't know?" I raged, running ahead of the two numbskulls, heading in the direction of the resort's emergency services cabin. "She better not be seriously injured, or I swear to God—"

I stopped short as we reached the door of the emergency services cabin. Yanking it open, I brushed past the person who'd been trying to exit and urgently looked around. I sighed, somewhat feeling relieved when I saw Deborah sitting up, talking with one of the workers of the resort.

I walked around the chairs that were lined up around the waiting area, to get to the cot where she was sitting.

"What happened?" I demanded as soon as I reached them.

"Robert," Deborah called, surprised.

I moved to her side, kneeling down. "What happened?"

She gave me an embarrassed smile.

"Deborah tried to bite off more than she could chew."

I looked to the far side of the cot to see a smiling Kimmy. Her blonde locks were pulled back in a long braid, and her black and blue ski outfit held splotches of dampness from melted snow.

"She tried to take on the bigger slopes."

I frowned, pinning Kimmy with my gaze. "You were supposed to be watching her." I'd given Kimmy specific instructions not to let Deborah get in over her head.

"Watching me? I'm not a child. We were having fun," Deborah insisted.

I returned my gaze to her but didn't respond. Instead, I let my eyes scan the entirety of Deborah's body. That was when I saw her injury. Propped up on a few pillows was her right leg, ice packs covering her ankle.

"It's just a sprain, looks like," the resort worker stated.

"Are you certified?" I questioned, glaring at him.

His eyes widened as if he was actually shocked that I'd ask his qualifications.

"Robert," Deborah called, tugging at my arm. "Let him do his job. John, has been very nice to me and my ankle isn't throbbing in pain any longer so he must be doing something right."

Reluctantly, I turned back to look at Deborah. "I knew I shouldn't have left you."

She tilted her head.

"Now that you're here, I'm going to head to the cabin to get some-thing to eat. Deb, do you want anything?" Kimmy asked, standing.

Deborah shook her head. "I'm fine. John says I'll be here another hour or so and then I get go back to the room."

"I'll take her back," I insisted, cutting off whatever Kimmy had been about to say.

Kimmy headed off.

"You were mean to her."

"She shouldn't have let you get on slopes you weren't ready for."

"She's not my babysitter, and like I said, we were having fun. I'm just upset I ruined it," she pouted.

"You didn't ruin anything," I reassured.

"The good news is I'll only have to be laid up for day and a half seeing as how we leave the day after tomorrow."

"You won't be by yourself."

"I can't ask you to stay inside with me. This is your last spring break of college. You should enjoy it."

"I *am* enjoying it." The only reason I'd had any fun on this trip at all was because I'd spent most of my time with Deborah, teaching her how to ski. I was way more advanced than she was and I loved skiing, and anything outdoors really, but seeing her eyes light up when she conquered a new slope had been the highlight of the entire trip. I didn't need much else, right then.

* * *

"You didn't have to stay with me this whole time. I bet you missed hitting the slopes one final time."

"Not even a little bit," I responded, sincerely, staring into Deborah's blue eyes. The blue in her eyes was illuminated even more due to the roaring fire behind us. We were sitting in the cozy lounge area of the cabin. Most of the others that'd come on this trip were on the slopes for one last time but I couldn't be bothered. Not when Deborah was here. The snow-covered mountains couldn't compare to this view.

"You say that as if you mean it." Her voice was softer than usual, almost unsure. She didn't usually display her vulnerability, which was probably why when she did it yanked at every nerve ending inside of my chest.

I inched closer to her, throwing my arm over the back of the love seat we sat on, facing one another.

"I do mean it."

Frowning, she dropped her gaze down toward the floor before peering up at me, out of the corner of her eye. "Don't try to woo me. I'm not Tracey or one of the other legions of women you've slept with."

I lifted an eyebrow. "Legions? My reputation precedes me, huh?"

Her gaze shifted back to me.

"Listen princess, I don't need to *woo* anyone. I damn sure don't need to buy a woman's interest by bringing her on a ski trip and ignoring all of my so-called friends. And I sure as hell don't need to be scared shitless when I hear that woman has been injured while skiing just to get in her pants." I moved closer, taking her chin between my thumb and forefinger. "So, you can drop the attitude, admit you like me as much as I like you, and we can get past all the pretense."

Her pink lips parted on a tiny gasp and I seized the moment.

Inching forward, I trapped her lips in a kiss that cemented my words. I felt the shiver that ran through Deborah's body and my cock instantly grew hard. I'd meant it when I said I didn't need to work hard to get a woman, but I've also never felt this intensely about *any* woman. Especially one I hadn't taken to bed yet.

Deborah's soft lips opened, on a sigh, surrendering to the kiss, to me. That awareness made me hotter than I'd ever been. I moved closer, trying to remind myself that, despite the fact we were alone, we were still in a public space. I couldn't take her right then and there. But dammit I wanted to.

I pulled back to tell her just that when I heard, "Isn't this quite cozy?"

My eyes instantly narrowed as I twisted around to see Jack Lassiter staring down on us. He was accompanied by a few of our other friends who'd gone out on the slopes with him. However, he was the only one who felt it necessary to interrupt an obviously private moment.

"Can I fucking help you?" I growled.

"Me?" he questioned, pressing a hand to his chest. "The guys and I were just wondering where you've been, and then we come in here and low and behold."

His tone immediately pissed me off. I stood up, getting closer, in his face. "Low and fucking behold," I repeated, my voice low, fists at my side, clenching. I knew Jack to be a pompous son of a bitch. Hell, we all were, but something about the way he looked at Deborah, the tone of his voice and that stupid fucking smirk he wore as if he had a secret only he knew. All of it made me want to put my fist through his face, but I restrained myself.

"Hey, man," he stated, stepping back and holding his hands up. He still wore that smirk, however. "I was just asking. You've been MIA most of this week. Then we come in here and find you lip locked with her." He gestured to Deborah.

"With her?" I repeated, again not liking his tone.

"Yeah, a fucking stripper no less."

The final word was barely out of his mouth before he was stumbling backward from a right hook I sent to his jaw. And just as I'd always suspected, Jack was a bigger pussy than most. He crumpled to the floor faster than a house of cards.

"What the hell?" he yelped, holding his jaw.

"Watch your fucking mouth," I growled.

"Robert!" I heard Deborah yell from behind me but I kept my gaze trained on Jack.

"Man, what the fuck is your problem?" Jack implored, stumbling as he rose from the floor. "She's—"

"You don't know when to fucking quit!" I grabbed Jack by the thick parka he had on and pushed him through the back door of the cabin until we were both out in the night air.

"What's your problem?" he shouted, stumbling in the snow.

"You. You're my fucking problem right now!" I growled.

"No, she's your problem!" He pointed inside. "She's not one of us, man! She's white trash!" he yelled, and ducked as I took another swing at him.

I missed his jaw that time because he covered his face, but the blow still sent him stumbling to the ground.

"Stay the fuck down!" I growled, lifting my booted foot to press against his chest, trapping him to the ground. "You talk too fucking much." Pressing my foot down harder, I leaned in closer. "I've threatened my own flesh and blood over that woman. Don't think I'll have any hesitation breaking everything you love over her, either."

"Robert, let him up. Come on, man, you know how Jack likes to mess around!" one of our friends, Brandon, said from behind me.

It wasn't Brandon's words that finally got me to release Jack. It was the fact that spending even another moment with him was taking away time that I could be spending gazing into Deborah's eyes. I had better things to do.

That reminder spurred me to remove my foot from Jack's chest, spin on my heels, and push past the group of four or five guys that'd followed us out of the cabin.

I turned toward the loveseat we'd been sitting on but she was gone. I looked around the room and my eyes landed on Kimmy.

"Where is she?" I questioned, moving over to Kimmy. Her startled expression didn't discourage me.

"Who— Oh, Deborah?"

I gave her a scowl. Who the hell else would I be talking about?

"I helped her up to our room after you got into it with Jack."

I didn't wait for her to finish her sentence. "You're going to have to sleep somewhere else tonight."

"What? That's my room!"

"Not tonight," I tossed over my shoulder as I headed in the direction of the stairs, taking them two at a time. For the past week, Deborah had been sharing a room with Kimmy. I'd kept my composure, made sure not to pressure her to share my room with me or vice versa, because I knew she wasn't ready for it, but all of that was over and done with. Kimmy would need to find another place to sleep that night because I had business to take care of.

"What do you want?" Deborah demanded as soon as I barged in the room, slamming and locking the door behind me. Her eyes narrowed to slits.

"What the hell are you pissed at me for?" I questioned just as angrily.

"For embarrassing the hell out of me like that!"

"*I* embarrassed *you*?" I pressed, moving closer and snatching the folded clothes she had in her hand, tossing them to the chair where her opened suitcase sat.

"Yes! You and Jackass!"

I almost grinned at the nickname she'd given Jack but I didn't.

"And just so we're clear, I'm not a damn stripper. I'm a cocktail waitress," she stated as if it made any difference to me.

"You could tell me you tamed lions for a living and I'd believe you," I responded, inching closer, wrapping my hands around her waist. It was a risky move. She was pissed. The tight set of her mouth and single wrinkle in her forehead told me that. However, she was also irresistible at that moment.

"I don't like cats."

At that I did respond with a chuckle.

"No cats, got it," I murmured, nuzzling the side of her neck with my nose. "What else don't you like?" I pressed my growing hard-on against her abdomen. A rush of energy shot through me when she responded by pressing her body against mine.

"Jackass. I don't like him." Her voice was airy, just above a whisper.

"Me either." I pressed a kiss to her neck and then another. "What else?"

"Um … sp-sprained ankles. I-I don't like those," she stammered as I continued to press kisses to the side of her neck and cupped her cheeks.

I brushed my lips against hers. A small sigh escaped her lips.

"Why not?"

"B-because it hurts to stand for too long."

I stepped back, remembering her injury. "That's not a problem."

Scooping her up in my arms, I swiftly carried her to the bottom bed of the bunk beds that were in the room. Wouldn't have been my first choice but I had to make due with what was available.

"How's your ankle?" I asked, staring down into her half-closed eyes, our lips barely touching as I hovered over her.

"Better." She surprised me by lifting her head and capturing my lips.

My surprise didn't last for too long, however, as I parted my lips, allowing myself to experience the feel of our mouths tasting one another. I reached down, moving my hand underneath the turtleneck shirt she wore, feeling the tender skin of her waist and abdomen.

"I'm going to take your shirt off now," I stated, pulling back from her lips. Kissing was no longer enough and I needed to make it clear my intentions for that night.

"The door—"

"Is locked. No one's walking in on us," I reassured. I paused for a moment, ensuring that she was okay with what was about to happen.

A slight tilt of her head gave me the go ahead.

"Fuck!" I cursed when I sat up and smacked my head against the wooden boards of the top bunk.

Deborah giggled, but then asked, "Are you okay?"

"I fucking hate bunk beds. Next time we'll have more room." The next time we were in this position, would be in my bed where we had more than enough room to explore one another's bodies. But I didn't have time to think about that. I needed to concentrate on the woman in front of me at that moment.

Reaching down, I pulled Deborah's shirt free from her body, leaving her nude from the waist up, save for the black bra she wore. I licked my lips before leaning down and outlining the tops of her breasts with my tongue. I moaned against the feel of her soft, supple skin.

Her chest rose as she arched her back slightly, obviously turned on.

"I'm going to take off your bra now," I informed her, looking up into her eyes.

She nodded, and I moved my hands around to the back clasp, undoing the bind that hid her breasts from me. I glanced up at her face. She bit her lower lip, uncertain. I swallowed, wanting to tell her she needn't be nervous. She was the most beautiful thing I'd ever seen. But words failed me. Action would have to do.

I lowered my head to her breast, encircling her taut nipple with my lips. Her body reacted instantly, jerking upward, her back arching, but I wouldn't let up. She tasted too sweet. The little moans that escaped her mouth were too enticing for me not to keep trying to pull them from her. I licked a line down the middle of her breasts before moving over to give the second one the same treatment as the first.

My cock attempted to bust through the zipper of my jeans and yet I couldn't stop. I squeezed with my hands, pleased to see her breasts fit perfectly into them.

"Robert," she let out on a whisper-moan, her head twisting from side to side against the pillows on the bed.

I heard the need in her voice. She needed more. I did too.

Forcing myself to pull away, I carefully sat back on my haunches, mindful of the damn top bunk. Next, I removed the sweater I'd been wearing along with the T-shirt I had on underneath before pressing our bodies together again, so I could capture her lips.

Deborah's hands went to my hair. Enjoying the feel of her hands on me, I groaned against her lips.

"Do you want me to make you feel good?" I questioned before dipping my head into the crook of her neck, nuzzling the sensitive skin there.

"Please," she begged.

My cock jumped against my pants, at the need and want I heard in her voice. At that point, it was either remove the rest of our clothing or come in my jeans.

I lifted, my hands going to the buttons of Deborah's jeans. I made quick work of undoing the button and zipper, pulling her pants down to reveal her smooth legs. The only thing that stood between me and ecstasy were the cotton panties she wore. My hands went to the waistband of her panties and she lifted her hips, aiding me in pulling them down to meet her jeans. After completely removing her clothing, I sat back again, admiring her taut body.

"I'm going to taste you."

Her eyes widened and forehead wrinkled. She was confused. Had no man ever gone down on her before? It would be my pleasure to be her first.

Running my hand over the wiry hairs that covered her mound, I noted they were the same brunette color as the hair on her head. I nudged her legs farther apart before throwing them over my shoulders as I bent down to get even with her weeping core.

"Rob—" Deborah called before breaking off into a loud moan when my tongue first brushed against her swollen nub.

A jolt of electricity pushed through my veins at hearing my name ripping from her lips only for it to break off into the sexiest moan I'd ever heard. My hunger increased tenfold and I refused to hold back any longer. I ate like a man starving, licking at the delicate folds of her pussy lips, savoring and memorizing each time her moans grew loud and insistent or soft and relaxed. I got into a rhythm, bringing her up high with the intensity of the way my tongue stroked her clitoris only to pull back before she got too close to the edge. Because while this woman made me wild with passion and need, I was running the show. She wouldn't come until I was good and ready for her to. I was ensuring she would never forget this night, nor would she ever think I paid this kind of attention to any other woman.

Try and fight it as I might, the fact that she was so aware of my reputation with other girls on campus bothered me. I didn't want her thinking of me and any other woman. Because the thought of her with any other guy, before or after me, nearly drove me crazy. Something had happened to me over the past week, and safe to say, that Deborah Tate had me completely under her spell.

Strange thing is, though, I highly doubt she even realized it.

Her moans grew insistent and I felt her thighs begin to tremble over my shoulders. She was ready. I inserted a finger into her wetness and captured her distended button with my lips, using my tongue to stroke her to her orgasm.

Her moans and screams were music to my ears. I hardly wanted to stop but I needed to. My cock was way past feeling uncomfortable still zipped up. Lowering her legs to the bed, I removed a latex condom from my wallet, which had been in my back pocket. I tossed my wallet to the floor and quickly undid my jeans, sliding them down along with my underwear.

"Wh-what is that?" Deborah questioned from her position on the bed.

My gaze went to what she was staring at in my hand. "Condom."

"Oh." She bit her lower lip. "For protection, right. So I won't get pregnant."

Shit. My cock actually jumped at the mention of her pregnant with my child. What the fuck was happening?

"Y-yes," I responded, ripping the condom wrapper open and placing it over the tip of my dick. I ran the condom down the stem of my cock before moving back to the bed.

I paused just after lining my cock up with her opening, and stared up into her eyes. "You know this makes you mine, right?" The words fell from my mouth before I even knew they were there.

"Yours?"

"Mine. As in no other fucking man can touch you." The first time in my life I'd made a declaration like that.

"That means your mine, too, then."

My dick jumped again. The idea of being hers was as enticing as she belonging to me. I didn't mind it at all.

Instead of responding verbally, I began sliding into her core, slowly at first, straining every muscle in my body, forcing myself to go slow. *I won't rush our first time together.* Just as I had that thought, I stilled completely when I met resistance.

I pinned Deborah with my eyes, our gazes meeting before she averted her eyes.

"Look at me," I ordered.

Her eyes slid back to me.

"Are … is this your first time?" I could barely get the question out.

She hesitated, but eventually nodded.

"Shit!"

"It's not—" She broke off, starting to sit up.

"No," I stopped her. "I wish I had known. I would've made this so much better for you." I wasn't a roses and chocolate kind of guy but for her I would've been.

"I-I don't need that other stuff," she said. Her hand went to cup my cheek, soothing me. I nuzzled my cheek against her hand. She was serious, but I still wished I would've known. I made a mental note for the next time to do this right.

"I'll take it slow."

I began sliding in, pushing through the resistance I felt. "Don't tighten up. Relax. Breathe, Princess," I cooed, working to ease her tension as well as mine. Eventually, she relaxed and I slid deeper inside of her until I was all of the way in.

I lowered my lips to hers, kissing her with all of the passion coursing through my body in that moment. "You feel so fucking good," I stated against her lips. "Am I hurting you?"

She shook her head. "N-no … Robert …" she called me, not knowing what she needed. Her hands went to my shoulders, pulling me into her. I knew what she needed. What we both needed.

I pulled halfway out of her before pushing back in.

"Oh!" she yelped, her back arching.

"Was that a scream of pleasure or pain?" I knew the answer already but needed to hear the words.

"Pl-pleasure," she panted.

"Good."

I pulled out, almost completely that time, and slowly pushed back in until our pelvises connected. I moved slowly before quickening my pace. My hands went to Deborah's small waist as my hips took control, pistoning in and out of her body, causing the entire bunk bed to shake.

Deborah's legs raised, circling my waist as I stared down at her. Our eyes never left one another's. We were communicating with our bodies and our gazes. This woman, the same one I'd watched from afar for four years, was mine now.

"Robert!" she shouted as she came.

"Goddamn!" I moaned when her pussy muscles clamped down

around my thrusting cock. Not long after her climax I was came furiously, harder than I'd ever come.

I grunted and convulsed, her pussy muscles milking every drop of semen from my loins. I spilled into the condom knowing one day that there would be no barrier between us and that Deborah Tate would eventually become Deborah Townsend.

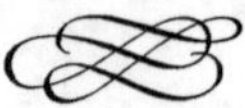

*R*obert

"Tell me about your parents."

Deborah lifted her head, giving me a quizzical look. We were still in bed, her closest to the wall, me on the outer edge. My arm was draped across her bare midsection, stroking her flat abdomen. Both naked as the day we were born. I was doing my best to refrain from taking her again. She'd be sore and I didn't want to cause her too much discomfort her first night.

"My parents?"

"Yeah, the people who raised you. Mom and dad."

She lowered her head back to my shoulder. "You first."

I chuckled. I didn't tell people about my parents. Most either thought they already knew everything there was to know given the status of my family's name. While others worked to get whatever inside information they'd think I'd give so they could run back to their own social circles or business associates with all of the nitty gritty details. Fuck that and fuck them.

But this was Deborah. The woman who would one day be my wife. She might as well learn the truth straight from me.

"My father's an asshole and my mother's a weak-willed social climber who thought she lucked out when he asked her to marry him. Aside from that, they're great."

Deborah lifted her head, staring at me, looking deeply into my eyes. I tucked my arm under my head.

I didn't shutter my gaze or close myself off from her like I did to the rest of the world. Like I'd learned to do from a very early age.

"He hit you."

I nodded even though it wasn't a question.

"Often," I replied.

"Does he still?"

I shook my head. "By the time I reached sixteen, I was two inches taller than he was. He's also slowed down and weakened from all of the extra weight he's put on over the years. One night he went to hit me and I caught his arm, twisting it until it nearly broke. That was the last time he tried to hit me or my brother."

"Jason, right? That's your brother's name."

I nodded again.

"Your mother never tried to stop him? Or leave him?"

I made a sound of disbelief at the back of my throat. "She might have tried a long time ago when we were young but I can't ever remember it. She's not a bad mother, per se, but was broken down by his verbal abuse long ago. She would stick up for us or try to keep us out of trouble from time to time."

"Then why do you call her a social climber?"

"Because as much as she might have disliked my father's treatment of all of us, she had no problem putting on a smile for all of her friends, throwing the most lavish events at Townsend Manor and all that shit."

It was silent for a few moments.

"Jason got it the worst, though." I looked up at Deborah. "My father targeted him."

"Why?"

I shrugged. "Who fucking knows. Jason always had trouble in school. He hated reading, got terrible grades, and our father never let up on him about it."

My chest tightened over the guilt I felt. Academics, sports, making friends had always come naturally to me. It was almost too easy, so much so, that I turned things like making friends or getting girls into a game just to make it fun. But Jason struggled in every area. He was almost my total opposite.

"My father died when I was just eleven years old."

It wasn't her words that surprised me but the way she'd said them. The tenderness she used when speaking the words *my father.* She'd loved him.

"How?"

"On the mountain there was very little work except working in the mines."

The mountain. It was how she referred to where she grew up.

"But it was dangerous work. I remember when the layoffs started happening. My mother was terrified Daddy would lose his job. But he got lucky … or so we thought. After the first round of layoffs, he still had a job. We were grateful. Unfortunately, it was short lived. A month later, there was an accident. My father and two other workers got caught in a collapse. It took them two weeks to dig their bodies out. We were comforted by the fact that he probably died immediately in the collapse, and didn't suffer."

Lifting my head, I pressed a kiss to her lips. Not from passion but to comfort her.

She blinked away the tears that had accumulated in her eyes and laid her head back on my chest. My hand rose to her hair, stroking it. This was the most intimacy I'd ever shared with a woman, and our being nude had nothing to do with it.

"What about your mother?"

"She was devastated after my father died. They'd been together since they were seventeen. But she knew she needed to take care of me. So she searched and searched for extra work, eventually getting a job at a store in the next town over. It took her forty-five minutes to walk there each day but she did it. She also took any odd jobs she could find. Babysitting, cleaning houses, selling things she'd made. Whatever she could do to make extra money for us, she did it."

"She sounds like an amazing woman."

I felt Deborah smile against my chest. "She was. She and my father always put me first. When I was really young, they would beg, borrow, or steal books they could find to help me learn to read. They always made sure I went to school because they saw it as a way off the mountain, as they used to say. It wasn't until just before the end of my junior year of high school that my mother revealed the biggest secret she'd kept for years."

"What was it?" I inquired, intrigued to learn about this obviously remarkable woman.

"After my father's death, every family member we had started coming around asking my mother what she was going to do with the life insurance money. She told them that they'd never gotten life insurance. A few weeks before the summer after junior year my mother told me the truth. She told me that they had in fact had a policy—albeit a small one, and when she'd received the check, she'd taken it to a bank to open a savings account in my name, depositing it all. For six years it just sat there. My senior year I did a sort of exchange program where I moved in with a family in a wealthier part of Kentucky to go to their high school. There I had access to guidance counselors who walked me through the process of applying to college and for scholarships.

"Once I was accepted to Stanford my mother told me I was going come hell or high water. The money from the insurance policy paid a monthly stipend to the family I stayed with, and was just enough for my plane ticket and incidentals to move to Palo Alto."

"I bet she's proud of you."

Deborah shrugged. "I hope so." She sat up again, peering down at me. "She died last year of lung cancer. I didn't even know she was sick. A relative of mine told me she made them promise not to tell me because she didn't want me going back home for anything."

I reached up and wiped away the tear that'd landed on her cheek. Swallowing I lifted my head and pressed a kiss to her forehead, pulling her back against my chest. Her silent cries against my chest tore me apart. I'd give anything to make her stop hurting. I didn't know what it was like to have parents who loved you so much they'd sacrifice their own happiness and well-being, but I was glad she did.

She deserved at least that much.

I held her until she stopped weeping, wiping away the tears on her cheeks. And because I needed to be inside of her again, I rotated our bodies so that she was on her back underneath me, her arms raised, clutching at my shoulders. She needed me as much as I needed her. Our second round of lovemaking wasn't hurried or rushed in the least. Once I sheathed myself with a second condom from my wallet, I slowly slid inside of her, watching her with every movement.

Even when it pained me, my body wanting to go deeper, harder, faster, I took my time, making sure I gave Deborah what she needed. I couldn't replace what she'd lost in the past, but I could show her that her parents' sacrifices had been worth it. That was because they drilled into her the value of education and put their money where their mouth was, she ended up at one of the most prestigious universities in the world. And more importantly, she'd run into me. The man who would spend the rest of my life making sure she never went without anything ever again. And that especially included feeling loved and adored.

We came together that second time, as well, and once we did, I slid from Deborah's body, but wrapped my arms around her, keeping her to my side.

That night I had the most vivid dream in my life. I dreamt of four little boys who grew into four dynamic and strong men. Men I'd be a fool not to be proud of.

* * *

Deborah

I felt him watching me before I even opened my eyes. Yet, I didn't feel creeped out. Slowly I blinked my eyes open, trying to adjust to the morning sun. I found those dark brown eyes of his and gasped. They were so intense. His eyes could tell an entire story without him having to open his mouth. That scared the hell out of me.

"Our oldest son will have your eyes."

It took way too long for me to even register what he'd just said.

I sat up on my elbow, the thin, white sheet slipping from my body, revealing my nakedness. "What?"

Robert's eyes had roamed down to my bared breasts, his face tightening with the same hunger that had been present the night before.

"What did you just say?" I insisted, covering myself, though that didn't deter his gaze at all. It was almost as if he could see right through the sheet.

Finally, his eyes rose to meet mine, again stealing air from my lungs with just a look. "I said, our eldest son will have your blue eyes."

"Oldest son?" He had to be crazy.

"Yes. Four boys altogether."

He was completely serious.

I jumped up from the bed, stumbling over his long, athletic build, frantically reaching for my black robe to cover myself. I couldn't be in the same room with him and naked without my body responding. And the absolute last thing I needed right then was for my body to betray me.

"What's wrong?" he questioned as if he hadn't just said the most insane thing in the world.

"You need to leave," I insisted.

He moved slowly but with intention, the tight muscles from all of the outdoor activities he'd told me he enjoyed evident on his frame.

Swallowing, I averted my eyes, taking a step back, until I bumped into the chair that held my suitcase.

"Why?"

"Because you're talking crazy. And put some clothes on!" I picked up his pants from the previous day and thrust them in his direction, still not looking at him.

I sighed in relief a little when he took the clothing from my hand. I heard rustling, indicating he was redressing himself. Of course, my relief wasn't to last too long.

"I'm not going anywhere until you explain yourself." His voice was so deep and domineering, I almost felt chastised and pulled to him at the same time. But I couldn't budge.

"Explain myself? I'm not your child and you are not my superior of any kind. I don't need to *explain* myself to you."

He shook his head. "Of course you're not my child. I just told you, you and I are going to have four children *together*. But that does make you my woman so I need an explanation."

My eyes widened. "Oh my god! Again with the children. What the hell is that about?"

He gave a casual shrug. "I had a dream."

"Dream? Seriously."

He nodded as if it were the most normal thing in the world.

"If you think I waited all of these years to lose my virginity just so I could throw away my Stanford education to settle down and be some rich guy's wife and a mother to his kids, you're sadly mistaken!" I protested angrily. It wasn't that I was opposed to marrying or becoming a mother, but I wasn't even twenty-two years old. We hadn't graduated college yet. And he was so sure. How could anyone be that damn sure of anything?

"You're overreacting."

The anger that moved through my body was uncanny. Not only had he said the worst thing you can say to any woman when we're upset, the cavalier and casual way he'd said it pissed me off even more.

"Get out!" I yelled.

Robert's scowl, while intimidating to most, I'm certain, did little to dissuade my anger.

"I'm not going any fucking where."

"Get the hell out! I am not talking to you about this anymore." I glanced at the clock on the wooden, circular table in the corner of the room. "We have to be on the bus in an hour. I need to pack and I don't want to look at you anymore." At that point, I wasn't even certain why I was so angry. I just knew I was.

"I said I'm not going any goddamn where. At no point did I ever say you needed to quit on your professional goals or sacrifice the education you've worked so diligently for."

I was too busy throwing clothes into my suitcase to respond to him.

"Deborah!" He reached for my wrist, halting my movements.

"I—"

"Robert!" someone called from the opposite end of the locked door, knocking loudly.

"Fuck! What?" he yelled, responding to the male on the other side.

I didn't recognize the voice.

"Open up, man. We've been looking for you. It's an emergency."

Robert growled, giving me one last glare, as if to say this wasn't over, before releasing his hold on my wrist and moving to the door. He yanked it open. "What?" he barked at the guy on the other side.

As soon as I saw his face, I recognized him. He was one of the freshman that'd accompanied us on the trip but I couldn't recall his name. I didn't waste time trying to, either; I went back to packing. Out of the corner of my eye I saw the guy lean in and say something low in Robert's ear.

"Shit!"

That one curse had me startled, alarm bells shooting through my body. Something wasn't right, and in spite of my earlier anger, I felt the deepest urge to comfort him. But he turned and gave me a sharp look, stopping me in my tracks.

"I have to go, but this isn't over." It sounded like a threat, a warning, and a promise.

My body shivered and my lips parted to ask him what it was that had him leaving so abruptly. Call me crazy, but my instincts were telling me that something was seriously wrong for him to drop the conversation we'd been having and to rush out. However, before any words could come out, he was gone and I was left standing in my empty room, missing his presence just that quickly.

I didn't know it then, but it would be another five years before I had contact with Robert Townsend again.

CHAPTER 9

*1*979
Deborah

"I don't understand why we had to have lunch here," Cohen stated as he glanced around at the crystal chandeliers lining the roof of the Crown Jewel hotel's restaurant we were sitting in.

I frowned, already annoyed by his tone. "Because this place is only a few blocks from my job and I love the food here," I retorted rather tersely.

However, Cohen didn't seem to pick up on it, or not care about my attitude at the moment.

"This place is ridiculously overpriced. The only people who come here are the ones who want to be seen or make everyone else believe they have money."

I narrowed my gaze, unsure of whether or not my boyfriend of the last two years had intentionally just called me some sort of social climber.

"Wasn't your sister's engagement party held here just a few months ago?" I sweetly reminded him, smiling as I stared into his hazel eyes.

His already present frown deepened as he shifted uncomfortably in his chair. "Don't remind me. Jonathan and his family just *had* to pay for the best," he scoffed.

"You know, for someone who supposedly doesn't like the well-to-do, you talk a lot about what other people do with their own money quite often," I noted out loud, while unfolding the white linen napkin and placing it in my lap.

Truth be told, Cohen's family wasn't poor by any means. His father had inherited his grandfather's luggage company, and while the company had taken a turn for the worst in recent years, Cohen had grown up in Williamsport's upper-middle class circles. But now, as a student teacher of economics at Williamsport University, he spent a great deal of his free time railing against the rich and elite society. And while the commonality of our views on issues of discrepancies in socioeconomics, education, and poverty in our society had originally drawn us together, I didn't need to hear about it when all I wanted to do was enjoy an hour-long lunch with my boyfriend. Especially, when I was in the middle of a hectic work day.

"Thank you," I lifted my head, telling the waiter who'd brought out our food.

Cohen waited until our waiter left to respond to my earlier comment. "I merely talk about the inequalities as I see them in society."

I lifted an eyebrow as my gaze dropped down to the sirloin steak on his plate, as he sliced through it before lifting it to his mouth. He talked a big game about hating disparity, poverty, and loathing everything he called *haughty,* but he had no problem indulging in those things when it suited him.

"You used to agree with me on these issues," he casually reminded me as he lifted a forkful of steamed, seasonal vegetable to his mouth.

I sighed. "I still agree."

"But you come to places like this for lunch."

"Like I already said, it's close to my job and I have to get back in …" I lifted my right wrist, peering at the time, "thirty minutes."

"Of course, your job," he muttered, but I heard the sneer in his voice.

"What's wrong with my job?" My hackles were up.

He shrugged, looking down at his plate. "Nothing. It's just that ever since you got that promotion and big raise you've changed."

I rolled my eyes but continued chewing the steamed trout I'd ordered for my lunch, before wiping my mouth with the napkin. I briefly debated on whether or not I should even respond. Ever since I'd been promoted six months prior to the supervisory role of heading up my own team in the finance department at Glamour Cosmetics, Cohen had been making little digs at every opportunity he could. At first I just shrugged it off as minor jealousy. I was moving along in my career while he was still working toward his PhD and teaching freshman-level macroeconomics classes. I didn't begrudge him his annoyance, in the beginning, but now it was getting real old.

"The only thing that's changed is my title at work." *And the amount of money in my paycheck, and the responsibilities of my job.* But I didn't feel like I needed to add that in.

"Exactly," he came back with. "Your *title* is oh so important now. It's like you feel like your *title* makes you better than everyone else. You're becoming one of *them.*"

I didn't have to ask who "them" were. When he said it in that tone, with that irritated expression on his face, he was referring to wealthy people.

"How so?" I questioned, needing him to give me an example of what he meant.

"Like the other night. We were supposed to go out to that jazz club you like but you stood me up."

"I didn't stand you up. I called you well ahead of time and informed you that our company's CFO personally invited me and a few others out to dinner. There was no way I could turn that down. He's the man who has the ability to influence my career for years to come." Standing up implied that I'd just not shown up ... at least, that's what it meant to me. That hadn't been the case at all.

"See what I mean? The Deborah Tate I met four years ago would've told the CFO to go screw himself."

I frowned as I stared across the table. Cohen and I had been friends for a couple of years before we started dating. I'd gone to an economics seminar on Williamsport University's campus about a year after moving to the city. I'd been invited by a work colleague. And while Cohen and I shared similar beliefs on inequality, I don't know what ever had given him the impression that I'd tell the head of my department to go screw himself.

"Maybe we just see things differently," I said, raising the glass of sweet tea to my lips, sipping from the plastic straw.

"What's that supposed to mean?" His tone was defensive, and while I hadn't meant to put him on the defense, I wouldn't back down from it either.

"Exactly what I said. I happen to like my job. And yes, I want to succeed in it and grow with my career, and increase my salary. Women throughout history did not fight for the right to vote, better work opportunities, and more equitable pay … hell, things we're *still* fighting for, just for me to be ashamed of my ambition." Unlike Cohen, I wasn't born with life handed to me. He was five years older than my nearly twenty-seven years. He'd been able to take time off between college and graduate school to backpack through Europe. From the moment I left Stanford, I'd hit the ground running, and as a result, had received two promotions within the last five years, and the salary increases to match. I would never be ashamed of my accomplishments.

"You're becoming one of them. Following the crowd."

I pushed out a puff of air, knowing this conversation was leading us nowhere. "Let's change the topic before we both end up saying something we don't mean. How is your research for your dissertation coming along?"

Cohen had finally gotten his dissertation topic approved and had begun formulating studies to carry out the necessary research to complete it. Obtaining one's PhD seemed like a grueling process, and he had at least another year to go before it was completed.

"It's taking too long to find the subjects for the study. Why these people won't just take what's being offered to them is beyond me," he responded, disgusted and pouting. He continued on, complaining about how all of his research participants were just looking for a hand out and therefore couldn't be trusted with his precious study.

Not for the first time, I stared across the table at Cohen and tried to remember what it was that had drawn me to him in the first place. He was handsome, I would give him that. With his somewhat shaggy blond hair, hazel eyes, and square jaw. And I wouldn't lie, I also liked the fact that he was six foot one, towering over me by a few inches. And like I said, we had some of the same values in common, but whereas I considered myself a go-getter, Cohen had a bad habit of complaining that the people around him were out to get him somehow. It was becoming a turnoff.

"Hey, I left my wallet back at the office. Can you get lunch this time?" he questioned as we finished up.

I refrained from displaying the frown that attempted to cover my face. This, too, was becoming something of a habit. And while I was a woman all about the progression of women's rights, and I *did* just get a promotion at work, granting me a much higher take home pay than what Cohen made on his student-teacher salary, I was getting a little tired of always footing the bill.

"Sure," I stated rather tersely, not wanting to make a fuss about it right then since I needed to get back to work.

"Thanks." He smiled and pressed a kiss to my cheek. "You're the best."

A year ago that little display of affection would have elicited a smile from me, but I felt nothing as I watched him out of the corner of my eye.

"I gotta go." He gave my left arm a squeeze before heading off, not even waiting for me to rise from the table after paying the check.

"See ya later," I mumbled and rolled my eyes. What was I doing with him? Maybe I was just being a bit cranky because of all of the extra hours I'd been putting in. Cohen hadn't been lying when he indicated my new promotion left me with less time for our relationship. There were weeks when I was clocking sixty or even up to seventy hours. But the cosmetic company I worked for had just acquired another smaller company, and we were working to integrate our two different systems, as well as train some of the employees of the other company on our systems. The acquisition was what had brought about the opportunity for my promotion, so I wouldn't shun it or the work. But it did leave me with less of a social life for the time being.

"Excuse me," I stated, startled. I had been so wrapped up in my own thoughts about work and Cohen that I walked right into someone. Oddly, a chill ran through me and I felt goosebumps rise along my arms. I was taken aback by my body's response, not having been cold at all in the restaurant. It was the middle of spring and a beautiful, sunny day out. It wasn't until he said my name that the puzzle pieces fell into place.

"Princess."

Not Deborah.

Princess. As if he'd been saying it regularly for the past five years.

My head snapped up and my throat constricted. "R-Robert," I stuttered. My voice was airy, just as it seemed to always be around him.

"What are you doing here?" he questioned, his dark brown eyes lingering on my face, as if trying to memorize a beautiful painting before the museum took the exhibit down.

"I-I live here," I blurted out.

His head lifted and he looked around the hotel's lobby which we were standing in.

"You live here?"

I shook my head, feeling silly. I tried to take a step back, seeing that we were nearly touching, chest to chest, but it was then I realized he still held my elbow in his grasp. Not too tightly, but firm enough that it would take a little bit of work for me to get away … if I'd wanted to. Strangely, I didn't have the inclination to move from his grasp.

"Yes, here in the city," I responded finally. "I've been here for a while."

"How long is a while?"

"Five years."

His eyebrows rose. "You moved to Williamsport right after graduation?" he surmised.

I swallowed, nodding. I glanced downward toward the floor, unwilling to allow him to see the anger in my eyes that rose when I remembered how long it'd been since I'd actually seen him. That final day of our ski trip. The morning after we'd slept together and he hurried out of the room for only God knew what.

"You've been under my nose this whole time."

The anger in his voice was what brought my gaze back to his. My head jutted backward in surprise. That was when I finally pulled myself from his embrace, stepping back in an attempt to break the spell he seemed to have me under.

"Under your nose?" I reiterated, partially to make him realize how ridiculous and possessive he sounded.

But in typical Robert Townsend fashion, shame was nowhere on his radar. He simply stared at me, nodding as if what he'd said made sense.

"Robert! We need to be going," the sharp edge of the male's voice grabbed both of our attentions.

I was able to catch an agitated expression marring Robert's handsome face before he turned, glancing over his shoulder at the man who stood a few feet behind him. The man was an inch or two shorter than Robert but much more robust. His face was reddened and looking just as agitated as Robert's had a moment ago. Despite the dissimilarities in build and age, I could see the resemblance between Robert and the man. This was Robert Townsend Sr. I'd seen his face many times in the business pages of the national and citywide newspapers.

"I'll be there in a moment."

I glanced back to Robert, whose voice had been just as short and terse as his father's. Robert Sr. didn't respond, simply turning toward the hostess.

"I need to go as well," I stated, secretly loathing the idea of parting ways with him, but also torn between the anger I felt.

"Take my card." He didn't even wait for me to respond when he grasped my hand with his and placed his business card in my palm.

"When you call just tell my assistant your name and she'll put you through."

I assumed with that he would turn and go to join his father. But I was wrong. He stood there, staring for a few heartbeats into my eyes. I was powerless to look away. And my breath hitched in my throat when a small smile touched his lips. For an instant, it felt as if I was viewing the sunrise after a long slumber. He bent low and pressed a kiss to my cheek. To any passerby it would appear innocent enough. However, the shiver that ran through my body when his lips touched my skin, and while he ran his thumb against the pulsing vein of my wrist, told an entirely different story. There was nothing innocent about this contact.

"I-I have a boyfriend," I blurted out for lack of anything else to say. I just needed to make it known that whatever he was thinking couldn't happen.

Robert pulled back, lifting an eyebrow, and an entirely different kind of smirk covered his face. "Not for much longer."

And with that, he released my hand, taking one last fill of me with his eyes before turning and strolling away to meet up with his father.

It felt like I stood there for minutes when in reality it was likely only a few seconds. At some point, my brain began functioning again and I remembered that I had a job I needed to get back to. It took the two-block walk back into my office building, a ride on the elevator up to the twelfth floor, and the three minute walk from the elevator doors, through the glass doors of the office and to my desk, for me to recall that I still held Robert's business card in my hand.

I placed the black card with silver lettering, which read Robert Townsend Vice President, Townsend Industries, on my desk. Below his name and title was his office number and extension. I ran my finger along the raised lettering on the card, and without a second thought, I brought it to my nose, secretly reveling in the faint smell of him. A mix of strength, cardamom, and cinnamon. I hadn't forgotten that smell in the half a decade that we'd been apart.

"Deborah."

I startled at the knock on my office door. Dropping the card and turning to the voice that called me, I gave a shaky, embarrassed smile.

"Jake, how can I help you?" I questioned my boss.

"Our meeting is in ten minutes. Making sure you have the files."

I nodded and smoothed down the side of my knee-length, black skirt. "Yes, they're right here." I tapped the manila folder that rested on my desk.

Jake mentioned a few more notes to be aware of for our meeting before departing. As soon as he did, I slid Robert's business card into the top drawer of my desk. I needed to focus on work and forget any notions I had of speaking to Robert Townsend again. He and I were long over.

Or so I thought.

* * *

Present

Deborah

"I don't like that Cohen guy," Destiny stated, frowning as we sat around the newly furnished conference room.

It was a Wednesday afternoon and Destiny, Michelle, Kayla, and Patience had taken time off from work or with the kids to help complete some of the last minute work that needed to get done for the shelter's soft opening the following week.

I stood from the cushioned armchair that I'd been sitting in to stretch.

"Trust me, you really won't like him once you hear the rest of the story."

"So tell us," Patience insisted.

I shook my head. "We don't have time. The story isn't going anywhere and we have a few applications to review."

Patience nodded. "I do need to complete the application for that state grant, as well as finish registering us with the local library for visits over the next few months. According to our last count, eight of the women who we'll be servicing have at least one child. We definitely want to get everyone registered for library cards."

"Of course you do," Michelle joked, teasing Patience because she was passionate about reading and starting children off with a book in their hand. "Also, there's an opening for an intern at my company. I wonder if any of the women would be interested in event planning?" Michelle mused out loud.

I shrugged. "I don't see why not. I've found that women who are down and out often want more for themselves. Usually, they just don't know how to get there and need to be presented with the opportunities."

"Amen," Kayla spoke up, waving her hand in the air, causing us all to giggle. Kayla was the most animated out of all of us.

"But before we get back to work, you could give us a little more of the scoop on Cohen, right? He really had you paying for his lunch?" Destiny questioned, sounding almost incredulous.

I chuckled, shaking my head at my own stupidity once upon a time. "He did."

"We've all done some sort of stupid for a man at one point in our lives," Patience stated. Again, we all laughed, recognizing the truth of her words.

"Hell, I married my first stupid." Destiny shuddered.

"It's okay. Tyler was only what? Twelve when you married your first husband, so he was much too young for you at the time," Kayla joked, referring to the nine year age difference between Destiny and Tyler.

Destiny swatted Kayla's hand away, laughing.

"We'll save the rest of the story for another day. We've got to finish this work day up by five or your father-in-law will be down here demanding I close up shop for the day." I rolled my eyes thinking about my husband. I'd said it jokingly but it was the truth. My husband was stingy with my time, always had been, and after forty years of marriage, I recognized he always would be.

"Heck, all five of them would be down here," Patience stated. "Especially Aaron, as if he doesn't work crazy hours."

I giggled. "He works hard so that you won't have to."

"I know it," Patience responded before covering her mouth as she yawned.

"See?" I nodded. "Being a mother of four is tiring enough."

She gave me a smile. "Excuse me, I need to use the restroom."

Rising, I watched her exit, heading toward the bathroom down the hall. I turned to see Michelle also watching Patience as she left. I didn't say anything, simply smiled and turned back to Destiny who was asking a question about the budget of our shelter.

CHAPTER 10

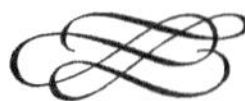

*P*atience

"Oh man," I groaned while covering my face again with my hand to smother my yawn. I was exhausted, as was typical for this particular stage in my pregnancy.

Just thinking about my pregnancy had me biting my lower lip. I still hadn't told Aaron yet, because I was not looking forward to his reaction. The fact that he'd had a business trip earlier in the week had made it a little easier to hide my exhaustion from him. But not much. We FaceTimed throughout the day, and he'd asked on multiple occasions if I wasn't feeling well. For once, it actually irritated me that he could not only run a multi-billion dollar corporation, and be the best father to our four children, but also be an extremely attentive and overprotective husband. Those were all traits I usually adored in him but not when I was holding in a secret.

Sighing, I stood from the bed and stretched, the cool material of the silk, magenta negligee I wore sliding over my sensitized nipples. I glanced down, realizing they were actually protruding through the thin material. Thoughts of my husband always elicited this type of reaction in my body. Probably why I was in my current predicament. But after missing him in our bed for two whole nights, I wasn't in a mood to ruin anything by telling him the news. That could wait for later. Right then, I needed him.

I smiled as soon as the door pushed open.

Our eyes connected. His ever present scowl had subsided to what appeared as a neutral expression to the outsider, but his eyes always told more of the story. His hazel pupils dilated and his chest fell and rose just slightly faster. His gaze dropped to my breasts, and I saw the moment he noticed my nipples. He hadn't even touched me—he was still on the far side of our bedroom and I already begun experiencing a pooling in the silk matching panties I wore.

"Kyle fall asleep?" I questioned, trying to sound casual.

Slowly, with the deliberate stalking speed of jaguar, he padded silently across the plush carpet of our bedroom. "Yes."

I swallowed. "Did he read to you tonight or you to him?" I questioned, pulling at the blanket that covered the bed.

My breath hitched when his hands clasped around my waist, tugging me backward so my body hit his chest.

"Both," he stated low, next to my ear before licking it.

I sighed and moaned, leaning back against his strength. "I missed you," I told him as my eyes floated closed while he continued to lick and bite at the column of my neck.

His left hand moved around the back of my waist, reaching underneath the negligee. "Why the fuck are you wearing underwear?" He growled, simultaneously pulling at the panties from behind, until his fingers reached my core.

I moaned.

Aaron reached up, taking a fistful of my locks into his hand and pulling them so my face turned upright to meet his.

"Answer me."

"I was checking on the babies." Andreas and Thiers, our two youngest sons, had been put down an hour prior to Kyle and Kennedy.

Aaron frowned, obviously still not liking the fact that I was wearing underwear. I was just relieved that he hadn't ripped this pair.

Lord knows I spent enough on panties because of all of the pairs he'd destroyed.

I began panting from the movement of his fingers inside of me, gliding in and out of my wetness. Reaching up on my tiptoes, I angled my face toward his. "Kiss me," I whispered.

He didn't hesitate, giving me what I want when he smashed our lips together, his hand still in my hair, holding me at just the angle he needed to take ownership of the kiss.

His hand slid from my hair to wrap my throat.

I grew wetter.

His fingers increased in speed, his thumb began gliding over my distended button, and within moments, I was coming. Just that quickly my orgasm had overwhelmed me, nearly causing my knees to buckle. Only when I was pregnant did I come that quickly.

Aaron pulled back, breaking the kiss to watch me. We both panted, needing oxygen after our exchange of energy.

"You missed me?" he questioned, his voice ragged.

"Of course."

My quick response satisfied something in his eyes. "Let me show you how much I missed you."

Within a half a breath, he'd bent me over the side of the bed, going to his knees, and I heard the distinct sound of tearing fabric.

"Dammit, Aaron!" I screeched at his impatience. He could've just pulled them down, no need to rip yet another pair of my underwear.

"Oh!" I yelped from the smack he'd given my ass.

"I told you to stop wearing underwear in the first damn place," he grunted.

I wasn't given time to respond when his strong hands spread the tops of my thighs and his mouth covered my sex. My arms folded, my head nearly hitting the mattress as my legs began trembling. His hold on the backs of my thighs was firm, not allowing me to move anywhere, even if I had wanted to. My hands twisted in the sheets, grasping for something to anchor myself to as he licked and lapped me up furiously.

I mumbled his name into the sheets of the bed, my hips thrusting backward, seeking more of the pleasure he was delivering. Again, just like the first time, my orgasm came upon me quickly. So fast, in fact, that I didn't have time to brace myself. I screeched and gasped for air as it singed the nerve endings in my body; all the while, Aaron continued to take his fill of my body, until the last tremble.

My entire body shook as I stood upright, Aaron using his hands to pull the negligee over my head. At least he didn't rip that.

He stared at the entirety of my frame, drinking me in with his eyes, adoringly. Even after four children, he still looked at my body as if it were the most precious thing in the world, and made solely for him.

"I love you," I murmured, moving closer to him and lifting the T-shirt he wore over his head. I ran my hands over the hard planes and contours of his chest, feeling the faded scars that'd been with him since his childhood. He no longer flinched when I touched them, and the tension in his body always subsided when I put my lips on them, which was what I did then.

As I kissed along the largest scar that ran across his chest, I felt his hand go to the back of my head. It was soon joined by his other hand, cupping the side of my face, pulling me to stare up at him.

"I love you so much it hurts." His voice was so hoarse, and I nearly wept at the vulnerability I saw in his eyes.

"Take me, Aaron," I begged, needing to be filled up by him.

I didn't need to ask twice. He lifted me up by the backs of my thighs, causing my legs to wrap around his waist, as he strolled over to the bed, laying both of us down. He moved fast, removing the plaid pajama bottoms he wore.

"Oohh!" I sang loudly as he penetrated me. My husband wasn't a small man by any stretch of the imagination. But, as it always did, my body adjusted to his size and girth.

I clawed at his back and shoulders as his hips created a rhythm for me to keep up with. My eyes rolled to the back of my head every time he pushed deeper inside of me. My back arched and my mouth became dry from moaning so much and calling his name. I couldn't believe I'd gone almost three days without this feeling of him being inside of me.

"No more business trips!" I managed to squeak out in between thrusts. He couldn't leave me alone for two days while I was this damn horny.

His head lifted, and without saying anything he crushed his lips to mine, his tongue and hard cock pushing in and out of my orifices. I dug my fingernails into the smooth skin of his back. He wouldn't let up; in fact, the little bit of pain urged him on. His hips began moving faster while he slipped his hand in between our bodies, again using it to manipulate clitoris.

Just when I felt my third orgasm rush me, he angled his hips, hitting my G-spot while continuing to use his hand to externally stimulate me. That was when I lost it completely. I'd tried to keep my screams to a minimum to not wake our children, but all rational thought was lost at that moment. My entire body pulsed and convulsed with the sensations of his movements as I clung to him.

He wasn't far behind either. He came with his lips covering mine. The convulsions of my inner muscles worked to milk him for every drop of semen his body could muster.

We continued kissing for a long while afterward. Eventually, our sweaty bodies were separated when he pulled back and out of me.

I groaned from the separation, wordlessly watching Aaron as he rounded the king-sized bed to head to the bathroom. A few seconds later, he returned with a wet, warm cloth, using it to wipe the evidence of our lovemaking from my body before tossing it on the nightstand.

I adjusted my body as he climbed back in the bed, his long arms reaching out and pulling me into his naked frame. I settled with my back against his chest, our breathing falling in sync with one another's. I felt like I could breathe easier for the first time in three days. It always felt like that when he went away for business.

"You could come with me," he said, his lips grazing my earlobe.

I frowned. We'd had this discussion at least a thousand times.

"I can't just go with you on every trip."

"Why not?"

I rolled my eyes. "Because we have four kids and someone needs to be here with them."

"They can come, too. We'd hire a full-time nanny and teacher for them."

"Aaron ..." I didn't say anything else because we'd been through this before.

His arms tightened around my waist and he was silent for a few moments before saying, "You came quickly."

My eyes widened, not expecting that. I should've known better. He always noticed even minute changes. Whereas most men barely noticed their wife's haircut, Aaron was keen to even slight changes in my mood, body, facial expressions, whatever it was. Like I said, the only reason I'd been able to hide this pregnancy for the last week and a half had been because of his travel.

"Did I?" I responded, lamely.

It obviously wasn't a convincing response, as evidenced by the way he removed his arms from my body, sitting up to stare down at me. His eyes did that searching thing they always did when he was figuring me out.

"Aaron—" I started.

"Tell me," he insisted, cutting me off.

I glanced out toward the corner of the room, unable to keep it together at the sight of the worry in his eyes. "It's not bad—"

"Then say it."

Pausing, I pushed out a breath before returning my eyes to his. "I'm pregnant."

His jaw tightened and a scowl covered his face. He began shaking his head. "No," he insisted, pulling back to stand.

"Aaron—"

"Don't Aaron me. How the hell are you pregnant?"

I sighed, glancing around at the wrinkled sheets of the bed we'd just made love in. "Uh, the sex might have something to do with it."

"Don't fucking joke."

My shoulders slumped. "I'm not joking. This is good news." I tried to sound cheery.

"Good news? How, Patience? How is it good news that my wife could possibly—" He cut himself off, slicing his hand through the air, shaking his head. "No. You're not doing this."

My eyes widened and I rose to my knees, allowing the sheet to fall completely from my body, exposing my nudity. "It's already done." I held out my arms but bit back the smile when I saw his cock jump as he stared at me. Even in his anger he couldn't turn his bodily response off.

"You almost died. Do you remember that?" he questioned, outraged. "I thought you were on birth control."

"Of course I remember. And I am … was. I missed a couple of days, and well …" I shrugged. Taking a pill at the same time every day while chasing after four children was a bit much. I'd forget for a day or two, and before I knew it, it'd be a week before I took a pill again. And hell, Aaron and I were like rabbits even with our crazy schedules. He was as much to blame for this as I was.

"You're not having this baby!" His face was set in stone.

I moved from the bed, standing before him, now almost as angry as he was. "What did you just say?"

"You heard me. You're. Not. Having. This. Baby."

My chest rose, my breathing increasing with my anger at the implication of his words.

"We're getting rid of it."

My mouth opened to tell him to go fuck himself but he quickly pivoted, turning his back on me and stomping off to the bathroom, slamming the door behind him. I jumped at the sound, my body shaking with fury. If he hadn't of stormed off, I might have tried to wrap my hands around his throat to strangle him for what he'd just said to me.

I growled, frustrated with that stubborn ass man. Against my better judgement, I started toward the bathroom door to pound on it and make him come out, but just then the baby monitor on Aaron's nightstand sounded, wailing coming through the speaker. One of the babies was up.

"You probably woke him with your door slamming," I yelled through the bathroom door before turning and moving to my dresser, pulling out a pair of panties and a long cotton nightgown, putting them both on before going to check on the baby.

As soon as I opened the door, I caught sight of Andreas kneeling up in his crib, crying. I moved swiftly to pick him up, hoping he wouldn't wake Thiers, who was on the other side of the room. I glanced over my shoulder and caught Thiers sleeping peacefully in his crib. While these two were identical twins, their personalities were very different. Thiers could sleep through anything, while Andreas needed the perfect conditions to get a good night's sleep. I was half convinced the little argument between Aaron and I had shifted the conditions in the house just enough to wake him and cause his grumpiness.

"What's the matter? Huh?" I cooed, cradling Andreas to my chest. As soon as I did his wails diminished to mini hiccups. "You're such a faker," I joked, bouncing him a little as I moved to the corner of his massive room where the light blue and wooden rocking chair sat. The room was lit by a soft light that the boys slept with every night. It allowed enough lighting for me to see my way around but wasn't disruptive to their sleep.

"Your brother's over there sleeping like a baby and you're making all of this noise."

Pressing a kiss to Andreas' forehead, I stared down into his eyes that were the same color as his father's. The twins looked even more like Aaron than Kyle did. But Andreas, I was certain had inherited his father's demeanor. His little face was scrunched into what could be interpreted as a scowl, even though he snuggled deeper into my chest.

"Okay," I sighed, grateful that the nightgown I'd chosen actually had buttons that secured it in the front. Usually, I left the buttons closed, opting to slip it on and off over my head. But Andreas was hungry as evident by the way his hand began fiddling with my shirt, his face searching for my nipple.

"You know you're going to have stop this pretty soon," I warned as if he could understand what I was saying. If he did, he obviously couldn't care less because as soon as I released my breast he took to it without a care in the world.

I ran my hand over his silky soft, tight curls, as he stared up into my gaze while he fed.

"You're going to be a handful, aren't you?" I laughed, then quieted down remembering a sleeping Thiers. "What am I saying? You're a Townsend. Of course you're going to be a handful," I whispered.

Just then I lifted my gaze to the opened door, noticing a shadow. My eyes collided with Aaron's as he stared at us from his position, arms folded over his chest. It was the same thing he always did when I was up with one of the children at night, even when I'd insisted he sleep because he had a long work day or needed to be up early in the morning. He always came to help or just watch over, especially when it came to handling Andreas.

While I couldn't fathom a better father for our children, even Aaron had trouble getting Andreas to settle down some nights. Most of the time, he refused to be held by his grandparents, and especially not strangers. At times, it felt like Andreas was attached to my hip because he only wanted to be held by me. Whereas Thiers had weaned himself at eight months, I'd had to work to get Andreas to reduce his feedings to nighttime only.

I looked back down at Andreas who was fighting to keep his eyes open. He'd fall asleep soon, but I knew better than to pull him from feeding just yet. He'd scream the whole house down.

I returned my gaze to Aaron who'd remained silent. Wordlessly, he stepped back from the doorframe and strode down the hall, his anger still apparent in the rigidity of his movements.

"You get your stubbornness from your daddy," I told Andreas before sighing.

Rocking us in the chair for a few minutes, encouraging Andreas back to sleep, I heard Aaron as he moved farther down the hallway. I knew he was headed down to the basement level where his home office sat. I shook my head, still pissed at his earlier comments. Aaron was the one who'd wanted more children in the first place. Immediately after the twins were born he'd informed me that he wanted at least two more. He was adamant. But that was before everything changed.

The first few hours after Andreas and Thiers' birth were okay, but as I laid in the hospital room, awaiting the nurses to bring me the babies for their next feeding, the pain in my body sharply rose. At first, the nurses told me to just relax, that it was normal to experience some cramping as my uterus contracted to shrink back to its original size. But this pain wasn't normal. It grew increasingly worse. My recollection of exactly what happened is hazy due to the pain and fear. I knew something wasn't right. It was confirmed when a nurse finally rolled me over onto my side to find a pool of blood.

It was at that moment, Aaron returned to the hospital room after having made a trip down to the nursery, and tend to Kyle and Kennedy who'd been taken home with his parents. I remember him yelling at the hospital staff, likely threatening their lives. Soon a doctor rushed in, giving me a shot of something, and not too long after the pain subsided along with the bleeding. But I wasn't out of the woods. I had to be given a blood transfusion due to the amount of blood I lost.

I shook my head, releasing that horrific memory. I almost didn't make it to see my boys grow up. I understood why my being pregnant frightened Aaron. Once I was home with the twins settled in, he insisted that we weren't having anymore children. At least not the traditional way. He was open to adoption, just not my getting pregnant. And since I'd just been terrified of dying after giving birth, I agreed, going back on birth control after the first six weeks. Obviously, that hadn't been fail proof.

I lifted from the rocking chair, cradling a now sleeping Andreas. I checked his diaper to make sure he wasn't wet before placing him back into the crib, lying him on his stomach and covering him with the embroidered blanket we'd been given as a gift.

I went over to check on a soundly sleeping Thiers, running my hand over his soft curls. While to outsiders the boys were difficult to tell apart, I noticed their slight differences. Thiers' curls were less tightly coiled than Andreas' and a little more coarser. Thiers' eyes, while still hazel, were a little more green in color. Running my hand down his plump cheek, I smiled and moved away from the crib, heading toward the door, closing it lightly behind me.

I wasn't surprised that our bedroom was empty. Aaron would be down in his office or working out. It was how he dealt with his anger. But I, for one, was too damn tired to go down there to continue our discussion from earlier. We'd just have to deal with it another time.

I laid down on my side of the bed, bringing my left hand to cover my abdomen.

"Your daddy will come around … Eventually."

I hoped.

CHAPTER 11

hen

Deborah

Frowning, I stared at the black phone on my desk that I'd just hung up. The call had been with Cohen. He was canceling on our lunch date.

Again.

The truth was, his canceling on me was actually a good thing. It'd allow me time to get through the paperwork I needed to read before my late afternoon meeting. While I'd read through them all already, I didn't see anything wrong with being overly prepared. Just as I plopped back down in my chair and opened the file, a knock sounded at my opened door.

I looked up, expecting to see my assistant asking if I wanted her to order my lunch in. She was good like that. But I was mistaken.

Instinctively, I shot up from my chair, eyes going wide at the sight of Robert casually standing in my doorway, flowers in hand, a magnetic grin spread across his face.

"Hi," I forced out, not knowing what else to say.

"Hi," he responded, his dark eyes circling my office, pausing on my

Stanford degree that I proudly displayed on the wall behind my desk. He entered my office, coming to a stop across from me.

"What are you doing here?" I racked my brain, trying to figure out if there was any possible way that the cosmetic company I worked for would be doing any work with Townsend Industries.

"Two reasons," he responded. "One, to give you these." He handed me the bouquet of long-stemmed, red roses.

They were absolutely gorgeous. I took the bouquet from his grasp, our fingers grazing one another's. I didn't miss the zap of electricity from that minor touch. Evidently, Robert didn't either as his eyes narrowed on our hands, his jaw clenching and releasing.

"And two," he began, his gaze coming back to my own, "to take you to lunch."

I twisted my head, furrowing my eyebrows in confusion. "Lunch? You came over here to take me to lunch? Wait, how did you even find out I worked here?" I knew I didn't give him the name of my employer when we literally bumped into one another at the Crown Jewel restaurant a week ago. I knew exactly how many days it'd been since we'd seen each other. Eight days. Because each day I took out his business card that I still hung on to and contemplated calling him but never did.

"I called around," he stated casually, his eyes landing on me.

"Called around? What does that mean?"

"It means exactly what I said. Where would you like to eat? The Crown Jewel again or someplace else? I have standing reservations at three restaurants not too far from here."

"I bet you do," I mumbled, still perplexed that he was standing in my office. Before I could utter another word, my stomach growled, embarrassingly loud. "Sorry, I skipped breakfast this morning," I admitted.

Robert frowned deeply, eyes narrowing. "You haven't eaten anything today?"

I thought about it and began shaking my head. "Oh no, I did have a granola bar this morning." It was the last one in my desk. I often kept them in my office since I had a tendency to skip meals throughout the day. It was a bad habit, I knew, but working long hours didn't exactly lend itself to being able to cook three meals a day, everyday.

"A granola bar ..." he uttered, sounding pissed.

"I was supposed to go to lunch with Cohen—"

"Cohen." He lifted a dark eyebrow.

"My, uh, boyfriend." Why did saying that to him feel like some sort of betrayal?

His frown deepened as he glanced around. "Looks like he's not here and you're hungry."

I didn't need much convincing after that. I was hungry and had been expecting to actually leave my office for lunch. Why not with Robert?

Because he's the man you've secretly pined over for five years.

"Everything alright?" he asked in my ear, as my own wayward thoughts had stopped me in my tracks.

I glanced back over my shoulder and nodded. "Yes, fine."

Fifteen minutes later, I found myself being seated in one of the finest French restaurants in downtown Williamsport. It was only a few blocks from my office building, but I was surprised to come out and find Robert had a car waiting for us. Like he'd already stated, he had a standing reservation, ensuring that we didn't have to wait in the crowded rush hour line to be seated.

"Thank you," I thanked Robert after he waved the host off to hold my chair out for me. I got comfortable in the soft cushioning of the cream-colored, wooden chair. I watched him as he rounded the table, taking his own seat. "I love the food here," I stated, covering my lap with the white linen napkin.

"You've been here before?"

I nodded, setting the glass of water back down that I'd just taken a sip of. "Yes, last year. The CEO of my company held a dinner here to celebrate the merger."

Robert nodded. "I read about that in the paper. Glamour Cosmetics bought Enchanted, making it the second largest cosmetics company in the nation."

I smiled, feeling proud even though the praise didn't belong to me at all.

"I received an invite to that dinner. If I had known you were there, I wouldn't have turned it down," he stated sincerely.

"Why did you turn it down?" I wanted to know even though I was surprised to hear that someone in his industry had been invited to the dinner. Though, I shouldn't have been. I was learning that many of those in the upper echelons of society often rubbed elbows with one another, no matter what industry they were in.

"I had another business engagement in Japan."

My eyebrows lifted. "Japan?"

He nodded.

"Are you working on a merger with a Japanese company?" I couldn't help but ask, knowing that even if he were he wouldn't be at liberty to tell me. Things like that were kept private until business insiders were given the heads up. And despite my movement up the ranks within my company, I was definitely not a business insider.

"No. Nothing like that. Not yet anyway. I just took a chance."

I tilted my head. "A chance?"

He nodded. "I have a suspicion technology will be the wave of the future."

"In energy?"

"In all fields," he stated confidently. "I want Townsend to be at the forefront of that wave. I am looking to diversify our assets so we're in position to grow even stronger once the technological changes come about."

"You seem confident in your assessment."

He leaned forward, forearms pressed against the table. "I have no reason not to be. But I'm not interested in talking about Townsend Industries."

"Oh no? What are you interested in talking about?"

"Us," came his one word reply, his dark eyes burrowing into mine.

I nearly choked on the water I'd taken another sip of.

He'd said it as if there really was an us.

"There is no *us*," I hissed, angrily pressing into the table, my voice going low so no one near our table heard us. The anger I'd felt over the last five years began to rise.

"You're angry."

My eyes doubled in size at the casual nature of his observation. "You think?"

He tilted his head and I tore my eyes away from him, hating how great he looked in his obviously tailored suit.

"Because I never contacted you."

It wasn't a question but I answered anyway. "Yes!"

"I'm sorry." It was a simple, albeit sincere apology. But I wanted more.

"You don't even know what you're apologizing for."

That was when he leaned across the table, his large hand covering my smaller one. I hated the fact that that sizzle of electricity whenever we touched ignited yet again. His hold on my hand was firm.

"I'm sorry for rushing off the way I did after our first night together. And for not contacting you afterward." He paused, glancing around either side of us before moving in closer. "My father had a massive stroke."

My eyes widened in surprise and I leaned closer as well. I'd heard all of those years ago that Robert Townsend Sr. had had a minor health issue but the news reports had made it seem like it wasn't that big of a deal, never going into full details of what the issue was.

Robert nodded, acknowledging my disbelief and unasked question. "The day before I left. That was what the emergency call was about."

"I read about something in the paper but they made it seem like—"

"We did that on purpose. All types of business snakes emerge from the grass when they think their rival has some sort of weakness. Townsend Industries was under immense pressure at the time, due to the oil crisis. Hell, we still are," he grunted, anger marring his face. "Anyway, we never wanted to show weakness. So I took over running the day-to-day operations at Townsend while he recuperated. It took nearly twelve months just for him to walk without a cane and talk without a slur. He's still not back to where he used to be."

At that, Robert closed up, evidently not wanting to reveal anymore about his father's health.

"I couldn't get back to campus even though I wanted to. The best I could do was finish our project from afar and get it to you."

I gave him a half smile at that. Robert had completed our World Mythologies project and had it especially delivered to my dorm room a week before it was due, saving me an immense amount of time.

"We got an A on the project, by the way," I stated, grinning.

He squeezed my hand. "I know."

"You didn't even make it to your own college graduation." I'd waited for him at graduation, certain that he would show up. I'd asked a few of his friends for weeks where he was when I didn't see him around campus. All they'd told me was that he was taking care of family business. That was when my anger started. But even then, I'd waited and looked for him at graduation, hoping he'd show up.

"My only regret is not getting to see you walk across that stage."

Why did his words feel genuine? Why had it been that aside from my own mother and father, my only regret was that he wasn't there to see me graduate—for us to graduate together.

"I completed all of my courses from afar. They had to mail me my degree. I was in a meeting with three other heads of energy companies, bargaining for lowered oil prices on the day of graduation. I would've loved nothing more than to have seen you in your cap and gown."

"You had family to take care of."

He snorted. "More like business."

I caught the bitterness in his tone but thought better of asking more about it. I'd spent five years rethinking the last conversation we had that night together. He'd shared with me the mistreatment from his own father. He didn't need to retell it.

"But I'm not here to talk about business."

"Than what are you here for?"

"To talk about you and I."

I pushed out a breath, shaking off the chill that ran through me at the mention of there being an *us.*

"There is no us. I told you, I—"

"Have a boyfriend," he stated on a flat tone, waving his hand dismissively.

"Yes."

"Then where is he?" he asked, glancing around the restaurant as if trying to find him.

I gave him a look. "Unlike you, he can't just take off whenever he wants. Cohen's working."

"Don't."

I wrinkled my brows. "Don't what?"

"Say his name again."

His voice dropped to that of a warning. It made the hairs on the back of my neck stand up and my nipples hardened. Thank God I was wearing a blazer over the thin blouse I wore to work that day, or else, I'd be in trouble.

"He's not here because he's not relevant. To you or to me."

I shook my head. "Don't say things like that."

He parted his lips but paused once our waiter brought our food to the table. I glanced down at the bowl of split pea soup I'd ordered with slices of the restaurant's freshly made baguettes on the side. It all smelled divine, but sitting across from Robert had done something to my appetite.

My appetite for food, at least.

"You're not eating," he stated, nonchalantly.

I suspected he knew exactly the thoughts that were running through my head.

Just to spite him, I picked up my spoon and began eating my soup with gusto. But when I lifted my gaze to peer across the table at him, the smirk on his face read, again, that he knew he was getting to me.

"It wouldn't work." I shook my head.

"It's already working."

"We haven't even seen each other in five years. We could be completely different people. You practically ran a multi-million dollar corporation."

In our time apart I'd done some thinking. I'd finally settled on the conclusion that Robert and I weren't meant to be. Yes, we'd shared a beautiful night together, but that was where it should end. We came from two entirely different worlds. For a woman like me, living the life I was living, making the money I was with the position I had in my company was practically a miracle. Few people ever made it off the mountain. Hell, I'd had a hard enough time adjusting to my life in Palo Alto and then again in Williamsport. There was no way I was ready or even willing to take a chance and enter Robert Townsend's world.

"Stop thinking that way."

I lifted my eyes to his again, surprised by the command in his voice. And turned on by it.

"How do you know what I'm thinking?"

"It's written all over your face."

I frowned. "Most people can't read my facial expressions." I wasn't particularly expressive. I knew it because I'd been told more than once at my job that it was one of my professional assets. In a corporate workplace where women were often still seen as too emotional, some of my male colleagues thought it was a compliment to commend me on not being like them.

"To others. But not to me. Just one look and I know what's going on in your head. I also know you're thinking bullshit about not belonging in my world."

"You don't know me."

He grinned. "Tell me I'm wrong and I'll get up and walk away for good."

"Really?" My heart rate increased.

He actually chuckled. "Fuck no. But I wanted to see what you'd say."

That elicited a giggle from me before I rolled my eyes at my own self. "We come from two different places."

"But we're in the same place now. It wasn't an accident that we ended up on the same college campus, being partnered together during our senior year, and living in the same city five years later. Mistakes like that just don't happen, princess."

I lowered my gaze, the butterflies in my belly fluttering from the term of endearment. Swallowing, I placed my spoon down next to my now empty soup bowl and took another sip of water while peering over the rim of the glass at him before responding. "Than what is this?"

"Fate. Destiny. Karma for something I did well in a past life. Whatever the hell you want to call it."

Pushing out a breath, I pressed my palms to the edge of the circular table, sitting back against my chair. His gaze, his words, his entire demeanor were all so intense. I tried to fit as much space between us as I could. Not because I didn't want to be near him. The opposite reason, actually.

"I have to get back to work," I finally stated. I was at a loss for words. Mostly, I was so perplexed on how a man I hadn't seen in half a decade could come in with one lunch and a few words and make me feel like he was turning my entire world upside down.

"This isn't over," he warned.

I didn't say anything as he stood and then moved around the table to hold the chair out for me.

Robert didn't hesitate to place his arm at the small of my back as we exited the restaurant once he paid the bill. And while a twinge of guilt formed in the pit of my stomach over the mounting feelings for Robert, at that moment, it felt good to not have to think about footing the bill for lunch. To not be chastised for wanting to enjoy a nice meal at a five-star restaurant every now and again.

"Thank you for lunch," Robert said as he helped me out of the back of his chauffeured car.

"I should be thanking you."

He shook his head. "I need your phone number."

Surprised, my head jutted backward. He hadn't formed it as a question. It was an order. I really should've been turned off. Instead, I took the pen and notepad he held out to me and wrote my home phone number down.

He took the notepad with my number on it and stuffed it in the inside pocket of his suit blazer. Moving closer to me, he lowered his face to mine, but just before he made contact with my lips, he pivoted his head, moving closer to my ear.

"I'll see you soon, princess." And with that, he pressed a kiss to the spot just beneath my earlobe.

My entire body tightened. He'd remembered one of the most sensitive places on my body.

As he stepped back, allowing me to pass by him toward the entrance of my office building, I fought hard to wipe away the thoughts of how after two years of being together Cohen still hadn't bothered to get to know my body as well as Robert had after just one night together.

CHAPTER 12

 *hen*

Robert

"Keep your guard up!" Buddy shouted from the side of the boxing ring.

I went to cut my eyes in his direction, and was almost knocked the hell over by a blow to my ribs. If I hadn't of pivoted at the last moment I would've easily had a bruised rib.

"Motherfuck!" I cursed, narrowing my eyes at my opponent, Thiers.

"Watch your back!" He chuckled as he hopped from one foot to the other, still on guard, his gloved hands raised in the air.

"You're unfocused," he stated, lowering his hands.

I pushed out a breath and grunted.

"Let's call it for this round, Buddy," Thiers, one of my closest friends, called to the owner of the boxing gym.

"You sure?" Buddy questioned.

I nodded.

"It's your money." He shrugged. Buddy was the youngest gym owner in the city of Williamsport. He'd become well known after his father, a famous trainer, opened the gym and he began working here as well. Eventually, he took over ownership after his father died, and he'd become even more successful than his father in a short period of time.

"What's going on?" Thiers questioned, tapping me on the arm as we stepped out of the ring and over to the metal folding chairs against the wall.

I sat, picking up the plastic water bottle I'd brought with me, and squirted water into my mouth, swallowing before I answered.

"These fucking leaks," I finally answered, gritting my teeth at just thinking about the problems occurring at work.

"That's still going on?" Thiers questioned.

"I just got a fucking call this morning from a reporter at the *Williamsport Gazette*. He asked about my trip to Japan last year that nobody outside of the company was supposed to know about. And then he asked about the health of my father."

Thiers sat back, whistling. "That's some shit. You all kept a tight lid on your father's condition for years now."

"It's somebody inside of the company. I can feel it. I just don't know who." I punched my fist into my hand. It was driving me a little stir crazy to go into an office day after day and not know who could be trusted.

"You know, I have more than one contact who could handle this whole thing for you. Get rid of your little problem and do so quietly."

I turned, looking into Thiers' dark eyes. Sweat glistened off of his dark, wrinkled forehead. He was completely serious. I'd known Thiers for years. His father had been my father's long time driver, along with a few other things. While Thiers never went on to become a driver like his father, he did take up the less legal side of his father's business. He had his hand in a little bit of everything. If he said he knew people, I was sure they were legit.

Briefly, I considered it. That's how pissed I was becoming over the constant leaks within the company. But I shook my head.

"I won't go down the same road as my father. I want to be as legit as possible."

Thiers, whose actual first name was Gary, made a disapproving noise with his mouth. "No one gets to the top of the food chain without getting a little dirt on their hands."

I nodded, conceding. But then turned to fully face Thiers so he knew how serious I was. "I want as little dirt on my hands as possible. Because when I do get my hands dirty I won't leave anyone breathing."

He nodded his head slowly. "I hear you. Now tell me about your woman."

And despite the dark mood that had begun to cover me at thinking about my work troubles, a lightness that I only felt when my thoughts turned to Deborah Tate made its way through the darkness.

"She's coming around," was all I said.

It'd been a week since I'd taken her out to lunch. The only reason I hadn't shown up at her office to take her out every day since was because of all of the problems at Townsend Industries. However, I made sure to call her every night. And each time she picked up. It wasn't lost on me that her so-called boyfriend was hardly ever around.

"Hey, careful with that."

I glanced down to see what Thiers was warning me about, only to notice that my grip on the water bottle had tightened so much, water had splashed out of the top. The thought of another man so much as breathing the same air as Deborah was too much.

"I need to go," I stated, standing.

"Go? We've still got another hour here." Thiers held out his hand to the empty boxing gym. We'd paid Buddy a nice amount for a private gym session. We did these sessions weekly. I worked hard to maintain my physique. No longer did I have as much free time to do all of the outdoor sports I loved as a teenager and in college. So now, I took it upon myself to make time when and where I could to get in a good sweat. Not only did it help in keeping me in shape but it aided in reducing stress and keeping my mind sharp.

"You take the hour. I'm going to go see my woman." I was tired of playing games. Five years of separation had been long enough. And it'd taught me a couple of things. First, it taught me that what I'd dreamt that night at the ski lodge wasn't just a dream. It had been a glimpse into my future. Me, Deborah, and our four sons.

It also taught me that we likely both needed that time apart. We'd been young, too young, to truly pursue what I knew was our future. We weren't children any longer. Boyfriend or no boyfriend, Deborah Tate was mine.

* * *

Deborah

"What the …" My question trailed off, as I peeked through the peephole of my apartment door. I'd only gotten in from work an hour ago after another long day of meetings. And just as I'd gotten settled into a pair of sweatpants and I started warming up a can of Campbell's tomato soup to have along with the grilled cheese sandwich I planned on making, a loud knock sounded at my door. At first I thought it might be Cohen, but as soon as I glanced through the peephole, I knew I was wrong.

"What are you doing here?" I questioned as soon as I opened the door for Robert.

He didn't even answer as he pushed past me, entering my apartment and taking it upon himself to shut the door, locking it.

"Break up with your boyfriend," he insisted.

"Well, hello to you, too." I folded my arms over my chest.

"Hi, princess."

I softened just a little bit at the moniker. Conceited bastard knew exactly what he was doing.

"Now break up with Colin."

"Co—"

His hand sliced through the air, indicating that it would not be in my best interest to complete his name.

"Robert, we—" Again my statement was cut off when Robert wrapped both of his hands around the sides of my face and pulled me into a kiss. Our first in five years.

I knew it was wrong. I was in a committed relationship. I loved Cohen. I thought.

But when Robert pressed our lips together, I released a breath that I felt like I'd been holding for eternity. Or for a half a decade.

I melted against his body, parting my lips and moaning when his tongue first made contact with mine. He tasted like a place I'd only been to once, but had always wanted to return to and bury myself into forever.

We kissed, forgetting our need for oxygen, while Robert's hands trailed up and down the sides of my waist. He was getting reacquainted with my body, and God if it didn't turn me the hell on. His kiss flowed between impatient and needy to slow and seductive. I reached up, wrapping my arms around his shoulders, pulling him into me.

I startled when my back was pressed against my door.

Robert's hands sunk to the tops of my sweatpants.

That was when my common sense returned. I covered his hands with mine, pulling away from the kiss, panting as my lungs desperately searched for air.

"Robert, we can't."

His jaw tightened, jaw flexing.

When I pushed away from him, my body was shaky and I hugged myself, running my hands up and down my arms, all of a sudden feeling cold without his embrace.

"I can't just break up with someone I've been with for two years just because you say so," I insisted, trying to sound confident in my decision. "It wouldn't be fair to him."

"Fuck fair," he growled.

My shoulders pulled downward as I dropped my hands to my sides. "What do you mean fuck fair? You can't always get what you want."

"I mean exactly what I said. Fuck fair."

"Robert."

"Fine. You want to talk about fairness. Is it fair to him that you're thinking of me whenever he kisses you, touches you? Does he know that even after five years, you still lay in bed at night thinking of me? Using those dainty little fingers of yours to make that pretty pussy come in only the way I can make it come? Does he know that?"

I gasped, my eyes going wide with embarrassment at his words. "Get out!" I yelled.

He'd made me feel completely exposed. Because as much as I hated to admit it, he was right, but my pride got in the way of me admitting it.

"He's fucking lame. Not half the man you deserve. You know it. I know it. And he knows it."

"Oh, and you're the whole man I deserve?"

"No ..." He replied, surprising me. "But I am the man that will have you screaming my name, calling out for me in the middle of the night, and wearing my ring and last name until we both take our final breath on this earth. I'm also the man who'll kill anyone who tries to get in the way of our future. So break up with him, for his sake, because he'd never survive my wrath."

I shook my head, not wanting to take in what he was saying. "You wouldn't."

He stepped closer, menacingly close. "Princess, not only would I, but I'd fucking enjoy it. How's that for fair?"

I closed my eyes, needing a moment to think because while I normally considered myself a morally upstanding citizen, the fact that Robert was standing in front of me declaring that he would literally take another man's life, was kind of a turn on.

It was right then that I started to realize I would likely be going to hell for this man.

I opened my eyes to find Robert's on me, peering down at me, through me. He was awaiting my decision.

"Okay." I nodded. "I-I'll break up with Co— him but we can't sleep together until I do."

I swallowed, relieved at having made that decision. Truth be told, Cohen and my relationship had been over for a while now. I wasn't sure exactly when it happened ... hell, truth be told, it was likely doomed from the very beginning. Because compared to Robert

Townsend there was no other man. He'd ruined me for everyone who came after him.

And as he moved closer like a panther stalking its prey, I knew he knew it.

"That's fair," he stated cockily while wrapping his left hand around the side of my face, pulling me into him for another kiss.

I wouldn't let my mind think about everything else he'd said. The mention he'd made about marrying me, or even the four children he spoke of having, after that first night together. No. I didn't need to think about all of that. For the moment, I could just soak up the beautiful feeling of his kiss, the embrace of his arms and being in his presence, and the strength and protection it afforded my own peace of mind.

"Are you hungry?" I asked as I pulled from his embrace. I needed to break the kiss because as much as I wanted to be fair to Cohen, I couldn't do so if he was going to keep kissing me.

Robert stared at me for a few heartbeats before finally releasing a breath. "Sure. What do you have?" He began removing his suit jacket.

"Campbell's tomato soup and grilled cheese."

I tilted my head when his forehead creased, looking disappointed. "What?"

"Campbell's soup? That's crap."

A laugh burst from my lips. "We weren't all raised with a silver spoon, Townsend."

He frowned.

"I'll pretty it up a little for you, and it pairs well with my grilled cheese. I'll even let you choose which cheese we'll have on our sandwiches." I glanced back over my shoulder before padding over my wooden floors toward my tiny kitchen.

My apartment wasn't too big, only about five hundred square feet. But I'd sacrificed size to be closer to my work. From my apartment to my job it only took about twenty minutes to walk—obviously, it was much shorter if I chose to drive, which I did only during inclement weather.

"You have more than one cheese option?" he asked from behind me, his warm breath moving over the back of my neck.

"Yes," I responded airily. Pulling the door of my ugly green refrigerator open, I bent over to seek out the cheese options I had. "There's a little grocer about halfway between my place and work. I stop there a couple of times a month. They have the best specialty foods, cheese being one of them." I placed the cheeses on the countertop. "I have goat cheese, havarti, gouda—"

"Gouda? For grilled cheese?"

"Don't knock it 'til you've tried it. But, in my opinion, you really can't go wrong with sharp cheddar." I held up the fresh round of cheddar I'd gotten on my way home from work just that evening.

"Cheddar."

I grinned. "I was hoping you'd say that." I loved the other options but had had my heart set on the cheddar.

"You need some help?"

I pivoted, looking back at him and pausing from slicing the cheddar cheese on my cutting board. "You cook?"

He shook his head. "No. Just thought I should ask to be polite."

I giggled. "Thanks for offering." I placed the remaining cheeses in the refrigerator and pulled out the European butter I'd also gotten from the grocer that evening.

"How's everything at work?" I asked, making conversation as my hands busily assembled our sandwiches and I began heating the cast iron skillet to melt the butter.

"There's another leak," he answered grimly.

I glanced back over my shoulder to see the hard expression that covered his face. Robert had told me about some of the leaks that had been plaguing Townsend Industries for some time now.

"You still have no idea who it is?"

"I have some names in mind. I'm going to have a guy I know look into it."

"A guy you know? That doesn't sound ominous at all," I teased.

Robert just shrugged. "It is what it is."

He moved closer to me as I began adding the Italian spices to the warming tomato soup.

"You buy high end cheeses and butter from a European grocer, high quality bread from its bakery, all to make your grill cheese and pair it with what? A ten cent can of soup?"

Smirking at his observation, I plated our sandwiches, cutting them on a diagonal, and poured the soup into two bowls before handing him his plate. I followed him to my dining space which was just off the kitchen, right next to the window that gave us a view of some of Williamsport downtown area.

"I guess my food is a reflection of my life."

Robert paused in chewing, giving me a curious stare.

I gestured with my head to the soup in front of him. "I grew up on Campbell's. When my mother could afford it, she would buy cans and cans of it. Only on a handful of occasions did we ever have enough for grilled cheese and soup, but I loved it when we did. Today, I can afford the soup and grilled cheese. I just get better quality cheese. I hated that rubbery American cheese the government sponsored programs would always give us." I made a disgusted face.

"It reminds you of home."

I looked out of the window. "A little, I guess." I'd never really even thought of it but it was true.

"You don't have to feel guilty for making it out of poverty."

I turned sharply to Robert, eyebrows furrowed. But he wasn't put off by my reaction to his statement.

"It's true. There's nothing to feel guilty about. Your parents worked and even died to give you a better life. You owe it to them to live it."

I placed my half a sandwich back down on my plate. I'd never revealed those feelings to anyone.

"I know that," I stated, my voice low. "But it feels odd or like I'm betraying them sometimes. I still haven't gone back home since I left. I've never been to the place where my mother is buried. I make in a month what my mother used to make in a year. Just saying that out loud almost takes my breath away. I sit in meetings with the CFO of our company and sometimes think, how did I get here?"

"It's where you were meant to be."

I swallowed, picking up my sandwich again and taking another bite. I didn't feel the need to fill the silence. Somehow, Robert just got me and that made it so much easier for me to relax. To not have to pretend to be one way or another. And while he was overbearing at some moments, at others, he gave me the space and freedom to be exactly whoever it was I needed to be.

"I have to head out of town tomorrow for an overnight work trip to New York. I'll be back Thursday evening. We'll have dinner," he stated, standing by the door. It was nearly ten o'clock at night, and while I didn't want him to go, I couldn't let him stay. Not like this. Not while I still had to deal with Cohen.

I nodded. "It's a date."

A smile touched his lips and he advanced on me, taking my lips in a sizzling kiss. Again his hands rose to cup my face. "Remind me again why I can't have you tonight."

Sighing, I wrapped my hands around his wrists. "Because it wouldn't be right."

A muscle in his jaw twitched. "I respect your loyalty. It makes me love you even more … but I loathe that your loyalty is to him."

"It's not to him. It's to us. We can't start our relationship off being deceitful."

Robert's response was quick. "Our relationship started over five years ago, so technically speaking, you *are* being disloyal to us."

I pulled back, grinning. "Like you haven't been with any other women in the past five years."

For the first time ever, I saw Robert's eyes shuttered and evade mine. "Point made," he finally responded.

"Dinner. Thursday. I'll pick you up."

I nodded, knowing what he was leaving unsaid: breakup with Cohen by the time he got back from his business trip.

* * *

Present

Kayla

"And did you? Break up with him?" I questioned as I walked my mother-in-law to the front door. She'd stopped by and had lunch with my mother and I while Josh had to go into the office for a few hours. My mother had left about thirty minutes ago, and I'd damn near begged Deborah to share more of her and Robert's story with me.

Deborah looked down at my daughter, Victoria, bouncing her on her hip, and replied, "I sure did."

We both laughed.

"Cohen was no match for Robert."

She shook her head. "None at all. But, surprisingly, it would take him a little while to learn that lesson."

I lifted an eyebrow. "Oh, what happened?" I squealed, wanting to hear the rest of this story.

"Unh unh." Deborah shook her head. "You've got enough of the story out of me. It's time for me to take my granddaughters out for our girls' day. I need to go pick up Kennedy and Annalise. Can you believe out of my ten grandchildren only three of them are girls?" She cooed to Victoria, tickling her under her plump cheek.

I smiled wide at the sounds of Victoria's laughter.

"I'm sure you'll have more granddaughters sometime soon."

Deborah's head popped up. "Are you? Have you heard something?" she questioned excitedly.

"No." I shook my head adamantly. "I'm not and I haven't heard. I was just saying …" I kept to myself that the way Joshua kept hounding me, I was sure we'd have another baby within the next year.

"Okay then. We'll be back in a couple of hours."

Smiling, I pressed a kiss to Victoria's caramel-colored cheek and ran my hand through her silky straight hair. After handing Deb the diaper bag, stuffed with everything she might need, I held the door open for them. I'd already told her how brave I thought she was going out alone with all three girls. Well, alone, aside from her security guard.

I shut the door behind them, and prepared to go up to my own office and read over some files before Joshua got home.

"Oh shit!" I startled, turning and swinging wildly at whoever was behind me. When I finally laid eyes on my handsome husband, instead of giving him a warm greeting, I punched his shoulder.

"Ouch!" he yelped. "Your right cross is getting better," he stated immediately after.

I bowed my head. "Thank you. I have a good teacher. But don't scare me like that again." I pointed at him before moving into his arms.

"Noted," he murmured in my ear and then pulling back to kiss my lips.

"Did you get that issue resolved?" I questioned on a raised eyebrow.

"The venue has finally been booked."

I clapped. "Good. The girls will be so happy once I tell them."

Josh nodded. "Thank you for loving my parents as much as I do."

I cupped my husband's cheek. "How could I not? They raised you and you are my everything."

His lips covered mine in an instant. I moaned into his mouth, feeling swept away. It took me a second to realize that I had literally been picked up off the ground and carried to my desk.

"Wait! No," I yelped when I heard papers and the files that'd been there hitting the floor.

"Kay—"

"No, wait. These are important," I stated, pushing an agitated Joshua away so that I could bend down to pick up the discarded files.

"What is all of this?" he asked, crouching low to help me pick everything up.

"It's reports and journal articles I've been gathering for my research on maternal mortality rates."

Josh looked puzzled as we both stood. "Mortality rates?"

I inclined my head. "Yes. After what happened to Patience when the twins were born I got to thinking. Hers wasn't the first story I heard either. Within the last year superstars like Serena Williams and even Beyoncé have spoken out on either almost dying or dealing with some sort of health scare while giving birth. From what I've read, it's no stretch to say that the U.S. has the worst maternal mortality rate in the developed world, and it's getting worse, not better."

I paused to breathe. Talking about this topic was something that got me really worked up. Not only as a new mother, but as a woman who almost lost her sister-in-law due to the same issue.

"I assume you're not researching just to research."

I smiled. "You assume correctly, husband of mine. I want … no, *need* to do something about it. Even if only in my neck of the woods. At the shelter I want to hire staff to give birthing classes, discuss maternal health, and provide prenatal care to some extent. And I've also been thinking of becoming certified as a doula."

"What the hell is a doula?"

"It's a person who acts as an advocate for a birthing mother. They help provide a calming atmosphere and tend to any needs of the woman in labor. Also, they can communicate the mother's wishes to the medical staff in the event that she can't. For example, many women want to have an unmedicated birth but sometimes they are pressured to be induced with medications by hospital staff that might be overworked and just want to deliver the baby to get it over with. The doula steps in so mom doesn't feel pressured to make a decision she doesn't want."

"Really?"

"Yeah. There's a lot more that goes into it also, but those are some of the basics."

"Sounds interesting. Would you need to go to school for this?"

I nodded. "There is no strict requirement for certification, but I would get certified and registered with one of the major doula organizations. While it takes some up to two years to get through all of the courses and become certified, my medical background would allow me to be fast tracked so it wouldn't take as long."

Josh glanced from the papers in his hand up to my face. "You've put a lot of thought into this."

"I have. Every time I looked at Victoria over the last few months, I kept thinking about the mothers who never make it home, or who die in the months after their baby is born, leaving them motherless. It makes my heart ache." I rubbed the left side of my chest, feeling that ache again from just talking about the subject.

Joshua placed the files down on my desk before moving to me, wrapping his strong arms around me. Melting into his body, I wrapped my arms around him and inhaled deeply.

"You know I'm with you a hundred percent of the way for anything you want to do. I'll move heaven and earth to get you whatever it is you need."

I smiled against his shoulder before pulling back. "Right now I need you to finish what we started a few minutes ago."

He sighed and his green eyes lit up in excitement. "God, I was so hoping you'd say that."

My laughter was cut short when Joshua pulled my mouth to his, covering it with his lips.

Mortality rates, doula certifications, and everything else could wait.

*P*resent

Joshua

"So you've known Buddy for a long time then, huh?" I questioned my father, just after we entered the dark basement area of the seemingly abandoned building. The sounds of the cheering crowd could be heard as soon as we stepped over the threshold of the metal door. We were in the underground fighting ring, simply known as The Underground. My father, of all people, had introduced me to fighting nearly nine years earlier, though he rarely came to these matches with me.

He nodded as I glanced over at him. "We go way back."

"Look what the wind blew in," Buddy greeted as he strolled over in our direction.

He was about a half a foot shorter than my father. He'd always said his height was the main reason he stuck to training and not getting into the ring himself. Though, I was sure he could handle himself if he needed to. You don't spend more than fifty years around a boxing gym, fighters, and training some of the best of the best, and not pick up on a few things yourself.

"Buddy," my father greeted, extending his hand to Buddy and pulling him into a short but warm embrace.

The many sides of my father often intrigued me. One minute he could blend in with a dingy fighting club and its trainer, and the next he could command the boardroom whose occupants combined for a net worth in the tens of billions. And a minute after that, he'd come home and be a doting, loving husband and father. He was a chameleon. But I wouldn't dare call him a jack-of-all-trades, because unlike that saying, he actually was a master at it all.

Do it a hundred percent or don't do it at all. Don't half ass anything.

I remembered that lesson he taught me when I first came to work at Townsend Industries. I'd made it clear from the beginning that I wasn't interested in the energy side of things but I was all in when it came to the real estate division. My father had told me those words and then got out of my way to let me sink or swim on my own.

"I know you're getting old, but are you getting senile on me? You came down here to fight?" Buddy questioned.

My father shook his head. "Just checking up on my third youngest. Seeing how this operation of his is running."

Buddy's gaze shifted to mine. "The kid's doing alright. A chip off the old block."

I grunted at Buddy. "Whatever. I didn't come here to talk and reminisce. You came to watch me fight or what?" I questioned my father.

"Let's see what you've got."

"Finally."

I parted ways with my father and Buddy to head to the bathroom to change into my fighting gear which was only a pair of boxing shorts, boxing shoes, and hand wraps. I waited until Buddy entered to tie my wraps.

"Damon's not here tonight," he informed me.

I nodded, already knowing he wouldn't be making it. "He's a newlywed. I don't expect him to be coming as often."

Buddy snorted and laughed. "Same with you. We're lucky if you make it out here once a month."

I shrugged. "I'd rather be at home in bed with my wife and daughter than looking at you all night."

"I'm hurt," Buddy stated, clutching his chest.

"You'll get over it."

I left out of the bathroom, chuckling as he retorted something to my back. I glanced up into the ring to see Doc inside. That was his nickname. He was actually a doctor, which, obviously, was how he got the name.

"What's up, pretty boy?" I taunted as I entered the ring.

"Townsend. Oh, how I'm going to enjoy this opportunity to mess up that grin of yours tonight."

I grunted. "Don't count on it."

"Alright, boys, you know the rules. I won't exhaust myself going over that shit again," Buddy yelled as he stood between us. "Let's go!" Stepping out of our way, he allowed us to do our thing.

Doc and I circled one another, and while I was certain he was the quietest one in the room, I could feel my father's eyes on me, watching me. It didn't make me nervous, however. It did the same it'd always done when I knew my father was observing. It made me brave.

"Shit!" Doc cursed when I saw an opening and landed a left hook to his right side ribs.

"That was just a fucking love tap. Don't be a pussy!" I taunted.

"Fuck you, Townsend," he retorted.

He swung and just narrowly missed clipping my chin. But I didn't let that near miss deter me. I went in for a sweep of his right leg, but he saw it coming and side hopped it. However, I caught him on my way up, sending a right cross to his chest, causing him to stumble backward. Nevertheless, Doc was no easy win. He wasn't too knocked out by my cross and quickly recovered, trapping my right hook in his grasp.

"Oh hell no," I blurted out, knowing he was going to try an arm lock move that he was known for. *Fuck that.*

I pivoted and kneed the same side of the ribs I'd punched earlier, causing him to loosen his grip on my arm just enough that I could free myself. We continued to go blow for blow for three more rounds before Buddy ended it. It was a draw.

"You went easy on me, Townsend," Doc stated angrily.

I shrugged. "Didn't want to end your career." It came across as a joke but I was partially serious. I still didn't fully comprehend why a doctor, a surgeon no less, would risk his livelihood by getting into an underground fighting ring that had few rules.

We slapped fives, and I hopped out of the ring, coming face-to-face with my father.

He patted me on the shoulder. "You half-assed it in there."

"How could you tell?"

My father lifted a brow. "I've seen you in action when you really want to take someone down."

I nodded. "Are you disappointed?"

He shook his head. "If you took it easy on him, you had a good reason."

I inclined my head, grateful that there were some things that my father just understood. He didn't require long explanations for everything. He had a sixth sense better than anyone I'd met in my entire life.

"Need someone to unwrap those gloves?"

"As a matter of fact, I do. While you're at it, you can tell me more of you and Mother's story."

"More?" he asked as if perplexed.

I gave him a deadpan expression. "Don't act like there isn't a shit ton more to the story. You didn't just sweep Mother off her feet, force her to break up with that Kaden guy, and live happily ever after."

Chuckling, my father lowered his head. He realized that I knew my mother's ex-boyfriend's name was Cohen, but I'd intentionally said the wrong name, as he'd done all of those years prior.

"I see your mother has been sharing more of our story with you."

"And now it's your turn to spill as well. What happened once Cory was out of the picture?"

He chuckled and held out his hands for my hand to begin unwrapping as I sat on the wooden bench in the bathroom.

"Let's see … a lot happened after that …" he began.

* * *

THEN

Robert

"You're shaking, princess," I stated, as I pressed my hands to cover Deborah's shoulders as I stood behind her. I squeezed the tops of her arms through her silk blouse, and ran my hands up and down them.

"I'm nervous," she admitted.

Leaning down, I pressed a kiss to the column of her neck, causing her to shiver. "Relax," I whispered in her ear.

It'd been two months since Deborah and I had officially begun dating. Eight weeks and four days since she'd broken up with Cameron or whatever the fuck his name was, and I'd claimed her as mine. That night, we were back at the same Crown Jewel restaurant where we'd originally bumped into one another over two and a half months ago. We were set to have dinner with my family. An event I didn't necessarily look forward to but I needed to get it out of the way in order for Deborah to know what she was getting herself into. My parents, in particular my father, weren't my favorite people in the world, though I worked with the man almost everyday. Or, truth be told, I was the one mainly running Townsend Industries and had been for the past five years, though to the outside world it looked as if he was still running the show.

He wasn't.

At least, not entirely. He still had enough sway with the board and the upper level management to prevent me from really delving into technology the way I wanted to.

"Hey, where'd you go? You can't zone out on me now."

I lowered my gaze back to Deborah, who had turned to face me.

The worry in her eyes unsettled me. I bent low, pressing a kiss to her naturally pink lips. "I'm right here, princess."

She pushed out a breath. "Good, because they're here."

I spun around to see my parents following behind the hostess as she walked toward us. I moved to Deborah's side, my hand resting at the small of her back reassuringly.

"Your brother's not with them," she whispered.

I frowned. "If there's one thing you can rely on Jason to be, it's late." And a complete let down in all areas of his life. But that's a story for another day.

"Son," my father greeted, a grim expression on his face as he huffed, sounding partially out of breath from the short distance of the restaurant's entrance to the table where we stood.

I nodded. "Father."

"Robert," my mother greeted more warmly.

I kissed my mother's cheek as she moved in for a hug.

I took a step back, again wrapping my arm around Deborah's waist again. "Mother, Father, please meet Deborah Tate, my girl—" I frowned, realizing how much I hated the word *girlfriend.* It sounded so juvenile. Like the word belonged on the lips of a teenage boy introducing his crush for the first time to his parents. That wasn't this. While the words went unsaid, I was introducing my future to my family.

"My woman."

I ignored the gasps from my mother and Deborah herself. However, I didn't ignore the dip that occurred in my father's eyebrows. My gaze narrowed on him as his eyes drifted downward, following the length of my arm as it stretched behind Deborah's back.

"Deborah, it's so nice to meet you," my mother stated, breaking the brief moment of tension.

"Pleasure to meet you, Mrs. Townsend." Deborah extended her hand.

My mother, on the other hand, opened both of her arms, pulled Deborah into a hug, and pressed a kiss to her cheek.

Deborah appeared surprised at first but soon leaned into the embrace.

My mother's response even surprised me a little but I realized this was the first time, ever, that I was introducing a woman to my family. She realized how serious this was.

"Deborah," my father began, a haughty tone in his voice.

"Thank you for taking the time from your busy schedule to have dinner with us, Mr. Townsend," Deborah stated.

He nodded curtly. "Let's sit, shall we?"

I moved around the table to hold out Deborah's chair for her. When I saw my father sit before my mother, I did the same for her. While I had some of my own hang-ups about my mother, she was actually a sweet woman. One who I never fully believed deserved the mistreatment by my father.

"So, Darlene—"

"Deborah," I growled, correcting my father. "Deborah Tate. Get it right." My voice was stern, and only when Deborah reached over, grabbing my balled up fist to loosen it, did I realize how tense my body had gone.

My father gave me a dirty look but cleared his throat and began again. "Deborah, do forgive me. I don't think I have heard your name before. Tell us, what is it that your family does?"

I opened my mouth to respond, but Deborah was faster than I was.

"Well, Mr. Townsend, both of my parents are deceased."

"I'm sorry to hear that," my mother chimed in, reaching her hand across the table to lightly cover Deborah's for a second before releasing it.

Deborah smiled at her. "Thank you, Mrs. Townsend."

"And what did they do before they died?"

"Excuse me?"

Deborah's hand went to my forearm, staying my anger. "My father was a coal miner and my mother worked a series of jobs in our little town of Beattyville, Kentucky."

My father's forehead wrinkled. "Beattyville. That doesn't ring a bell. And what is it that you do for a living?"

"Are you serious with this line of questioning?"

"Robert, calm down. I'm sure your father's just trying to get to know me."

"Don't be so sure," I responded while glaring at my father across the table.

"Son, am I not supposed to question the first woman you've invited to dinner to meet your mother and I? Surely, that makes no sense."

"Having a discussion is fine, but interrogating her to discern pedigree and status is *not*. She's not a show pony."

"Robert, calm down," my mother added. "We just want to get to know the woman who obviously has so much of your attention." My mother looked across the table to Deborah. "It's lovely to meet you. I've noticed for some time now that my oldest son seems less stressed and happier. I suspect you have something to do with that."

Deborah turned to me and smiled, her hand still in mine. "My coworkers have said the same thing about me. Even with all of the craziness going on at the office, they say I seem more relaxed."

My mother lifted an eyebrow. "Oh? And where do you work?" The question was casual enough, but due to my father's questioning I was already on edge.

"I work for Glamour Cosmetics."

"Oh!" My mother's face lit up like a Christmas tree. "I love Glamour. Their foundation and blushes match my skin perfectly. Do you work directly with developing makeup lines?" my mother inquired, genuinely interested.

Deborah placed the glass of water she'd just taken a sip of back on the table, shaking her head. "Not directly. I work in the finance department."

"Finance?"

Deborah nodded. "That's right, Mr. Townsend. I studied mathematics at Stanford."

"Is that where you two originally met?" my mother asked, looking between the two of us.

"Yes, Mother. We were in the same class."

"Though our first introduction was a bit unorthodox," Deborah joked, glancing in my direction.

It helped to lighten my own mood, and I reached over and pressed a kiss to her cheek and whispered, "I've more than made up for that little indiscretion." If we hadn't been sitting around a dinner table with my parents, I would've done a hell of a lot more than whisper in her ear.

Deborah gave me a sly grin.

My mother went on to say something about Glamour Cosmetics,

and she and Deborah broke off into a conversation. I mostly remained silent, letting the women talk, but I kept an eye on my father. His face read displeasure, which wasn't uncommon at all. However, the way his eyes kept drifting to Deborah's clasped hand in mine, spoke to how he really felt about our union.

"Sorry I'm late."

Four heads peered up from the table where we'd been eating our meal to find my brother, Jason, staring down at us, a stupid smirk covering his face.

I frowned as the odor from whatever cheap alcohol he'd gotten his hands on practically punched me in the nose. And while that was bad enough, it was the sight of the woman in a leather jacket, tight, ripped jeans, and a half shirt who he had his arm wrapped around that really pissed me off.

"Jason." My father's voice was clipped as he glared at my younger brother and the woman he'd shown up with.

Jason's smirk widened. "Oh, thank you," he said to the hostess, who'd brought over two extra chairs for he and his date. He made a big show of making space for himself and the woman at the table. "Here, Lydia. This is Lydia, by the way," he introduced, glancing around.

"Hey," she responded waving at everyone at the table.

My father huffed. "You're nearly an hour late and you make this spectacle?" my father stated in a hushed tone across the table toward my brother.

"What? I apologized. You want me to do so again? Fine. I'm sorry, big brother, for arriving late to your dinner to introduce us to your …" He paused when he finally looked at Deborah. His eyes narrowed. "You look familiar. I'm Jason—"

"Don't fucking touch her," I growled as he reached his arm out for her to shake.

"Robert—" Deborah began, but I shook my head.

"No. We have no idea where his hands have been." I glanced at the woman next to him whose eyes were halfway closed. "Keep your hands to yourself."

"We're all just happy you could finally make it, Jason," my mother spoke up, trying to smooth things over. "Jason's been doing a lot of traveling," she said to Deborah, likely because she believed Deborah was the only one who didn't know the truth.

For her part, Deborah smiled and nodded.

What my mother was unaware of was the fact that I'd already told Deborah that Jason had been in yet another rehab facility for the past three months. He'd barely gotten out two weeks ago and here he was, drunk again.

"I think we need to order a drink to celebrate Robert's relationship."

"Put your fucking hand down," I ordered to Jason as he lifted his hand to call over a waiter. "You've obviously been drinking already. And I don't give a damn what you do once you leave here, but while you're at this table you will not be drinking anything except water."

Jason's dark eyes, which were similar to my own, enlarged.

"Maybe you're the one who needs a drink. You're starting to remind me of someone else I know." He eyes glided from me to our father, obviously letting it be known who he was referring to.

"Robert," Deborah stated in a hushed tone, pulling me by the arm as I halfway stood up to reach my brother to throttle him.

He knew, more than anything, what comparison to our father did to me. I may be a lot of things, but Robert Townsend Sr. I was not.

My father kept mostly silent. Jason was just twenty-five years old, but my father had already given up on him. Sure, he'd fund his life-style—which included his growing number of stints in and out of rehab facilities—but that was as far as it went. In my opinion, much of Jason's defiance was an obvious attempt to get some type of reaction from our father. I would've told him it wasn't worth it, nor should he even bother, if I thought he'd actually listen to me. But what Jason, myself, and our father all had in common was our stubbornness.

It was a Townsend male trait.

One I was certain wouldn't be broken in this generation or the next.

CHAPTER 14

 *hen*

Deborah

"I'm sorry about this evening." Robert's voice was heavy with concern as we approached my apartment door.

I turned to him, hating to hear that defeated edge in his voice. It was the same tone he used whenever the subject of his family came up.

"And I thought my family was bad," I joked, but Robert didn't find it funny. "Hey," I cupped his face, lifting on my tiptoes even though I wore three-inch pumps, just to be level with his face, and pressed a kiss to his lips, "that was a joke."

Turning his head, he pressed a kiss to the inside of my right palm. "I know."

"Then why the long face?"

"Because I don't want to scare you off with my ridiculous family."

I grinned. "Scare me off?"

He nodded.

"I don't think that's possible."

"Are you sure?"

Damn, why do I find him so irresistible? Just when I thought I couldn't fall for him anymore, he showed me another layer of his vulnerability that made me love him even more.

"I'm sure."

"Good, because I wasn't letting you go no matter what you thought of my dysfunctional family."

I turned my head upward, letting out a laugh.

"I just needed you to see what you were getting yourself into."

"Getting myself into?"

"Yes, when you marry me."

"Robert …" I sighed. Not a week went by that he didn't bring up the mention of marriage and our future together. At first, I thought he was just teasing, but I quickly learned that he was one hundred percent serious.

"I know, us Townsends have our issues. Trust me, I know, and it's actually selfish of me to ask you to be a part of that, but I'm a selfish bastard when it comes to you, princess." His hands moved to my waist and he dipped his head, letting his lips graze mine.

I couldn't respond to his words because his kiss had stolen mine. My arms wrapped around his shoulders, pulling him to me. Robert's family had been exactly the level of dysfunction I had anticipated thanks to his many warnings. But if he thought that was enough to scare me off or give me doubts about our relationship, he had another thing coming.

"Keys," he said against my lips.

I blinked, confused. "Oh!" I suddenly stated, realizing he was telling me to take out my key to my apartment so we could get inside.

As soon as I pulled the key from my purse, he plucked it from my hand, stuck it in the lock, and opened my door, ushering us both inside in a manner of seconds.

The door was barely closed before he pounced on me. My core began to weep with need for him. His hands were pulling at the tucked in silk blouse, searching for the soft skin underneath. As soon as his calloused hands made contact, my body temperature started to rise even more.

His lips were demanding against mine, searching, prodding for mine to open, to let him enter. I moaned into the kiss, allowing him entrance into my mouth, our tongues finding one another's.

Robert walked us down my short hallway toward my bedroom, pressing the door open and then turning the light on. All without breaking the kiss. His lips began trailing down from my mouth, over the line of my jaw, and down my neck until he reached the sensitive spot that always sent me into overdrive when he kissed it, just underneath my earlobe.

"Robert," I whispered breathlessly.

"Tell me you're mine, princess," he demanded.

I had no choice but to comply. When in this position, with all of these feelings running through me, I would say or do whatever it is he asked. "I'm yours."

"Huh!" I gasped at the loud tearing sounds that I heard. I pulled back to see a tear in my blouse.

Robert didn't even stop to acknowledge it, his hands going to my skirt, pulling at it.

"Robert, you ripped my blouse!"

"I'll buy you another," he responded urgently, while his hands easily found the back zipper of my skirt, slipping it down my hips and legs, leaving me in a torn shirt, bra, and panties.

"You better!" I responded, trying to sound angry but the airy tone of my voice spoke more to how turned on I was in that moment, than upset over a shirt. Besides, it wasn't the first time he'd torn an item of clothing of mine in his rush to get me undressed.

"It'd be better if you stopped wearing clothes altogether." His lips closed in on mine again, halting any reply I might've had.

I began hurriedly unbuttoning the collared shirt he'd worn to dinner while loosening the tie. As soon as his buttons were free, I pushed the shirt over and down his shoulders, exposing his broad, sculpted chest. I licked my lips as he let me stare at his body in amazement. I admired how, despite the fact that he often worked sixty-plus hour weeks, he found the time to keep in shape all while still being an attentive boyfriend.

"Come here," he growled, wrapping his right hand around the back of my head and neck, pulling me to him, collapsing his mouth to mine again. He would only let me stare for so long before he needed to touch, to finish what he'd started.

Finding myself pressed against the cool sheets of my full size mattress, I arched my back, pressing my still covered breasts against his bare chest as his body covered mine. His hands went around my back, undoing the clasp of my bra and quickly discarding it. His head dipped low and he ran his tongue down the center of my chest before moving to my left breast, covering it with his mouth.

"Ah!" I let out on a heaving breath when his tongue ran along my turgid nipple.

He did it again and again, sending my body to higher and higher levels of pleasure, but just prior to the peak he would back off, delaying the ultimate gratification. He used his hand to pinch my other nipple before he trailed a line of kisses down my belly, pausing for a moment to dip his tongue into the folds of my belly button before continuing on.

With insistent hands he tugged at my panties, pulling them down my thighs and over my knees until he removed them completely. He then forced my knees apart with his hands, his eyes glittering in hunger as he stared at my sopping wet sex.

Instinctively, my knees tried to tighten, but Robert held firm, keeping them apart.

"I told you, your body belongs to me. Every inch of you is mine. Don't ever try to hide this pretty pussy from me, princess."

I sighed, tossing my head against the pillow, still unable to believe the impact his words could have on me, when I felt the wetness between my legs increasing. Oral sex was something I was still getting used to. The only man to have ever done it to me was Robert. Cohen had believed that it was unsanitary. Of course, that hadn't stopped him from requesting I use my mouth on him. But that wasn't the case with Robert. He gave as if his own life depended on it, and rarely asked for the return favor. It was as if seeing me pleasured gave him his own pleasure and he didn't need to ask for more.

Any coherent thoughts I'd been able to have up until that moment, were cut short when Robert dipped his head and ran his tongue up and down the entirety of my labia. Again, my back arched and I planted my elbows into the mattress, my toes digging into the bed as well. Robert's hands moved under my buttocks to my waist, essentially lifting me off of the bed, bringing my core closer to his mouth. The moans that poured from his mouth as he sexually stimulated me with that same mouth turned me on that much more. I'd never felt so desired and wanted as the times when he and I made love.

The tingling first started in my toes before working its way up my legs, down my thighs, until finally exploding in my core. I lifted my hips as the powerful shockwaves of my orgasm took a hold of my body. My fists tightened and I threw my head back against the pillow, all the while calling his name.

It took me a while to reorient myself after that explosive orgasm. When I did, I came to to see Robert hovering over me.

"I'll make you come like this every night." His words were so full of promise. "Marry me."

I went to respond, but my breath was stolen once again as he began to ease his thick erection inside of me. He lifted my right leg over his left forearm, opening me up and exposing me even more to his entry.

Panting, I lifted my hips, wrapping my arms around his shoulders, pulling him closer.

"Marry me," he insisted again at the same time he fully seated himself inside of me.

"Robert," I sighed out, not knowing what else to say. I could barely register the words he was saying. "Oh!" I yelled when he tilted his hips, allowing his penetrating cock to hit the sensitive nerve endings that composed my G-spot. My eyes crossed and head fell back when he did it over and over again.

"Be my wife, Deborah," he demanded.

"Yes!" I shouted, ready to agree to anything at that point.

He rewarded me by reaching down and rubbing his thumb against my clitoris while continuing his penetrations, sending me into my second orgasm of the night.

I didn't yell this time around. I was too spent. Instead, I let the orgasm have its way with my body as I convulsed and tightened up. I felt the inner walls of my sex clamping down around Robert's still thrusting cock. Finally, I felt his body stiffen in my arms, the veins popping out of the side of his neck as he came.

But something was different.

I felt the gush of his explosion inside of me for the first time ever. It was then I realized why this time had felt so much more intense, so heightened. Because we hadn't used protection.

At the same time that realization struck me, Robert began easing out of me.

"W-we didn't use protection," I stated just above a whisper.

His eyes scoured the length of my naked body before finally resting on my own gaze. "We don't need to. You're going to be my wife."

I blinked at the cavalier way he'd said those words, as if completely unfazed. That was when it hit me—I had agreed to being Robert's wife and he was completely serious about it.

*P*resent
    Aaron

"You don't sound like yourself."

My jaw flexed upon hearing my mother's words on the other end of the phone. I still hated when other people were easily able to read my emotions. Even if that someone was my own mother.

"I'm fine, Mother," I replied as I glanced out the window of the backseat of the town car I was riding in. It was early morning, and I'd just finished dropping off my oldest two children, Kyle and Kennedy, at school, while Patience stayed home with Andreas and Thiers. Now, I was on my way to a breakfast meeting, more than a half an hour away from my office.

"Whenever somebody says *I'm fine* that's a clear indication that they are not fine."

I remained silent because there was no response I was ready to give to that. I heard my mother sigh on the other end of the phone, obviously growing impatient with my lack of response.

"Did Kyle and Kennedy get to school, okay?"

"Yes."

"Good. Ken was so excited about the diorama she made depicting a scene from the latest book she read."

I snorted, a small smile covering my face at the memory of Kennedy showing me her school project.

"I'm sure she'll get an A on it." And if she didn't, her teacher and I would definitely have a talk about it.

"Don't go bullying her teachers, Aaron," my mother stated, guessing my intent without my opening my mouth.

"I'm not a bully."

She made a disproving sound with her mouth. "If you say so. How's Patience feeling?"

I sat up straighter, my hand tightened around the phone that I held to my ear. "Did she tell you she wasn't feeling well?" I questioned. I knew she hadn't told anyone else about the pregnancy yet. Again my hand tightened around the phone at the fear that ran through my belly when I thought about my wife being pregnant. I was such a fucking greedy asshole. I should've made sure she was properly protected.

"No, I just saw her yawning a little the other day at the shelter. She told me Andreas is still waking up a couple of times throughout the night to feed."

I relaxed slightly, releasing the breath I'd been holding. "Yes, he is."

"You know, I think he's even more like you than Kyle."

"How so?"

"Well, he *only* wants Patience, he lets it be known when he doesn't want to be around or held by someone, he rarely smiles, except of course when he's with his mother. Hell, I've seen him nearly hit you a couple of times when you tried to give her a kiss while she was holding him."

I actually chuckled at that because it was true. Andreas had certainly inherited my surliness and my near borderline obsession with his mother. He hated for her to even hold his own twin at times.

"You might be right."

"I am. I'll let you go. Enjoy your breakfast. Hope your meeting goes over well."

"Thank you, Mother." With that, we disconnected the call and I continued to stare out the window instead of down at the papers in the file that sat next to me. I'd been over the files numerous times, had memorized the information inside. This breakfast was just a formality to meet with the heads of a local finance company Townsend may've been interested in acquiring. I needed to go over it with the board first in order to get the ball really rolling.

But business wasn't the prevailing thought in my mind as I rode closer to the restaurant. I could conduct that meeting in my sleep. What had me on edge, and what my mother had heard in my voice, was the tension that coursed through me whenever I thought of my wife. My body tightened again as I thought about her pregnancy. It'd been two weeks since she told me and I still couldn't come to terms with it.

Just as we passed another street the hairs on the back of my neck stood up, a tingling sensation moving down my spine. My gaze narrowed and I refused to turn my head to the right of me, already knowing what I'd see.

"I don't even get a hello?"

My frown deepened. "I was hoping if I ignored you, you'd go away."

Emma giggled. "Since when has that ever worked, Aaron? Come on, you know how this goes. I show up when you need me the most."

I pushed out a breath on a sigh. "I don't need you."

"I thought we were passed this by now."

I didn't respond.

"You know you're being bullheaded."

I finally turned my head slowly in her direction.

Emma.

There she sat in the long, white nightgown she always seemed to have on whenever she appeared out of nowhere. Emma was my guardian angel or whatever the fuck you wanted to call it. She was my person from beyond. A distant family relative who had lived and died long before I was born. And yes, she always seemed to pop up when life presented its most difficult challenges.

"By not talking to you?" I questioned, finally responding to her statement about my stubbornness.

She shook her head, her long, brown locks moving about her shoulders. "No. I'm used to it by now. I'm talking about your wife. You're being borderline unreasonable about this baby."

"It's not about the baby," I insisted. "It's about my wife. Her life."

She tilted her head, giving me a sympathetic nod. "I'm sure you believe that."

"It's not what I believe, it's what I know. Are you here to give me advice?" My tone was harsh, dismissive.

"No. I've learned better than to give you advice. You'd never take it. My job is to help you see where you're making a mistake so that you can fix it before it's too late."

I turned to her sharply. "Don't use ominous language like that." My tone was threatening.

"It's not a threat, Aaron. You know I don't do threats. I am simply asking you to think about what it is you're doing and how you're treating your wife before you do irreparable harm to your relationship."

"I'm not doing anything harmful."

She gave me a *get real* expression. "Aaron, you've practically demanded that your wife get an abortion."

"To save her life!" I yelled before I could catch myself. I glanced up ahead, glad to see that the partition was already up. I wasn't a fool. I knew what it would look like to an outsider, me sitting in the backseat screaming at a woman only I could see.

"Worry less about what the driver thinks of you and more about what your wife thinks," Emma insisted.

I fucking loathed when she read my thoughts.

"I don't give a shit what the driver thinks of me. And I am thinking of my wife. She might not like it now but she will come around."

I grabbed the file I had been ignoring moments before and tore it open, as if I was really reading through the pages.

"I see you've closed yourself off. I know when I'm being dismissed."

I grunted.

"This conversation isn't over."

I stared at the papers in my hands for a moment before looking over to my right. When I did, she was gone. I mulled her words over for another minute but then pushed them out of my mind. I was doing the right thing. Patience would eventually get on board with my decision.

Without even realizing what I was doing, I pressed the button to talk to the one man I owed my life to.

"Didn't you just hang up the phone with my wife?"

"Good morning, Father," I responded.

"Morning, son. You're headed to the breakfast meeting with Truth Financials?"

I nodded even though he couldn't see me through the phone. "Yes, I'll have a full report to the board by the end of the week."

"I'm certain you will. But you didn't call to discuss business."

"I didn't." I paused. "When you were courting Mother, was there anything or anyone that stood in your way?" I didn't understand why I wanted to know the answer to that question but I did.

"Have you met me?"

I let out a small chuckle.

"There were a few that tried, however."

Raising my right wrist to my face, I saw that I had another twenty minutes before we would arrive at the restaurant. With that knowledge, I sat back against the seat and began listening, undistracted, to my father's story.

* * *

Then

    Robert

"This is not the best time to be doing something like this, son." My father's voice was thick with agitation.

I gave him a deadpan expression, refusing to allow myself to give into the anger that consumed me whenever he dared to speak of my and Deborah's relationship. It was, after all, our engagement party, and the last thing Deborah would want is for me to make a scene.

"Something like this?" I questioned, lifting an eyebrow.

"Yes, this." He nodded, looking around the expansive space of the foyer we stood in. We were in Townsend Manor, the home I'd grown up in and that my parents currently lived in. The Manor, as it was often referred to, was a ten-thousand-square-foot mansion which resided on over six acres of land. My father's father had purchased the property when my father was still a teenager, and began building Townsend Manor once my father took over Townsend Industries. It was the only home I'd ever known before moving away to go to college. And while it had been large enough, I refused to move back in once I returned to Williamsport, much to both of my parents' dismay.

Townsend Manor hadn't been my first choice to host our engagement party, but my mother had insisted. And Deborah had been pleased at her invitation, thereby practically twisting my arm to agree. Now, here we were, two months after announcing our engagement and my father was in my face about it.

"*This*," I began, "is my fucking engagement party, in case you failed to understand."

"I recognize that, and I am asking you if you believe this is the right time to be getting married? Townsend Industries is still mired in all of these leaks, the board keeps on my ass about our stock prices, and this damn energy crisis won't let up." His voice was tense and full of the stress of everything he'd just mentioned. I watched as he ran his forefinger along the collar of his tuxedo shirt, to provide space between the collar and his thick neck, obviously overheating.

I stepped closer. "You don't think I've been working on everything you've just mentioned? How many times have I told you that Townsend needs to expand our product and services line? The energy markets are too tumultuous with everything going on internationally, for us to be so reliant on oil. Technology is the wave of the future, and you keep getting in the fucking way of—"

"Now you listen, son. You might have done a good job helping to run Townsend while I was ill—"

"Helping? Is that what you fucking call it?" I questioned, moving even closer. "I did more than *help*. I've been running this goddamn company for the better part of five years. You know it and I know it. The only people who don't know it is the board, and I know how much you don't want them to find out."

He grunted, rolling his eyes. "Yeah, once they do find out, we'll see how much they think of you running the company with falling stock prices and a decreasing market reach."

"Because you won't take your foot all of the way off the gas. You won't fully implement any of my suggestions nor will you allow our R&D division to fully pursue alternative energies. You're the one getting in the way of progress, and once you're removed from position as CEO, I will be able to take Townsend into the next decade and century to reach its full potential."

I started to walk away, done with my father and the conversation for the time being, but his words pulled me back.

"She's not right for you, son!" he hissed.

I spun around, glaring at my father. "You don't get to decide who is and who isn't right for me."

"She's not one of us."

My entire body stiffened and I advanced on my father. "The last man who said those words to me, ended up on his ass."

My father's eyes widened, mouth going ajar. "You would turn on me for her? On your family?"

"In a fucking heartbeat." Tightening my fists at my side, I stepped back, fearing that I really would hit my father in that instant. How dare he try to hold the title of family over my head? The only time he'd treated his own sons like family was when he needed one of us to do something for him, or to look good in front of others. We were related by blood and linked forever by the legacy of Townsend Industries but we weren't a family. At least, not in the truest sense of the word.

"She is my family. And with her, I will raise our children to know the meaning of the word family. To look out for one another first and foremost, business will come second. They will turn out nothing like you." I meant what I said with every fiber of my being.

I stepped away from my father and the ghosted expression he now wore, and turned to walk away, going to look for my future bride.

* * *

Deborah

"That ring is gorgeous," Robert's aunt stated, holding my left hand out in her hand as she gazed at the princess cut diamond ring Robert had given me two days after he'd proposed. "I always looked forward to the day I'd meet the woman who captured Robert's heart. You have to tell us how he proposed?" his aunt, Nancy, gushed as she stood beside Robert's mother, his younger cousin, and two friends of his mother's.

I glanced around the circle of women, who were all a part of high society. Their eyes were glued to me, anxiously awaiting for my retelling of how Robert asked me to marry him. Obviously, I wasn't about to inform this group of women that my now fiancé proposed while he was deep inside of me, bringing me to my second climax of the night.

No.

That was a story I should probably keep to myself.

"Well," I paused, clearing my throat and cupping the champagne flute I held with both hands, "it was very romantic. Just after dinner at my place. He pulled out the ring and asked."

"Did he get down on one knee?" his cousin, Laura, questioned.

I took a sip of champagne and nodded. "Mhmm, I believe he did."

Laura frowned. "Believe?"

"Oh well, you know, I was so emotional and everything, my recollection is a little hazy," I laughed it off.

"Oh, don't I know it. When my Harold finally proposed to me after our long courtship, I was over the moon," Robert's aunt stated, her eyes looking wistfully upward as if remembering that day. "I couldn't wait to pick out a dress and design our wedding cake, and book the caterers for the food. It was such a spectacular time."

I wrinkled my forehead.

Her daughter, Rachel, spoke up. "Oh yes, when Andrew asked me to be his bride I felt the same way. Luckily, I was able to take days off from the job I had at the time to work closely with my wedding planner and get everything done just the way I liked it. Hopefully, your job will let you take off," she finished, looking toward me as if I should've been in agreement.

"Well, I don't think I'll need to take many days off to plan the wedding. We'll just have to work around my schedule. It's a very busy time at work right now."

Rachel and Nancy frowned.

"They'll have to learn to make due without you, hun. Besides, once you and Robert marry and begin having children, you'll have to resign anyway. They might as well start looking for someone to fill your role now." That statement had come from one of Robert's mother's friends. Suzanne, I think her name was but couldn't recall.

I didn't know what surprised me more—the fact that she'd actually said those words to me with a straight face, or the fact that every other woman in the circle nodded their heads in agreement.

"Quit my job?" I questioned, looking around the circle.

"Yes, of course," Robert's mother answered. "There's no way you can work full time, be a mother, and hold up your duties as a wife to a man in a position such as Robert's."

"What position is that?"

"There's all types of events and charity organizations that will need your time or request for you to make an appearance." Janet shook her head. "Robert should've gone over all of this with you." She moved closer, taking my left hand into both of hers. "We've all been through it, dear. It's a bit of a shock in the beginning, but we get used to it. Besides, no woman attends a prestigious school like Stanford not to find a husband. Am I right?"

I glanced around to find the rest of the women nodding their heads in agreement.

Pulling my hand from hers, I opened my mouth to tell her that she had this all wrong, but that's when I was saved by my fiancé.

"Excuse me, ladies. If you don't mind, I need to steal my fiancée." Robert didn't wait for any of the women to respond, including myself. With his arm around my waist, he led me away from the other women.

I was more than happy to leave their presence, still stupefied at their beliefs.

Robert led me down a long wall that turned off from the mansion's dining space where most of the engagement party was being held.

I stopped abruptly and turned to face him. "I did not go to Stanford just to marry a rich guy!" I insisted.

He paused, obviously stunned at my outburst.

His eyes read mine. "Okay," he stated cautiously.

"And I am not quitting my job, Robert."

His forehead wrinkled. "Did I ever ask you to quit your job?"

"No, but just in case you had those thoughts. You can just discard them right now. I'm not leaving Glamour Cosmetics. I will continue to work."

He nodded. "Okay, anything else you need to get off your chest?"

I thought for a few seconds, my eyes roving up toward the vaulted ceilings before they landed back on him. "No, that's it for now."

He nodded sharply. "Good. Now that that's settled, let's get married."

I gave him a wary look. "It's way too early for you to be going senile, sweetie. You've already asked me to marry you. And I agreed. I know this because otherwise, I wouldn't be standing in your parents home, wearing this pink sequined gown—"

"You look delicious by the way," he growled as his eyes roamed up and down my body in the fitted, floor-length gown.

"Thank you, but back to what I was saying. We're already getting married."

"Right. Tonight."

My eyes doubled and mouth fell open. "Robert, where is this coming from?" He'd never shied away from the fact that he desired a short engagement, but we had originally planned for our wedding to be six months out from the night of our engagement party.

"From the fact that we've waited long enough."

"We haven't even been dating six months." How he had managed to get me to say yes to marrying him in such a short amount of time, I didn't know. I'd dated Cohen for two years, was friends with him for two years prior to that, and the idea of marrying him had never entered my mind.

"What's your point?"

I sighed.

"Additionally, this is coming from the fact that you nor I even like half of these people here."

"Half?" I questioned, giving him a look.

"Okay, ninety-nine percent of these people. And yes, it's mostly me who doesn't like them. You hardly know anyone here."

I snorted. A handful of my friends had come to the party to congratulate Robert and I, but the bulk of the people in attendance had been invited by Robert's parents. Needless to say, I didn't know any of them.

"And what does that have to do with us getting married tonight?"

"Because these same people will be at our wedding if my parents have anything to do with it. And look, I'm willing to give you the wedding you want. Anything you want. If you want the big, fancy dress with a long train and all that shit, I'll do it. But all I need is for you to be my wife. Tonight. We can still plan a big, opulent ordeal if you—"

"Yes."

His mouth hung ajar as if he was ready to keep making his argument.

I moved closer, hands cupping his face. "I'll marry you. Tonight. You know more than anyone, I don't need a big wedding. Hell, this engagement party was enou—" My words were captured by his lips covering mine.

Abruptly, he pulled back from the kiss, grabbed my left hand, and I found myself having to run in heels just to keep up with his long strides.

"Robert, slow down," I hissed. "I'm in heels."

I went to protest more, but almost ran right into him when he stopped short.

"What the hell are you doing here?" His voice was low, a tone I recognized he spoke when he was attempting to stave his anger.

"Just here to say congratulations."

A voice I hadn't heard in years, but recognized immediately had the hairs on the back of my neck standing. On its own accord, my face formed into a scowl at the sound of Jack Lassiter's voice. I peered over Robert's shoulder to see my suspicions confirmed. It'd been over five years since I'd seen Jack's face, but he still wore that same cocky grin he always seemed to have in college.

His eyes moved over Robert's shoulder to find me. His eyelids rose slightly, that grin widening. "To give you both my congratulations."

"You weren't on the invitee list."

Jack looked back to Robert. "My father was. He believed it was a mere oversight that I wasn't invited to the engagement party of an old college friend. And when I heard it was to the one and only Ms. Deborah Tate, I just had to be here."

"Thanks for coming to celebrate with us, Jack," I managed to say. "But we have an important engagement to make." I decided to speak because I could feel the growing tension in Robert's body with each word Jack spoke.

"Now, what could be more important than welcoming an old friend at a party to celebrate your love. Am I right?" Jack's gaze shifted from me to Robert and back to me again. That was when he held up the champagne flute he held in his right hand. "I mean, kudos to you, Deborah. The girl from Kentucky scored big with the Townsend from Williamsport. You're a long—"

"Robert, no!" I implored in a hushed tone, trying not to draw attention to the fact that Robert had literally just wrapped his hand around Jack Lassiter's throat. Thank God we were still in the hallway, apart from most of the partygoers.

"Did you think I was fucking kidding when I told you I'd kill you five years ago?" Robert questioned through gritted teeth.

I moved closer, squeezing his free hand in mine.

"Robert," I whispered. "Don't do this here. Don't let him ruin our wedding night." I said it low enough so only he could here. I watched as his grip on Jack's throat loosened slightly.

Robert glanced down at his arm then back up to Jack. "You spilled champagne on my tuxedo. Apologize."

"L-let g-go," Jack struggled to get out.

"Apologize."

"S-sorry."

Slowly, Robert released Jack, leaving him coughing and struggling for enough oxygen to restore his normal breathing pattern. With one last glare at his former friend, Robert wrapped his arm around my waist and led us through the throngs of partygoers toward the front door.

Unfortunately, Jack wasn't the only hassle that stood in between Robert and I getting married that night.

* * *

Then

    Robert

"I can't believe we're going to do this," Deborah stated as we exited the front door of Townsend Manor. "Are you one hundred percent sure about this?"

I paused, turning to her as we reached the driveway of the Manor. Staring into those blue eyes, I briefly thanked my stars that I would be able to look into those same eyes every night before I went to sleep. "I've never been more sure of anything in my entire life." I froze, not wanting to ask my next question but also needing to. "Are you having doubts?"

She paused and it felt like my whole world stopped spinning, as if my very fate rested in her response ... because it did.

I only resumed breathing when she shook her head. "No." It wasn't the word but the assuredness I heard in her voice that had my world spinning again.

"Okay, than let's catch a flight to Vegas and get married."

Deborah began giggling in excitement.

"Whoa! Tonight, big brother?"

I pivoted to see Jason, arm wrapped around yet another woman, staring between Deborah and I.

"I came to surprise you, but I guess you two are full of your own surprises, huh?" he questioned, chuckling.

"You're two hours late to my engagement party but you were coming to surprise *me?*"

"That's right," Jason responded as if that answer made any sense at all. "We wanted to share our good news."

My eyes went to the woman he had his arm draped around. The one he was staring down at as if they shared some big, important secret. For her part, the woman's eyes skittered between Deborah and I before looking back to Jason. She wasn't the same woman he'd brought to dinner a couple of months ago. This woman had long, brown hair and wore a long, black sleeveless dress, appropriate for an engagement party. Her eyes didn't have that glossed-over look from whatever drugs or alcohol most of Jason's dates usually consumed.

"We're married," Jason added without preamble.

"Oh," Deborah finally stated in the face of my own silence.

I looked from Jason to the woman and back to Jason again.

"And does your *wife* have a name?"

"Jesse. Her name is Jesse."

"Jesse," I repeated, my eyes going to the woman, who couldn't keep her eyes on me.

"And ..." Jason continued.

I looked back to him and the sparkle in his eyes told me he still felt like he had another surprise up his sleeve.

"We're expecting."

Deborah gasped.

My eyebrows dipped to a V. "Expecting what?"

Jesse nervously looked to Jason.

"A baby."

The chuckle that burst from my lips was unintentional but well deserved due to the ludicrousness of the moment.

"Robert," Deborah whispered in a warning tone before saying, "Congratulations, Jesse and Jason. We're sure you both are so happy about the baby and your nuptials." She sounded so elegant and genuine.

I, on the other hand, didn't give a shit. "How the hell are you going to raise a baby, let alone provide for a wife? You can barely wash your own ass."

"Fu—"

"Robert, that's enough. We're sorry, Jason. We'd love to stick around and talk more about everything but we have a really important thing to get to. I'm sure your parents will be thrilled to hear your good news."

I let myself be pulled away from my moronic brother and his seemingly ditzy bride by my soon-to-be wife. Once we reached the town car we'd arrived in, Deborah began scolding my response.

"You could've been nicer."

"Nicer?" I questioned while simultaneously waving the driver off. "We're going to the airport," I told him, before getting in the backseat of the car behind Deborah. "How do you expect me to be nicer? Two months ago he was attending our dinner with a completely different woman on his arm. Now he's married to a another woman we've never met and she's expecting his child. The child of a guy who's never put in a day of work his whole pathetic life."

Deborah frowned as she glared at me. "He was trying to upstage you."

I snorted. "You think I don't realize that?"

"Of course you realize it but you don't understand it. He actually looks up to you, wishes he could be more like you. You said yourself, your whole lives, your father constantly compared you two and he always came up short. Jason's just doing what he can to prove to your father, you, and most importantly, himself that he's just as good as you are."

"And getting married and having a baby proves that how?"

She angled her head, giving me a leveling look. "Come on. Do you think your parents would've thrown this lavish engagement party for him? Even though you didn't want all of the pomp and circumstance, they still did it. If for no other reason than to show you off. They wouldn't have done the same for Jason. You and I both know that. And so does he. He probably felt like he had to make a splash or some sort of impact on his own."

I ran my hand over my chin, thinking about her words. This was yet another reason why I loved this woman. She made me consider things that would've never crossed my mind. To me, Jason was just a screw up I'd had to cover for or protect my entire life. But Deborah's words helped me to put some things into perspective.

"You might have a point."

"You know I have a point."

"Great. Point made. But I'm done thinking about my brother for the time being. We have more important things to worry about."

"Such as?" She smiled, lifting an eyebrow.

"Is that going to be your wedding dress or will we have to buy a different dress for the ceremony?"

CHAPTER 16

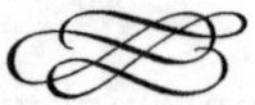

hen

Deborah

"You're shaking."

I glanced over and laughed, again, taken aback by the huge dark hair, sunglasses, and sideburns of the Elvis impersonator who was going to be walking me down the aisle.

"I'm sorry," I stated before covering my mouth to smother the giggles. "I just never thought I'd be getting married like this."

I saw a dark eyebrow raise over the brim of the sunglasses. "You know it's not too late to cut and run."

I shook my head immediately. "No, it's not that. I love Robert. He's the man I'm going to spend the rest of my life with. And have children with. It's just that one minute we were at our engagement party, and the next minute, I'm here. Standing at the edge of the altar, ready to be walked down by an—" I burst out laughing as I stared at the man in the tight, light blue, bell bottom bodysuit. "An Elvis impersonator."

I glanced at the man, whose real name I didn't know. He was staring down at me with a small smirk on his face. Somehow, I managed to sober up.

"My daddy liked Elvis," I blurted out, reliving a memory of him

148

dancing to an Elvis Presley song one night. We didn't have any type of music player. My father sang the song out loud as he danced. Suddenly, a wave of sadness hit me.

"Your parents aren't here."

I looked up, blinking at the man next to me. "They're gone," I stated softly.

"I'm sorry to hear that, little lady." He glanced down the aisle toward the front of the red and white chapel.

I followed his eyes and smiled as I saw Robert emerge from behind the side door and take his position. A bubble of laughter moved up my chest, expressing itself through my lips.

"I knew he wouldn't wear that powder blue tux." It'd been offered to him by the chapel, a powder blue and ruffled tux that'd been worn by God only knew how many other men. Instead, he wore the same tux he'd worn to our engagement part, but it looked as if it'd been freshened since we'd departed Williamsport.

I don't know how he'd done it, but Robert had someone meet us as soon as we'd landed in Vegas, the night before, with a beautiful, shimmering white gown that I was wearing at that moment. I couldn't have picked out a better wedding dress.

"You sure he's the one?"

I glanced to my left at Elvis. "Never been more sure about anything in my entire life."

He nodded. "That's what I love to hear. Let's get you hitched, beautiful."

I wrapped my left arm around the bulky arm he held out to me, and a second later music began playing. Holding up the bouquet of fake flowers I'd been given at the registry desk of the chapel, I proceeded to fall in line with Elvis and the music as we made our way down the aisle.

"I've got it from here," Robert told Elvis as soon as we made it to him. He took my hand in his, guiding us closer to the second Elvis impersonator, who would be reciting our vows.

"We are here today, to join this man and this woman ..." the officiant began.

I didn't hear much of what he said. The only thing I was aware of was the promise in Robert's eyes as he stared at me, my hands in his.

"I understand the groom has a few words he'd like to say."

I looked to the officiant and then to Robert. "I didn't know we were supposed to write out our own vows," I whispered as if there was a room full of people who could overhear.

"We weren't but I had something I wanted to add."

I stood upright, inhaling deeply as Robert squeezed both of my hands in his. "Deborah, from the first time we kissed I knew you were going to be my wife. There was no amount of time, doubt, or distance that ever made me waver in that knowledge. What I understood then, and am thankful for now, is that we needed those five years apart. I needed to grow into a better man for you. A man you would be proud to call your husband. I have taken that time to grow up, to understand who and what matters to me most. And I promise you that no one and nothing will ever come before you and our future children. This I vow to you on this day and forever more."

"Robert," I whispered his name, barely able to get it out through all of the emotion swelling in my body. I blinked a few times, to prevent the tears from falling. I was at a loss for words. I hadn't been prepared to say any vows of my own.

"You don't need to say anything, princess." Reaching up, he wiped away a tear from under my eyes. "Just say I do."

I nodded. "I do."

A heart-stopping smile covered his face. Elvis said a few more words that I couldn't make out because my emotions were running all over the place. I hardly remembered Robert slipping the wedding band around my ring finger. But I clearly recalled the kiss he planted on my lips once Elvis finally pronounced us husband and wife.

He kissed me with every bit of passion that was contained in his body, and I gave as much as I got.

"No backing out now," he said when he finally pulled away.

"I would never dream of it."

"Good." He lifted our clasped hands to his lips, pressing a kiss to mine just before we proceeded to walk down the aisle for the first time as man and wife. I let out a round of laughter when Elvis number one began tossing rice at us as we passed through the doors of the chapel.

We were official.

That smiling, laughing couple had no idea that back home, there was more than one figure plotting against our demise.

CHAPTER 17

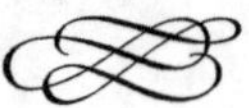

resent
    Tyler

"You never told me that that fucking Elvis tried to get you to run away," my father stated sharply from the head of the table.

The entire family, including all of the grandchildren, were seated in the dining area of my parents' home, Townsend Manor. The same place they'd run away from, the night of their engagement party.

"He was just making sure I really wanted to get married," my mother soothed, taking my father's hand in hers.

"Wait a minute," I spoke up, all eyes turning to me.

Before I could even say anything, my father groaned loudly.

"I told you he was going to pick up on it," my mother told him.

I lifted an eyebrow, looking between my parents. "You gave me … us," I corrected, taking Destiny's hand in mine, placing them on the dark wood of the table, "shit for eloping on a yacht when you two ran off and got married in Vegas? By an Elvis Presley impersonator, no less? You always told us you'd both gotten married here at Townsend Manor."

"We did," my mother quickly responded.

"A year after our Vegas wedding," my father clarified.

152

"So your anniversary date *isn't* September 19th, 1979."

"It is. We always told you the right date, just not the right location."

There was a collective sigh around the table. The wrong date would've thrown a monkey wrench into my brothers' and my plans.

"Anyway, back to my original question. What was with you giving me crap for our quickie wedding when you'd done it yourselves?"

"Tyler, watch your language at the dinner table," my mother scolded.

"Apologies."

"And please, I didn't give you half the sh—" My father paused, looking toward my mother who glared at him, eyebrow raised. "... difficulty my father gave me. Not that it made a difference either way," he added coolly.

We'd always known that my father hadn't had a great relationship with his own father. My grandfather had passed before I was born, so I never met the man, but from the little I did know about him, I wasn't a fan. However, I do know that some things he'd taught my father had stuck with him until this day. He'd even passed some of those lessons on to us.

"They really didn't give us a hard time, babe," my wife interjected. "Resha was more upset than your parents when she found out we'd gotten married."

I glanced down, grinning at Destiny. Her cousin and best friend, Resha, had indeed been pissed off when she found out Destiny and I had married, just the two of us, on a yacht in the Bahamas.

"I can't believe you kept that secret from us all of these years," Joshua added, the rest of the family nodding their heads in agreement.

"Some things aren't your business," my father stated with a shrug.

"Your wedding day isn't one of those things, Father," Aaron added, surprising most of us.

He of all people was one to talk about secrets. The man had had an ongoing relationship with his wife that produced two children long before any of us knew about it. Granted, he didn't even know about the children until they were five years old, but still.

"We're not the only one with secrets." My father's eyes narrowed on Aaron and then on the rest of us. "What happens in your relationship is best left between you and your spouse. Remember that, boys. It's okay to share some things with the outside world, but at the end of the day, remember who it is you come home to at night. Who you curl up next to in the bed before you go to sleep, and who you open your eyes to every morning. Your loyalty, first and foremost, is to your wife. A man who can't be faithful to his family is a man who can't be trusted, period, point blank."

We were all silent for a good thirty seconds, ingesting and digesting my father's words. I couldn't see them, because I was too busy looking at my own wife, but I was certain my three brothers were also looking at their wives, delivering silent promises with their gazes that lined up with my father's words, as I was.

An hour and a half later, I found myself trailing behind my wife, watching the sway of her ass in the knee-length, sleeveless, floral dress she wore, as she strolled down the hall, carrying Travis, our youngest triplet, in her arms. I firmly held Annalise and Tristan at either one of my sides.

We both worked to change the children's diapers, dress them in their pajamas for the evening and warm their bottles to give them before putting them down to sleep. With three babies, all eight months old, it was a task to get everyone to bed on time but it was one we were getting better at.

"Stop!" Destiny, whisper yelled, swatting at my hand after I'd just pinched her ass on the way out of our children's bedroom. We kept them all in the same room, for now, since the room was directly across the hall from our bedroom.

I frowned and then growled, grabbing the slip of a woman I'd married, pulling her soft body to my hard frame.

Giggling, she wrapped her arms around my neck. "You're incorrigible."

I grinned. "You know I love it when you use big words like that." I dipped my head, biting her chin before licking her neck. I lifted my head with her still in my arms. "We should have another baby."

Destiny sucked her teeth and pushed from my embrace, turning her back on me to head into our bedroom. I was expecting that exact response.

"Tyler Townsend, are you out of your mind?" she began as I entered the bedroom behind her.

I pulled open the top drawer of the mirrored nightstand that sat next to my side of the bed, reaching for a remote, before plopping down on the bed.

"Yup. Any other questions?" I pressed the power button on the remote, and the familiar noise of the retractable mirror that was above our bed sounded as it began to emerge from it concealment.

"Don't you dare," Destiny warned but she was much too late.

My gaze trailed down the length of her five-foot-two-inch frame. I licked my lips as the sight of the smooth, chestnut skin of her legs, anticipating having those legs locked around my waist.

"I'm going to take a shower."

"Let me get you dirty first," I growled, moving so quickly from my position on the bed to the other side of the room, she startled when I grabbed her from behind, spinning her around to face me.

My hand went to her left shoulder, slowly guiding the material of sleeveless dress down her arm along with the strap of her bra.

"We're not making another baby tonight."

"Says who?"

"Says this IUD I had inserted."

I frowned, my face morphing into a scowl at the remembrance of the copper hindrance to my impregnating my wife.

"Get it taken out," I ordered.

"No." She shook her head at the same time the back of her legs hit the bed.

"Why not?" I demanded.

"Tyler, how many children do we have?"

I lifted my face toward the ceiling. "Here we go."

"No, answer the question. How many children do we have?"

"Three, Destiny."

"And how many times have I been pregnant with *your* children?"

"Once."

"Exactly. I gave you not *one,* not *two,* but *three* whole children at one time. And now, you're begging for another."

I smirked. "Yes."

She rolled her eyes again. "See? Incorrigible."

I growled deep in my throat before cupping her face, bringing her lips to mine. Her lips parted instantly, as they always did when we kissed, because no matter how much she protested or how irredeemable she found me, she still knew who she belonged to. Her body knew, her mind knew, and her soul knew.

I tugged on the drawstring at the back of her dress, releasing it. The top half floated down to her waist and I wasted no time, quickly pushing the offending fabric the rest of the way down, leaving her clad in the silk bra and panty set she wore beneath. I knew the set well. It was a pair I'd purchased for her a few months back. She had made some ridiculous comment about not feeling sexy after giving birth to three children.

"Three is not enough," I growled, unclasping the bra.

"Tyler." She let out on a sigh while I pushed her back against the bed, moving over top of her.

"We deserve more babies. Another son or daughter that looks like you with your sharp wit and attitude." I pressed a kiss to the side of her neck before moving down to her chest, licking the tops of her breasts.

"I don't have an attitu— Oooh!" Her comment broke off on a moan when I pushed her breasts together and licked them.

I moaned, sounds of satisfaction emerging from the back of my throat as if I was savoring the best meal I'd ever had in my life. Because I was. Nothing tasted better than my wife.

I pulled at her panties, removing them from her legs before spreading them wide to give myself a full view of the prettiest pussy I'd ever had the pleasure of seeing.

"You do have an attitude but I have a remedy for that." I lowered my body until my mouth was even with her sex.

Destiny's thighs immediately clamped around the sides of my head but I wasn't deterred in the least. If anything, I was more turned on.

The more aroused she became the more I fucking became. No one sent me into overdrive like my wife could with just a moan or a look.

I lapped at her pussy like a dog who'd been out in the Texas sun all day without any water. It didn't matter that I'd had her just that morning. Going twelve hours without being inside of her, sometimes felt like the cruelest form of torture.

I inserted my fore and middle fingers into her wet core, and within seconds she was coming from the ministrations of my mouth and fingers.

But I gave her little time to recover, when I made quick work of stripping before moving back to the bed and turning her over so she was on all fours.

"Arch your back for daddy," I growled, pressing my palm to the center of her back. I began sliding in when her back curved downward, causing her ass to press backward into me.

"Shit! Tyler!" she screamed.

"Language, precious," I chided, using the pet name I'd given her, while smacking the back of her ass.

I licked my lips at watching her butt jiggle from my hand. So much so, I smacked her again, causing her to jump and press back against me, all while moaning my name.

Damn, nothing sounded sweeter than hearing her moan my name as I rode her into climax.

I bent over her body and reached my arms underneath her to pull her up so that her back pressed against my chest.

"I'd hate to have to remind you of the consequences of your foul language, precious."

"Screw you, Tyler!"

My cock jumped inside of her. Damn I loved it when she defied me. I knew she loved it, too.

Wrapping my hand around her throat, just under her chin, I forced her head to turn upward toward me. I crashed my lips over hers, and pushed her knees farther apart with my own, allowing me to slide in deeper from behind her. My hips sped up at the same time my free hand wrapped her body to allow my fingers to play with her clitoris.

She reached her hands up, one going to the back of my head, her fingers playing in my hair. Her other hand cupped my tricep. The little moans that poured from her mouth were swallowed down my throat.

I felt her thighs begin to tremble.

"Are you about to come for me, baby?" I pulled back and whispered low in her ear.

"Y-yes!" she hissed.

"No, you're not," I retorted, abruptly halting the movements of my hips and hands, pulling away from her body.

"What the fuck?" Destiny yelped.

I had to fight with all of the strength I had in my body not to bend her over again and plunge my cock as deep as I could get it inside of her core. I knew she was right on the brink of coming. But my darling little wife needed to learn a lesson.

"Tyler," she growled from the bed as I strode, on shaky legs, toward our bathroom. "Get your ass back here!"

I glanced over my shoulder, my entire body going rigid at the sight of her naked and wanting on our bed. But I held firm.

"Shhh, precious. You don't want to wake up the children, do you?" I turned and entered the bathroom, just managing to hold on to my own sanity. My body wanted nothing more than to come inside of my wife.

"Oh they need to wake up," she stated a few moments later, entering our bathroom behind me. "Because it might just be the last time they see their father before I kill him."

I chuckled, turning to her to see her frowning, eyebrows narrowed, her beautiful face full of scorn. Damn she was gorgeous and hot as hell when pissed. And with the ache in my cock growing, my resolve didn't stand a chance.

She gasped when I grabbed her by the waist, spinning her to face our huge mirror over the countertop. I planted her hands against the granite counter, pushed her knees apart with my own, and plunged deep inside of the walls of her pussy.

The moan she let out was fierce, and I really did fear she might wake the children. But all of my common sense was lost by then.

"Are you going to give me another baby, Destiny?" I groaned loudly in her ear.

"Ty-Tyler … don't stop," she pleaded instead of answering.

A smack to her ass had her pounding against the countertop with her fist.

"That wasn't the answer I was looking for. Try again." I smacked her ass once more and plunged deeper, causing her to rise on her tiptoes.

"Shit!" She leaned over the counter, her arms growing weak.

"Destiny, are you going to give me another baby?" I demanded.

"Fuck! Yesss!" she screamed. Simultaneously, her pussy muscles clenched, legs trembled, and she began milking my cock for every ounce of my life-producing fluid.

The orgasm ripped through my body, ferociously. I came for what felt like forever, all the while pumping into my wife as if my body was desperately trying to override the offending birth control that was imbedded into her womb.

Not until the last drop of semen poured from me, did I finally unseat myself from inside of her. We both collapsed into a sweaty heap onto the cool, marble flooring of our bathroom.

All that could be heard was the sound of the both of us, catching our breaths until I finally said, "When can we get started on making the next one?"

* * *

Destiny

"What am I going to do with you?" I questioned, out loud in the dark bedroom as I laid in our massive bed, facing my husband. I ran my hand down the side of his face, lightly running my fingers through the short hairs of the auburn-colored beard that was only a few days old. His eyes were closed but he wasn't sleeping.

He turned his head, planting a kiss to the inside of my palm before opening his eyelids to stare directly into mine. "Love me."

My heart squeezed in my chest. "I already do."

All thirty-two of his pearly whites could be seen with the smile he expressed.

"Give me a few months. Until the triplets are one."

He frowned.

"Tyler, they're almost eight months. That's only four months away. Then I'll get the IUD removed and we can start trying."

Sighing, he rolled over onto his back, pulling me by the arm to move closer into his body. I did so, until my head was on his chest.

"It's a deal."

I pressed a kiss to his chest. "Are you okay?" I questioned, knowing something else was bothering him. Something he'd been carrying around for a while now.

"Would you be okay if I retired from the NFL?"

I lifted my head to be able to see his face. The dimness of the low lighting of his nightstand allowed me to see him just enough to see the question in those hazel-green eyes of his.

"You're still considering it?"

He nodded.

After the triplets were born, and all of the upheaval that'd surrounded their birth, Tyler had decided to take a leave of absence from the National Football League where he was one of the top quarterbacks. Needless to say, it was a controversial decision for a man in his position. Some in the public eye had said that his actions served as proof that he wasn't really committed to his profession, echoing the sentiments that plagued his collegiate and professional careers. Because he'd been born into wealth, many outsiders didn't believe he'd had to work as hard to earn his position.

I knew those claims were bullshit.

My husband busted his ass every time he put on the jersey for his team.

But I also knew that dedication, times ten, was what he carried off the field for his family. Most of the idiots talking didn't know the story behind the birth of our children. The fact that I was attacked and almost killed which led to my needing to give birth while our babies were only thirty-one weeks. It was a scary time and Tyler had been our rock through it all.

I reached up to cup his cheek. "You know I've got no problem being your sugar mama," I teased.

He smirked a little.

"Are you still thinking of coaching?"

"A little. Coaching requires a lot of time and travel, also."

"But it's something you've always wanted to do. And it won't be as taxing on you physically, as playing. You'd be home more with the kids and I. And trust me, if I'm giving you a fourth baby, your ass better be home," I stated, sternly.

I yelped when I suddenly found myself flat on my back, my husband's long, solid frame hovering over me, his arms wrapped around my waist. Dipping his head, he planted a quick kiss to my lips.

"There's no *if*, precious. We're having number four. And I could play one more season and then take one to two years off, still working with sponsors and sports camps before I jump full-time into coaching."

I smiled. "Sounds like you've got it all worked out."

"Mostly. The only other thing I have to work out is how to get my wife to come on the road with me when I am traveling."

I gave him a deadpan look. "Tyler—"

"Your podcast with Resha can be broadcast from anywhere. You've already got the technology set up for that since she travels for work. Most of your business clients would have zero problem working with you remotely, and the kids could come with us, when they're not in school. When they are in school, we'd have a full-time nanny, and not to mention, we live in the same neighborhood as my entire family. They could stay with them, and we both know your mom wouldn't mind staying with them while we're out of town."

I shook my head, laughing. He'd really worked it all out in his mind before talking to me. That's how he was. The consummate problem solver. Never liking to approach me with a problem until he'd figured out the solution. As much as it bothered me at times, it also aided in making me feel cared for, and know that I was married to a man who would do whatever to protect and provide for our family.

"She does love that room," I said, referring to the room Tyler had especially added to the plans of the house when it was being built. It was for my mother, and was on the first floor, so she wouldn't have to climb the stairs of our home, given her Parkinson's.

"She loves her grandchildren even more."

I nodded. That was the truth, and my mother would be elated to spend more time with them.

"I could probably take some time off, too," I mused out loud.

Tyler lifted his head to stare down at me, raising an eyebrow.

I shrugged. "I could take fewer clients and continue doing the podcast with Resha."

"Are you sure?"

Smiling, I leaned closer to kiss Tyler's lips. I loved that he appreciated my desire to work and make my own money. Considering his wealth from birth, and the money he'd accumulated in the NFL, our children's children wouldn't have to work a day in their lives. But my career provided me with more than just money. It gave me the deep satisfaction of knowing I was making an impact on people's lives by helping organize their finances in a way that served them. But I was ready to be more present with my family.

"I am. And given the fact that I'll be working more with your mom and the ladies at the shelter, I'll still get to provide my knowledge of personal finance to women who need it. And I'll get to take the kids with me to spend time in the daycare. It's a win-win."

"The shelter's really turning out to be a family affair." His fingers trailed slowly up and down my bare arm.

"It is," I added wistfully on a sigh. "Resha's even going to help by giving fashion pointers for interviews, makeup tips for the workplace, and how to carry yourself with confidence." I was excited that Deborah had been open to allowing my cousin to join us in helping the women who would be entering the shelter.

"I'm so proud of you all."

I moved closer to plant another kiss to his lips. "Thank you, baby. Oh, speaking of your parents, did you book the hotel rooms for all of us?"

He nodded. "Of course. Five days, four nights in the luxury suite. Aaron, Josh, and Carter booked as well, and Mother and Father's tickets were booked well in advance."

I sat up, clapping in excitement. "This trip is going to be epic. I can't wait to see the expressions on their faces."

Tyler's long arms reached for my waist, moving to position me over his body. He had that gleam in his eyes. The one that always sent a current of electricity through my body and caused a flood at my center.

"I'm more interested in the look I'm about to put on your face right now."

I moaned, throwing my head back as I slipped down onto his erection. "You shouldn't feel this damn good after all of this time," I murmured.

Tyler chuckled. "Precious, it's only going to get better and better from here."

His hands tightened around my hips, and together we began moving into a rhythm that I was certain, had it not been for my IUD, would've resulted in another child. Hell, in between gasps and moans, I silently prayed my birth control was strong enough to stand up to the pleasure my husband was unleashing.

CHAPTER 18

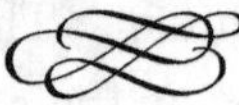

*P*resent
Robert

I glanced at the name flashing across the screen of my cell phone. I pressed the button, and a second later my oldest son's face appeared.

"Shouldn't you be in bed next to your wife?"

He frowned, and his blue eyes—which mirrored his mother's—narrowed. "She's with Sam. I swear that kid just knows we're trying to make another baby."

I chuckled deep in my throat. "Just like you were when I was trying to make your brothers." I laughed harder when Carter's face crumpled up in disgust.

"The last thing I ever need to hear about is you and my mother ..." He broke off, shaking his head.

"Grow up, son. You're a father and husband yourself. You know what it takes to make babies. Your mother and I—"

"Lalalala," he began singing, sticking his fingers in his ears.

"Alright, alright," I stated in between laughs. "What are you calling me for while your wife's taking care of your youngest?"

"I know there's more."

I lifted an eyebrow.

"Don't give me that look. More to your and mother's relationship. You both said at dinner the other night that while you were getting married there were those plotting against you. I want the details."

Insistent little fucker. All of my boys were. Aaron had called me earlier that morning with the same question, but he'd quickly been called away for a work issue before I could get the story out.

"How do you know we weren't just making that up?"

He gave me a *get real* expression. "I know there's something more to that Jack guy. And Cohen. I know Mother's ex just didn't walk away so easily."

I nodded. He'd hit the nail on the head.

"It's why you taught all of us to kill a motherfucker if he threatens our family."

I pitched forward in my chair, my arms folding over one another on the hardwood desk I sat at in my home office.

"You bet your ass it is."

"Then spill."

I narrowed my eyes. "I don't take orders from you."

"Father—"

"Alright, alright." I nodded. "Here's the story …"

* * *

Then

Robert

"The leaks are still happening," my father snapped, his voice pissed off, as he stood at the corner of the room. He stared down at the city some twenty floors below us.

I cut my eyes in his direction. "What did you expect?" I was beginning to loathe my father.

"Not this!" He grunted, turning to face me.

I was unfazed by his antics. He was an empty suit. I'd been the one running the company over the last few years. But I was powerless when it came to implementing the changes I really wanted to make. Which included getting to the bottom of the leaks, and tapping the board to let us pursue greater research and development funds in new technological advances and different forms of energy. However, they all saw my father as the helm of the company still, and they deferred to his assessments when it came to what changes to approve.

The problem was, my father was envious of me. I'd felt it all along, since I was a teenager, really. I was smarter than he was. I had more insight into the future. But instead of being proud of that fact and letting me pursue my ideals, he held the reins of the company tighter. At least, he tried to.

"This is your fault," he charged, jabbing his finger in my direction.

I sunk my hands into the pockets of my suit pants because they were growing itchy at the sight of his fucking face. And while the thought of punching my father didn't necessarily repulse me, I would not do it in the office.

"How is this my fault?"

"Because your focus has been off. Ever since you married that—"

"Choose your words with extreme care," I threatened.

My father stopped short, his face reddening, but he wasn't deterred for too long. "Your wife. Ever since you ran off and got married like some commoner, things have been falling apart. Your head's not in the game."

It'd been six months since Deb and I had flown to Vegas and gotten married. Obviously my father still wasn't over it. And I didn't give a shit, either.

"Like some commoner? Do you hear yourself? Speaking as if we're royalty or something."

"We might as well be!" He slammed his fist into his open palm.

I rolled my eyes away from his, shaking my head. My father always had an enormous inferiority complex that masqueraded as his need to feel and tell everyone how superior he was to them.

"The leaks are happening because you won't let me get to the bottom of it. It's affecting our stock prices, and I just got a call this morning from a partner of ours who is growing concerned with everything he keeps hearing in the papers."

"Did you tell him what I told you to tell him?"

The scowl I wore whenever I was in the presence of my father deepened. "No one is buying that bullshit *'we're looking into the leaks and doing everything we can to stop them'* line anymore. It's been well over a year since the leaks began. Our investors are getting antsy. And you know what happens when investors get antsy."

My father's expression turned grim, and for a second it seemed like he was actually beginning to understand how deep this problem ran. But then he opened his mouth and said, "No, just stick to what I instructed you to tell everyone. This will eventually blow over."

My shoulders sagged. I knew he didn't have the fucking heart to make the right decision. To put his ego to the side and do what was right for the company. He needed to feel like he was in charge, when the truth of the matter was, it had been that way since his stroke.

I was done playing games. I didn't say anything—I simply nodded and turned on my heels, to exit my father's office. I strode down the hall to my office, shutting my door behind me before I picked up the phone on my desk.

"Hello?"

"Thiers." I was relieved to hear his voice at the other end.

"Robert? Calling in the middle of the day? Must be serious."

"It is. I'm tired of these fucking leaks and I need your help to get to the bottom of it all."

* * *

"Is this like the last job?" the behemoth of a man standing in front of me questioned.

Even at my six-foot-three height, I had to look up to meet the gaze of the six-foot-seven former Vietnam vet, turned private investigator, who Thiers had connected me with months ago.

We were standing in the Buddy's gym. This was the spot Thiers and I met when we needed to meet during the day.

Shaking my head, I folded my arms over my chest. "No, that was personal. This is business."

His lifted a dark blond brow; his face looked as if it was set in stone. "There's a difference?"

I pivoted, turning toward Thiers. He just shrugged and looked between the two of us.

"In this case, yes," I responded.

"How'd you make out with that little filly, anyway?"

"Little what?" I questioned sternly, my top lip curling.

"The little filly you had me look into a few months back. She was a looker—"

"Hey, Rick, I'd calm all that down if I were you. This man's married to her now," Thiers interjected.

Rick turned to me, brows raised, shocked.

"And her name's Deborah."

He nodded slowly, his lips moving into a smirk. "Well, congratulations. My invite must've gotten lost in the mail."

Thiers chuckled. "All of ours did. This fucker flew to Vegas and got married by an Elvis impersonator."

The big fuck let out a guffaw right along with Thiers. "That must've been a sight."

"It was. Look, we're not here to talk about my wife, my marriage, or anything else that doesn't have to do with getting to the bottom of the bullshit going on with Townsend Industries."

Rick sobered up and nodded, his face quickly morphing into a serious expression. "You've been having some trouble."

"That's right."

"So what are you coming to me for? Townsend has some of the best security around from what I hear."

I nodded. "That's the exact reason I need you. We have state of the art security and a hiring process that is meant to weed out potential corporate spies, and yet we're still dealing with this shit."

"You're thinking it's an inside job?"

"I know it is."

"Then why not go to daddy and have him hire new staff?"

I curled my top lip upward, scowling, but breathed deeply to calm my growing irritation at this line of questioning. I knew Rick was trying to goad me, to feel me out and see what I was really after. This wasn't the simple 'look up a person, find out their address and where they worked' type of thing I had him do with Deborah. This was possible corporate espionage which could be a federal offense.

"Because his head is too far up his ass."

That caught Ricker's attention. Folding his arms over his broad chest, he stared at me, his sharp hazel eyes assessing me.

"My father's an empty suit. He knows it and I know it. But the board isn't willing to oust him yet, and it'll be a cold day in hell before he turns the reins of Townsend Industries over to me."

"Why?"

"Because he knows I'll do a better job than he ever could. And legally … for the most part."

Rick looked to Thiers. "He's serious."

"As a heart attack," Thiers quickly retorted. "I wouldn't fuck with him if I were you."

Rick turned back to me. "What do you need?"

I nodded. "I need to know where these leaks are coming from. Who at Townsend is behind it, who on the outside is gaining from these leaks, and …"

"And then you need to know how to fix it."

I shook my head. "No, I know some guys at the Justice Department, SEC, and the FBI. Once we find out who is behind this, I know who to contact to make sure they're put behind bars."

Rick nodded. "Sounds like a job I'd be willing to take on. I'm always up for a good corporate espionage case. Give me a minute, while I make a call to my office to reschedule an appointment, and I'll be back to talk to you about some more of the details."

I nodded and watched as he strolled off in the direction of the gym's office to make his call.

"You trust that guy?" I questioned, turning to Thiers.

"I do." He nodded. "He served with my cousin in 'Nam. Saved his life. He's been back over five years now, and started working as a PI four and a half years ago. He's done a couple of jobs for me. Helped you find Deborah when you first discovered she was here in Williamsport."

I tilted my head. Thiers was right about that, and it was something I'd always be grateful to Rick Kennedy for.

"He ever take on anything this big?"

Thiers shrugged. "Not sure but you can ask him. He's up to the job, you saw him."

I pushed out a full breath. Thiers was right. Rick, for whatever reason, felt like the right person to handle this. He was an outsider, didn't have any ties to Townsend Industries, my father, or the high society world I came from. He didn't have skin in the game, and he was sharp. He knew his stuff, and from Thiers and other clients of his I'd talked to, he was highly intelligent and capable. All of the traits I would need to get to the bottom of these leaks and stomp them out.

CHAPTER 19

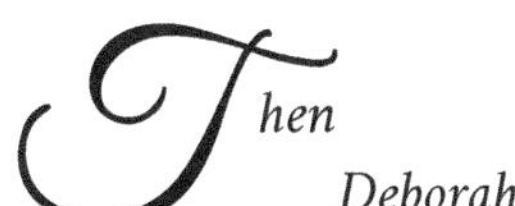

hen
Deborah

"And have you had a chance to look over the finances for the new Enchanted line?" my manager, Steve, questioned as we sat down to lunch. We were back at the Crown Jewel restaurant. I'd grown a little nostalgic for this place since it was the first time I'd seen Robert again after five years.

I briefly thought about how much had changed in the past eight months since that day. Not only had I reunited with Robert but he and I were *married.* A little over six months now.

"Deborah."

I blinked and looked across the round table at Steve who was staring at me, a knowing grin on his face.

"I'm sorry, what did you say?"

"Marital bliss, huh?" His eyes moved from mine, lowering to my hands as I held them in front of me.

I glanced down and realized I'd been twisting my wedding ring as I stared off into space, daydreaming about my husband. This was becoming somewhat of a habit.

"Is it obvious?" I asked. I tried to keep my marriage to myself while at work. Not only did I not want to talk too much about Robert, knowing everyone was interested because of his last name, but I also didn't want to give my supervisors any ammunition to look me over when it came time for promotions. While women in the corporate world had come a long way, there was still much left to be desired when it came to breaking through the glass ceiling, so to speak. The fact that I was now married to an extremely wealthy man, felt like it had almost everyone I worked with making bets as to when I would announce my resignation. They had another thing coming.

"Oh, only to someone who is looking at you," Steve said.

I ducked my head.

"Don't be ashamed," he quickly added. "This world is too small and too crazy to pretend like you're not happy."

An odd feeling came over me at the sadness I saw in his face, but it quickly disappeared, and his friendly smile returned.

"Back to the Enchanted line."

I pulled out the file I'd brought with me to lunch, and we began discussing the financial issues surrounding the production of this new cosmetic line for our company. We spent the hour talking about financial projections, marketing strategies, and the cost of branding and advertisement.

"We'll need to meet with marketing and advertising next week to nail down these numbers. You know they do not enjoy this kind of stuff."

Laughing a little, I shook my head. "I'm well aware. But it's a necessity."

"If you don't mind, I'm going over to the building next door for a meeting."

I quickly nodded and waved Steve off. "No problem. I'm just going to head back to the office."

We parted ways, and I checked the time on my watch to see it was only about ten of one. I'd make it back to the office by one and would give Robert a call. We often talked at some point during the afternoon, if only for a few minutes since both of us were busy at work.

"Still eating at the Crown Jewel? Must be why you dumped me for your rich boyfriend."

I turned, the hairs on the back of my neck raising at the sneer I heard in Cohen's voice. I faced him to see a deep frown marring his usually handsome face.

"Cohen ..." I was a little stunned at the almost menacing glare he was giving me.

He blinked and his features seemed to relax but only slightly. "Deborah Tate, how nice of you to join us peasants at the Crown Jewel of all places. How is your boyfriend doing? What was his name? Randy? Roy—"

"Robert," I stated firmly, knowing full well he knew the name. "Robert Townsend, and he's *not* my boyfriend."

"Oh?" he questioned, lifting an eyebrow, a sardonic smile creasing his lips.

"No. He's my husband." To add to my statement, I waved my left hand in front of my face so Cohen could see the diamond and gold wedding band on my ring finger.

His smile instantly dropped. "He married you?"

My head jutted backward at the incredulity I heard in Cohen's voice. As if he was completely knocked over by the fact that Robert would marry me.

"He must be trying to get back at his father."

"Excuse me?"

Cohen looked at me, his eyes narrowing. "Come on, Deborah. You can't think a guy like Robert Townsend is actually serious about *you*."

"*Me?*"

"Yes. I mean, get real. You're beautiful and all, but you come from nowhere Kentucky. You have no social standing. What would Robert Townsend want with—"

"Cohen, I think it would be best if you didn't finish that sentence. I'm going to walk away now. Don't ever speak to me again. If you see me walking down the street, cross it."

Spinning around, I made a beeline for the door of the restaurant to head back to work. I was so angry, I was sure steam was coming out of my head. I couldn't believe Cohen's words. They were like a slap to the face. I'd spent time telling him how I felt like an outcast at times. Like I sometimes wasn't meant to be in the role I was in at my job. Cohen was the one who first introduced me to the term imposter syndrome. And there he was, throwing it all in my face by telling me someone like Robert only married me to score points in a feud with his father.

"Hi," I answered the phone in my office, breathless and a little agitated.

"Hey. Everything alright?" Robert's voice was on high alert. I could just picture his cinnamon-colored eyes moving from side to side, trying to mull over what had me so worked up.

"I'm fine. Just ran into someone on my way back from lunch."

"Who?"

"Co—" I paused, knowing that name would not go over well with my jealous husband. "Cochren, a former manager in our finance department. He lost his job after the merger last year and he's still a little bitter about it."

"He was making trouble for you?"

I blinked, internally chastising myself for getting Robert worked up. If I knew my husband as well as I thought I did, I had no doubt that he'd be looking Cochren up to give him a piece of his mind.

"No, he just said a few words to Steve. But Steve took care of it. No big deal."

"Then why did you sound upset?"

I rolled my eyes. Sometimes I wished I had a husband who wasn't so damn observant.

"Hey, you know what I was thinking for dinner? Grilled cheese and tomato soup. The grocer not too far from my job just started selling this amazing tomato bisque. I had it for lunch yesterday. It should be much more pleasing to your palette than Campbell's."

I sighed when he chuckled on the other end of the line.

"Only if you're making grilled cheese with gouda."

"I told you you would like it," I said in a 'gotcha' voice.

"You were right. But how about this time I'll try to make it? You just bring the soup."

Tilting my head, I briefly pulled the phone from my ear. "Robert Townsend is going to try his hand at cooking? Well I'll be—"

"That's enough of that."

I giggled, covering my mouth so my coworkers wouldn't overhear me too much. Robert wasn't one for cooking, having dealt with hired staff his entire life for that purpose. But I loved that he was open to learning. He kept saying that his sons would need to know how to cook, just in case. He was adamant about this four sons thing. Speaking of …

"Hey, have you spoken to Jason?"

There was a brief pause on the other end.

"I called yesterday but they didn't answer."

"It's been a couple of months now."

He sighed. "I know."

Jason and his wife, Jesse, had lost the baby she'd been pregnant with. While Robert still had his doubts that the baby was even Jason's, we had tried to be there for the couple. Unfortunately, it appeared Jason was dealing with the loss in the usual destructive ways he dealt with life. Only this time, Jesse was along for the ride, seeming to stick by his side.

"Maybe we should invite them over this weekend."

"Deborah—"

"Hear me out, Robert. Jason obviously envies you and was trying to one up you. But he and his wife are dealing with a loss. She was five months pregnant. I remember when they came over a few weeks before it happened. Jesse was so happy to feel the baby kicking inside of her. I can't imagine the pain she must be feeling. Surely, you can put aside whatever anger you have toward your brother to comfort him and his wife."

It took a while for Robert to respond. Finally, he pushed out a heavy breath and said, "I'll invite them over. We'll have dinner together this weekend, whether he wants to or not."

I nodded even though he couldn't see me.

"I love you."

"You're really going to love me after this gouda grilled cheese I prepare tonight."

I giggled just before hanging up the phone.

Minutes later, I realized that my mood had shifted entirely. That short conversation with Robert had been enough to lighten my spirits and shrug off what Cohen had said earlier.

I didn't need to concern myself with what Cohen or anyone else thought of Robert and my relationship. In my heart, I knew we were made for each other.

* * *

Then

Robert

"It's not looking good," Rick stated as I sat across from him at a local dive diner we'd designated as our meeting spot. The diner was located on the outskirts of Williamsport, far from Townsend Industries.

"What's not looking good?"

Rick parted his mouth but then quickly closed it when the waitress brought us the meals we'd ordered. I immediately pushed my plate aside, wanting to know more about what he'd found in his investigation so far, than in any food.

I watched as he cut into the T-bone steak he'd ordered with eggs and biscuits. How anyone could eat steak at seven in the morning was beyond me. But that wasn't my concern at the moment.

"None of it," he answered after swallowing his food. He wiped his hands before sliding a manila envelope across the cracked wood of the table.

Taking the envelope, I pulled out the photos that were inside. I looked them over, as Rick continued to eat. The first three or four photos were of men who worked for Townsend as execs. The photos were of them getting in and out of cars, or meeting with my father or another coworker over lunch. The final photo was what had shocked me. I paused, holding it up, examining every angle of the picture.

"Is this Deborah?" My eyes went to Rick. It was a stupid question. The image was of a woman from behind, but I knew my wife. I knew what she looked like from every angle. I didn't need to see her face to know it was her.

"She look familiar?"

"Don't get fucking coy."

Rick slowly placed the knife and fork he'd been using to cut his food down, and wiped his mouth with one of the paper napkins before peering across the table at me.

"Look, this is what the investigation has turned up so far. That looks eerily similar to a woman fitting your wife's description. And they," he nodded toward the picture, "are two men standing to greet her. Two men who work for Townsend Industries. One is high up in Townsend's security staff, and the other is—"

"Will Chisolm. He's a top exec in the finance department."

"You know your employees better than I do."

I nodded. "What is this supposed to prove?"

"Nothing so far, but I think we're getting somewhere. I believe the leaks are coming from the finance department of Townsend. I've been able to track them down that much, so far."

"Deborah has nothing to do with this," I sneered.

Rick held up his large hands in a surrendering fashion. "I'm not saying she does. I'd hate to be the one to tell another man his wife is screwing him behind his back. I'm just saying, I've tracked the breaches to the finance department in your company. Will is one of your top guys in that department. He also is pretty close with your father, so one could speculate that means he has insider information that no one else would have. He knew about your father's stroke … one of the few who did. Doesn't Deborah work in finance for—"

"Don't question me about my wife. Ever." My voice was coated in steel.

Rick stared at me, pausing for a moment, before proceeding to pick up his knife and fork, cutting into the remainder of his food.

"Just remember, you hired me to get to the bottom of this. And you paid upfront. Cash. So it's my job to deliver. No matter where the twists and turns lead, I will track them down until I get the answers you asked me to get. Just brace yourself because those answers could end you up in a world of hurt if you're not prepared for them."

I watched as he casually bit into his last piece of steak, savoring it as if he hadn't just delivered me with the possibility that my wife was in some way connected to the deception threatening to take down Townsend Industries.

CHAPTER 20

*A*aron

"Mark, hold my calls for the next hour," I barked out as I passed my head assistant's desk, striding down the hallway toward the glass door.

"Your meeting with Merc is at two," he called after me.

"Shit," I grunted, having forgotten all about the meeting with my vice president. My head was too occupied with outside distractions. Glancing at my watch, I discovered it was just after one in the afternoon. "Reschedule it."

"What time?" he called again to my back as I'd already pivoted to head for the door.

"Any other day besides today."

"Okay, and—"

"Mark, if you ask me one more thing before I walk out of this door, I assure you you will not have a job to come back to tomorrow."

Mark's lips clamped shut and he didn't even flinch as he placed his attention on the computer screen in front of him.

With that I turned and walked out of the door, pressing the button on the elevator that led to the private garage where the town car that'd brought me into work was parked. I should've felt guilty for threatening Mark, but as the longest assistant I've ever had—with close to two years—he understood me. Truth was, I wouldn't really fire him … well, not over asking another question. Either way, my focus was off at work and I needed to talk to someone about it, so I headed to the one place I thought I might get a little perspective.

"I think this might be the first time you've ever been down to the station," Carter greeted, a stunned expression on his face as he came down the stairs of the fire station. He was dressed in the dark, navy blue pants, and short-sleeve shirt that was his uniform. My eyes drifted down to the bright, white and golden patch that read Lieutenant Townsend, distinguishing him from the rest of his squad. A swell of pride hit my chest, not for the first time, at the sight of him in his newly minted position.

"I was here a few years ago when you were first assigned to Rescue Four."

His forehead creased, eyebrows dipping, and then rose. "That's right." He snapped his fingers, pointing at me. "I recall. That was a long time ago."

I nodded. Long before either one of us were husbands or fathers.

"What's up, bro?" he questioned, giving me a wary look. "Everything okay?"

I shrugged. "Not quite. Do you have a lunch break or something?"

He frowned. "I'm on a twenty-four hour shift. We don't have lunch breaks during those."

I narrowed my gaze on him.

Slowly, a grin spread across his face and he patted me on the shoulder.

"Calm down, I'm messing with you. I actually just clocked out when Captain came up and told me you were here to see me."

"You don't need to get home?"

He shook his head. "Michelle's still at work. Diego's in school for the next couple of hours, and Sam's with the sitter. What's up?"

I pushed out a breath. "I'm starving, let's get something to eat."

"There's that Italian place you like that's not too far from here."

"Buona Sera."

Carter glanced over at me.

"Let's eat somewhere else." That restaurant was where I'd had my first unofficial date with my wife. The place I took her while courting, and when we first married. It was a place for just she and I. I wasn't in the mood to share it with anyone else, even if that someone else was my brother.

"Cool. Let's check out the new Asian fusion place down the street."

I refrained from frowning, hating the concept of Asian fusion anything, but I was hungry and I hadn't come here to spend an hour deciding where to eat.

Fifteen minutes later, Carter and I were sitting across from one another, while our waitress brought our glasses of water with lemon.

"Do you need more time to order or are you ready now?" she questioned through a wide smile as she looked between the two of us.

We ordered our food, and I waited until the waitress left, not missing the extra glances she tossed our way, before turning my attention to my brother.

"I need to talk to you."

Carter gave me a deadpan expression. "I assume that's why we're here. What's up?"

"I, uh …" I paused, not even knowing where to begin. For the first time in a long time I found myself stumped.

"How bad did you fuck up?"

My shoulders sagged. "Bad."

He whistled low.

"Patience is pregnant."

"Whoop!" he cheered, clapping, genuinely excited by the news.

As I glared at him, I'm sure my face was turning red with the anger that was starting to well up in me.

Carter suddenly quieted upon seeing my expression. "Wait … you're saying that was your fuck up? Getting your wife pregnant?"

I took a sip of my water before answering. "Do I need to remind you of what happened the last time she gave birth?" I fucking hoped I didn't.

"Of course I remember. But, Aaron—"

"It's not uncommon. Women die carrying and birthing children almost every fucking day. And it's not just women who don't have healthcare. And I won't go into the stats for women of color …" My voice trailed off, my hands balling into fists at the tension this particular conversation always brought up in me.

"You've been doing your research."

"Of course. I'm preparing a chart to show Patience to explain to her why getting an abortion is the right thi—"

"Wait. Stop. Don't say another word. Did you just fucking say what I think you did?" He didn't even bother to hold his question until our waitress finished placing our plates in front of us and left.

I remained silent, my jaw flexing as I grinded my teeth together, waiting for the waitress to leave. When she did, I looked back to the brother who was only older than me by a few months.

"I did," I said, in response to his question.

"Start from the beginning. I've gotta hear this."

I hesitated, but finally pushed out a breath, and told Carter what happened the evening Patience first told me she was pregnant.

"She hasn't really spoken to me in the last two weeks."

"I bet," Carter stated, shaking his head as if he agreed with my wife.

"She can't have this baby. All she needs to do is understand the possible consequences and why she cannot have this cannot happen. I am more than open to adoption. I've made that—"

"Adoption?" He pulled a face, frowning at me over the forkful of food he'd brought halfway to his mouth. His blue eyes, just like Mother's, narrowed in the same way hers did when she gave me one of her disapproving expressions.

I didn't get those looks too often, but when I did I had to avert my eyes. But I refused to turn away from Carter. I wasn't in the wrong here.

"Aaron, you just asked … no, excuse me, you *demanded* that your wife get an abortion. Can you take a second to pause and think about how that made her feel?"

I rolled my eyes up toward the ceiling. "I know she was upset."

"Upset? Upset?"

I lowered my gaze when I heard his fork clink against the porcelain dish in front of him.

"The kids spill their juice on a white sofa, expect your wife to be upset. You come home an hour late to a romantic dinner she had planned, expect her to be a little upset. You come too quick and she doesn't get off—"

"She always gets off first," I interrupted sternly.

Carter rolled his eyes. "You know what the fuck I mean. When you demand that your *wife,* whom you have four kids with already, get an abortion—not because you can't adequately take care of the child in some way but because you're scared of what might happen, you need to expect she'll be way passed *upset.*"

"She almost died!" I yelled, slamming my fist on the table. I ignored the onlookers who I could see out of my peripheral looking our way.

Carter, however, wasn't disturbed in the least. My anger rarely bothered him.

"Get pissed all you want, but just know, you fucked up." He shook his head. "I can't fucking believe you," he said before stick a forkful of food in his mouth.

We were silent for a few minutes as we both ate. I didn't even taste the steamed red snapper and sautéed vegetables I'd ordered. At that point, I was just eating for sustenance, having not eaten since the night before. I had all types of tension coursing through my body. I hadn't touched my wife in two weeks. The longest we'd ever gone since the twins were born and she'd been cleared after the six week check up. I was horny, agitated, and though I loathed to admit it, scared shitless.

"Did you even stop once to consider she might be scared?"

My eye rose to meet Carter's as he stared at me.

I sat back in my wooden chair, knowing he had more to say.

"Have you? I mean, yes, you were there. You walked into the hospital room to find her being worked on by nurses and doctors. I'm sure that was terrifying. I couldn't even ima—" His voice broke off as he shook his head. "But Patience was the one who went through it. She was the one who bled out minutes after delivering her two children. Did you once stop to ask her how she felt about being pregnant?"

I opened my mouth to respond but no words came out. Clamping my mouth shut, I wiped my lips with the linen napkin that had sat in my lap.

I shrugged off Carter's words. "After we brought Thiers and Andreas home, she agreed that we were done having children. We'd consider adoption in the future but her getting pregnant wasn't an option."

"I'm sure this was right after she got out of the hospital and you did most of the talking in that conversation."

My scowl deepened as I narrowed my eyes on Carter. "I didn't force her to agree."

"You probably didn't." He tilted his head, conceding that point. "I'm sure if Patience didn't want that she would have made her disagreement vocal enough. But it's what? A year later, and here she is pregnant. So what changed?"

"Nothing. She simply forgot to take her birth control."

Carter grunted. "So you made the decision to not have anymore kids but you left the birth control up to her?"

"She agreed, asshole. And I didn't leave it up to her the way you're implying. She chose to get on the pill."

Carter wiped his mouth, nodding. "I'm sure."

He didn't sound too sure.

"And now, things have changed." He set his finished plate to the side and leaned in, arms folded over the table. "Look, I'm not telling you what to do. But you came to me for a reason. I'm certain Father would just tell you to get your head out of your ass and stand by your wife, holding her hand, and to take your ass out to the store to get whatever weird shit she's craving."

"Hostess cupcakes," I supplied.

He paused looking at me, questioningly.

"She craves them when she's pregnant." I'd already seen a few wrappers in the kitchen's garbage can a few days prior. A small form of guilt hit my belly when I realized I wasn't the one who had made the grocery store run to get what she'd been craving.

"Yeah, well, Father would likely tell you to quit your whining and head to the store to stock up on Hostess cupcakes. But, you didn't go to Father. You came to me. And my advice will be a little different. I'm Patience in your marriage."

I gave Carter a look like he was crazy. "You're two months pregnant?"

He huffed rolling his eyes. "Screw you, asswipe. Anyway … I go to a job everyday that could kill me. Hell, given all of the shit that's happened with the squad and department lately, I was closer to death than ever, remember?"

I nodded solemnly, hating that I did remember.

"Yeah, and through all of that, and my subsequent promotion, Michelle has never, not once, asked me to quit. She's not even hinted at it. She hasn't asked me to try to transfer to a station with fewer and less dangerous calls. None of that. And if she did, I wouldn't hesitate to oblige her. Deep down, I'd fucking hate it, but I'd do it. You know why?"

I pushed out a breath but didn't say anything. I didn't need to.

"Because family over everything. If my wife needed me to be in a safer role so she could sleep better at night, that's what I would do. But that's not the heroic part. The real hero in this scenario is my wife. *Because* she's never asked me to change. She knows me better than anyone on this planet, and she knows I'd do it for her. But she also knows it'd go against who I am at my core. Protecting, serving, and saving people is the cornerstone of who I am. Not who I choose to be but who I was born to be. It's the same reason I left for the military at eighteen without a second thought. Same reason I quit, too. I was tired of killing people. I chose to save them instead. It's how I met my wife. And she knows asking me to go against my base instinct would be her asking me to betray myself."

Turning to stare out of the window, I inhaled deeply and exhaled. I wasn't asking Patience to betray herself. I was just asking her to put our family first. The faces of our four children came to mind. I couldn't imagine a world in which they didn't have their mother to raise them. No. The deeper truth was, I couldn't imagine a world where *I* didn't have her with me, always. To raise our children, to grow old with, to fight with, and then make up with. That was a world that just couldn't exist.

"No," I shook my head. "She's not you, Carter."

"Aaron—"

"No," I said more firmly, to the reception of more stares from around the restaurant. "Patience is not you. Our children, the ones who are already here, need her. I need her. She can't have this baby."

I was adamant in my decision. Nothing was changing my mind. Not even my stubborn wife.

CHAPTER 21

"You know they're all up to something, right?" I said, looking over my shoulder as I sat on my side of the sleigh bed in our master bedroom. A smile blossomed on my lips when I found Robert's sizzling gaze on me.

His smoldering eyes ran over my shoulder, up my neck, and to my face until he met my eyes.

"They're always up to something. Little shits."

I giggled. "It was you who decided to have four of them."

He shook his head. "No, that was decided by something greater than me, princess."

I let out a sigh. How that pet name could still sound so damned good from his mouth after forty years of marriage was beyond me.

"C'mere," he growled.

I yelped when he moved quicker than a man his damn age should be allowed to move, and I found myself on my back, my husband hovering above me. I lifted my hand and ran is through his greying hair. The color might've been different but it still felt soft and silky to the touch.

"Can I tell you something?"

"You better talk fast."

I let out a sigh when he buried his face into the crook of my neck. "I really liked the shaggy look on you when we first met."

His head popped up. "At Stanford?"

"That is where we first met, right?"

"Princess, you and I met even before we got to this place. But yeah, that was where we reunited in this lifetime."

The butterflies in my belly flapped as they normally did whenever he made some mention of us being "written in the stars" as he put it.

"You liked my hair long?"

I nodded. "I did. I love it short, too, but you were so damn handsome with that long, seventies look. Even though every other guy had the same long hair, you stood out above them all."

He kissed my bare shoulder before pulling down the strap of the dark blue negligee I wore. He pressed another kiss to my shoulder, and then to my lips, allowing his lips to linger over mine, savoring the moment.

Pulling back, I laid my head against the cool, Egyptian cotton bed sheets. "Did you ever doubt us? Me?"

He paused before looking me in the eye. "Not for a second."

* * *

Then

Robert

I strolled into the usual diner where Rick and I met, nodded at the waitress who'd become used to seeing my face—every Wednesday morning at seven a.m. I'd been doing this same routine for the last three months. Meeting with Rick to get what new information he'd been able to uncover. It seemed like every time we parted ways I grew more and more pissed off and tense. Even Deborah was beginning to ask why I was so damn agitated while at home. This shit needed to end soon.

"Look, man," Rick began as soon as I sat down across from him.

That wasn't a good sign.

"I told you I hated to be the one to bring you this type of information, but I caught something else."

"What now?" I questioned, angered already but needing to know what the fuck was going on at Townsend.

"Your father's into some odd shit."

I snorted. That news was nothing new.

"I uncovered at least three different houses that he owns under subsidiary companies in the Townsend name."

"Houses?"

Nodding, Rick slid a folder across the table. That was the signal that he was done talking for the moment and it was my turn to do some viewing or reading. Or in this case, both.

I slid the papers out of the folder to find images of what appeared to be rather unkempt homes. But behind the photos was a stack of papers. The dates on the papers went back years. It looked like a number of different wire transfers, purchases of goods and services. Some I recognized were for Townsend, while some I didn't recognize at all. There were a number of real estate forms which didn't make any sense.

"My father has sat on Townsend's real estate division for years. Why is he acquiring these properties? And what reason on Earth would he have to acquire these run-down homes?"

"Those aren't for Townsend business. At least, not in the way you're thinking about it. Those homes," he motioned his head toward the photos while chewing his steak, swallowed, and said, "are where he conducts the business he'd rather no one found out about."

Quirking an eyebrow, I redirected my attention at the photos again. "Tell me more," I demanded, still staring at the images.

I heard Rick's knife and fork hit the plate, and a rustling of the paper napkin as he presumably wiped his mouth before speaking. "Your father isn't one hundred percent on the up and up."

"No one who runs a nearly billion dollar company is," I retorted.

Rick nodded. "True that. But your father's hands are a little dirtier than most. Some of those houses, I believe, hold evidence of your father shaking down company owners and sellers of energy products and services to get them to work with Townsend, or to sell to Townsend at cheaper prices than your competitors."

"Why wouldn't they just go to the police? Surely, they'd be able to prove what he was up to."

"They would've, which was why your father always held something over their heads. An illicit affair—"

I snorted. "An affair? What man lets another man shake him down over an affair?"

"One whose mistress isn't a mistress but a mister."

I pinned Rick with my gaze.

His gaze went to the file again. "Page six of the documents. Third column down."

I looked to where he'd just said. "Larry McStephens," I read out loud. I knew the name well. His gas and oil company had merged with Townsend nearly twenty years ago.

"He was having an affair with his assistant's husband. It's true," Rick added when I gave him a disbelieving look. "I've got the information to prove that as well. But Larry has since died, of natural causes, and Townsend has owned his company for two decades. There are more instances such as that. I've checked into all of the people your father shook down to make Townsend what it is today. Most are either dead or on their way to it. They're not the ones behind these leaks."

"So who is?"

He sighed, his expression turning grim as he pushed his plate to the side and planted his elbows on the table.

My heartbeat quickened. I knew I wasn't going to want to hear this part, but I needed to.

"This is where it gets ugly. In every one of these instances, your father had a select few who knew what he was doing. There's Ben Jones, John Lassiter, and Mitch Colon."

"Jones and Colon still sit on the board."

Rick nodded. "The same board who makes the decision whether or not to oust a CEO."

I quickly saw where Rick was going with this but it didn't make sense.

"But what incentive would they have to leak private information to give our competition a leg up? Their interest would be in ensuring Townsend's secrets stay buried."

"I was wrong. That last part wasn't the ugly part. This is." From the briefcase he often carried, he pulled out another folder and slid it across to my hands.

I hesitated before even touching the folder. I knew I wasn't going to like what was in there. I just fucking knew it. But I couldn't avoid it. All of the secrets needed to be out on the table if I was going to clean house.

Like removing a band-aid from a cut, I quickly opened the folder … and the face of my wife stared back at me. I took my time assessing the photo, examining every nuance and angle. She was on the sidewalk close to her job, looking up into the eyes of her ex-boyfriend, Cohen Walker. His arms were draped around her arm, as they faced one another.

I narrowed my eyes before returning my attention to Rick. "One, how do I know this is a recent photo? They dated for two years. Second, what the hell does this have to do with the leaks at Townsend Industries?"

"Good." Rick nodded. "You're asking the right questions. I wondered if this information would cloud your judgment so much you'd shut down and fire me before I could explain."

"So start fucking explaining," I demanded through gritted teeth.

Rick took his time, wiping his hands with his napkin before discarding it on his empty plate, planted his elbows on the table, and said, "Cohen Walker is John Lassiter's nephew."

I lifted an eyebrow. "Keep talking."

"Oh, I intend to. Cohen's mother's sister is married to John. He's his uncle via marriage. Now, here is my theory according to the files I've been able to dig up and the images. Cohen and Deborah were dating.

It's widely known that Cohen has this moral high ground in which supposedly hates the wealthy and all of the inequality it creates, or whatever." Rick waved his hand dismissively. "In fact, that is something he and Deborah connected on when they first met. She is from one of the poorest counties in the nation. I speculate they got together based on that shared belief. Somehow, John recruited Cohen to aid in his plot to take down Townsend Industries, using his nephew's distrust and disdain for all things wealthy. Cohen then roped Deborah into the plan, and once you two started seeing one another again and then fucking got married, she had closer access to Townsend Industries than anyone."

I shook my head. "That makes no sense. Deborah rarely asks me about Townsend Industries. She has not now or ever plied me for information on the company."

"She wouldn't. No real spy asks these questions directly. They wait until you're sleeping to dig around in the work files you've brought home, or call out of work sick so they can stay home while you're at work to dig around, have secret meetings, and make calls."

I pushed out a heaving breath. It felt like the four walls of the diner were closing in on me. None of this made sense. I thought back to all of the late nights Deborah and I shared together, talking into the wee hours of the morning. I shared intimate details of my life, Townsend Industries, and about my family. But she'd always reciprocated. It wasn't a one-way street. I knew her just as well as I let her know me.

"This doesn't make any sense. Why would Deborah help Cohen?"

Rick shrugged. "Why do people do eighty percent of this shit they do? Money," he answered his own question.

I leaned in closer. "I have more money than I could spend in a lifetime. Deborah knows she has access to more wealth than she could ever imagine. She doesn't even have to ask, so why would she betray me just for money?" Not to mention the fact that she hardly ever showed much of an interest in money. She continued to work at her full-time job as diligently as she had before we married, and she was adamant about not quitting, either. The very notion that I would demand she quit once we were married completely freaked her out.

"Hell, we all need more money. She's a chick—"

"Woman. Don't ever fucking refer to my wife as a *chick* again."

Rick stared at me, unflinching before slowly nodding. "Woman. She's a *woman* in corporate America. And she's from Beattyville, Kentucky at that. Deep down somewhere, she's gotta believe it's all a dream or that one day it'll all blow up in her face. Maybe this thing with Cohen is her way of cashing in before that happens. A sort of insurance policy, if you will. Or maybe she's truly in love with him and will do—"

"Don't fucking finish."

Rick's words halted on the spot.

I shook my head. "This isn't right. Something's not adding up. My wife isn't involved."

"Look, I've worked with plenty of spouses who refused to believe their—"

"I don't give a damn about any of them. My wife, Deborah Townsend, *isn't* involved in this shit." I slapped the opened file and papers before pushing it all back across the table toward Rick. "Keep digging and come back to me with the truth or I'll find someone who will!"

I stood up so abruptly, I knocked my own chair over. Buttoned my suit jacket while staring down at Rick, threw a couple of bills on the table to cover the tab, and wordlessly walked out of the diner.

* * *

"WHAT?" I answered the buzzing phone on my desk, pissed off from my early morning meeting with Rick. It was just after noon and I still hadn't calmed down.

"Mr. Townsend, you have a call from a Jack Lassiter. Shall I patch him through?" My secretary, Cindy questioned, in the neutral, professional tone she always used.

My eyes lifted as I rose from my chair and stared at the far wall of my office.

"He says he's a friend from college," Cindy continued, mistaking my silence for my trying to recall the name.

"No. Yes, yes, I know Jack well. Put him through."

A few seconds later, the phone beeped and I heard, "I wasn't sure if you were going to tell your secretary to put me through, take a message or just hang up on me."

I grunted. "What are you calling about, Jack?"

There was a moment of hesitation on the other end. "Well, uh, I recognize the last time we talked, I was rude and a bit of an ass to you and Deborah. I was thinking we could possibly have lunch together and catch up. There are some things I've been meaning to say to you."

"Is that right?" I rocked back on my heels, still standing and staring at the far wall in my office.

"Yes."

"That's good, Jack, because there are some things I've wanted to discuss with you as well. I have a lunch meeting today, but are you available this time tomorrow?"

"Yeah sure, buddy. I'll meet you at the Crown Jewel. My treat."

My frown deepened. I hated his use of the word *buddy* but I kept my composure, in spite of myself. "I'll see you there."

I hung up the phone, still staring off into space. The hairs on the back of my neck were standing up. My instincts were in overdrive. The conversation I'd had that morning with Rick played over and over in my head. Something big was coming. I could feel it in my body. I glanced down at the picture on the corner of my desk. It was of Deborah and I the night we got married. I lifted the frame to stare at it more closely. In the picture, Deborah was laughing, mouth wide, eyes staring up into mine with her arms thrown around my neck. I had the biggest smile on my face as I gazed down into her blue orbs, my arms locked around her waist. It was a completely candid photo. Not one that had been posed for. A raw, real moment that we shared moments after promising one another forever.

I placed the photo down when my phone rang. I lifted it to my ear, to hear Cindy informing me that the person I'd scheduled my lunch meeting with had arrived. I instructed her to send them to the conference room where the catered lunch had already been set up. After that, I took the time to gather my files, phone my father to let him know the meeting was set to begin, and then proceeded to head out. I took one last look at my wife and I. The twisting that occurred in my gut nearly had me doubling over.

Rick's words and photos were still running rampant through my brain.

CHAPTER 22

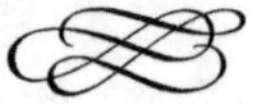

hen
Deborah

Sighing, I placed my hand over my belly, before continuing down the hall from the doctor's office. Not only was the nausea I'd been experiencing for well over a week still getting to me, but the news my doctor had given me could've knocked me over with a feather. What I had suspected as a bout of the flu was much more.

Because my symptoms hadn't seemed to be improving, I'd left work early to get in an appointment with my primary doctor. Now, I was headed home. If I could make it without having to stop and throw up every fifty feet.

Thankfully, I was able to make it to the parking garage of my doctor's office, in my car, and complete the twenty-five minute drive back to the luxury condo that Robert and I shared without too many problems. I entered the three-thousand-square-foot condo, with nearly panoramic views of the city of Williamsport, and fell back against the closed door. A wistful smile touched my lips at the memory of Robert bringing me back here after we'd married in Vegas. To my surprise, he'd arranged for all of my belongings to be moved into his place before we even arrived home. It took a couple of weeks for us to decide which of my belongings we'd keep and which ones of his. Granted, most of his stuff was more modern, higher quality, and definitely more expensive, but I still coveted everything I'd been able to purchase myself, with my own money.

"Oh no!" I blurted out, covering my mouth and running as fast as my legs would carry me to our first floor guest bathroom. As soon as I made it inside, and lifted the toilet seat, the contents of my lunch from earlier in the day spilled out of my mouth. I'd only managed to have some chicken noodle soup and a small piece of bread for lunch, thinking that was all I could keep down. Yet, that was a lie, because I'd just heaved it all up.

I cleaned up the bathroom, flushed the toilet, and slowly made my way upstairs to the master bedroom that Robert and I shared. I entered to our adjoining bathroom to brush my teeth first, to get rid of that awful taste of vomit in my mouth. Next, I headed straight to the bed, work clothes and all. The only thing I managed to remove were the three-inch black pumps I'd worn to work that day. I let them sit right by the side of the bed, not bothering to neatly store them in the closet with my other shoes, as I often chastised my husband for not doing. Pulling back the blanket, I sighed deeply in relief as my tired body burrowed into the coolness of the sheets. I was out like a light. I had the best sleep I'd had in quite a few weeks.

Suddenly, I awakened without opening my eyes. The room was completely silent. There was no hint or sign that I wasn't alone, yet somehow, I knew I wasn't. Someone was watching me. Intently.

Slowly, I peeled my eyes open. I had to blink a few times to adjust to the low lighting in the room. The sunlight that had been highly visible prior to my nap was no longer there. I couldn't tell if it was because the shades were drawn or if I had managed to sleep well past my anticipated twenty or thirty minutes. When I turned my head, my eyes collided with the dark brown eyes that I didn't need more light to recognize.

However, the look in those eyes stole my breath. Robert stared at me as if assessing my every move. Methodically, his eyes trailed from my face, down my body that was mostly still covered by the blanket.

When his eyes met mine again, he rose from the low-sitting, cushioned chair that was positioned in the far corner of our bedroom. I could hear his footsteps as he padded across the carpeted floor.

When he reached the bed, his hand moved, pushing a stray lock of my hair out of my face.

For some reason, I was held spellbound. Unable to push out any words as he glared down at me, his gaze both hungry, protective, and questioning. Three emotions that I wasn't sure how to take all at once. Robert slowly leaned down and pressed his lips to mine.

He pulled back. "Tell me that I can trust you, princess."

He didn't yell the words. They didn't come out as demanding. But there was an order behind them.

"You can trust me," I responded, feeling that he needed to hear those exact words.

He leaned down, his hand going to the back of my head, pulling me to him. Our lips clashed and the kiss and contact sent chills throughout my entire body. I felt the weight of Robert's body moving over top of me, as my back was pushed against the bed. Our lips never disconnected.

In the darkness I heard the rustling of clothing and then the warm air of the bedroom touched the skin of my bared shoulders. He was undressing me at such a rapid pace, I barely had time to catch my breath. Within minutes, Robert and I were both naked, my arms around his neck as he stared down at me, his eyes still searching mine.

"You're my wife. Mine," he said harshly as if trying to prove it to the both of us.

I nodded. "Until my last breath."

His lips covered mine and his knee pushed my knee wider, opening my body up to him. I was already primed for his entrance when he began sliding his thick cock deep inside of me. My back arched off the bed, pressing my sensitive nipples against his firm chest. The sensations were all too much.

I threw my head back against the pillow, moaning out his name. Robert's lips made a trail of kisses up and down the column of my neck, as his hips continued penetrating me deeper and deeper. I wrapped my legs around his back, fusing our bodies together while he buried his face into the crook of my neck.

For some reason, this time was different. It wasn't frenzied or hurried. There was passion but it wasn't the all-consuming, overwhelming passion that I'd become used to from my husband. His strokes were almost lazy, as he dragged his long length in and out of my body. Every few strokes, he'd adjust his hips to reach contact with a different angle inside of me. He hit my G-spot over and over, making just enough contact each time to send chills throughout the entirety of my body, but pulling back before he pushed too far and made me come.

It was a dizzying experience. One that had my eyes rolling to the back of my head.

"Come for me, princess." The magic words.

He loved it when I came on his orders. I'd managed to stave off my orgasm for those exact instructions. And I let the feelings overcome me until I was coming. Toes curled, heart racing, thighs tightening around his hips coming.

By the time my body let up, my arms felt like Jell-O as they fell to the side of the bed and I laid back against the pillows, still working hard to control my breathing.

Robert pulled out from inside of me, but still remained over top of me, staring down at me.

"Are you still not feeling well?"

I wrinkled my forehead in confusion before remembering that I had indeed not been feeling well. That morning I'd told him I might make a trip to the doctor's office due to what I'd thought was the flu.

Reaching up with my arms again, I circled his broad, sweaty shoulders.

"I'm feeling better, but it turns out there is something the doctors found."

His head jutted backwards and he gave me a curious look.

"It's the kind of something that lasts for nine months," was all I said before clamping my lips shut, letting the words I'd just shared ferment in his mind. It took a little longer than I thought, but I guessed that was what happened when you told your husband that you were pregnant for the first time.

I saw the exact moment he caught on. His face changed, eyes widened just a little and there was a glint in them that I'd never seen before. He pulled back and his hand went down to cover my still flat abdomen.

"How far along are you?"

"The doctor thinks I'm around six weeks or so. But I made an appointment with my Ob-Gyn for next week to confirm that."

He sat up completely, eyes still glued to me.

I wanted more of a reaction. From almost day one of our relationship he'd been telling me about having children. To be more precise, that we'd have four children, all boys, who'd be a handful. If they were *anything* like their father, I didn't have a hard time imagining that fact at all.

"Are you going to say something?"

His brows spiked. "You need to eat."

I frowned as I watched him quickly dismount from the bed, pull on a pair of running shorts, and head out of the room, presumably to get some food. Looking around the room, I saw the shadows of our clothing on the floor but still couldn't make out what time it was. Robert didn't believe in having a clock in the bedroom, preferring to let his body wake up naturally. I thought it was a ridiculous notion, but it worked for him. He woke up around five a.m. every morning, with no clock and no need to set an alarm. So I let it go.

I padded over to our shared closet and pulled down the silk robe he'd purchased for me a few months earlier. After slipping my arms into the light blue robe, I tightened the belt before heading out to go search for my husband. I found him in the kitchen; the smell of butter burning on the stove stopped me in my tracks.

"What are you doing?"

He glanced over his shoulder. "Shit," he growled when I began coughing from the smoke.

"Take that off the stove," I told him, pointing at the frying pan he was using.

Upon moving closer, I could see that he'd sliced a few squares of the cheddar cheese I'd purchased earlier in the week. Next to the cutting board were a couple of slices of French bread along with the butter.

"I could go to the store to pick up some of that tomato bisque soup. Or Campbell's," he mumbled the last part, obviously hating the brand name soup I still had an affinity for.

I shook my head. "The grilled cheese is good enough. I'm not even sure how long I'll be able to keep it down."

I quickly finished what he'd started, making two grilled cheese sandwiches and plating them before carrying them over to the large table where he sat. Instead of finding my own chair, I opted to sit in his lap. His arm went around my back, leaving his other hand free to pick up his sandwich. I watched as he took the first bite, chewing and savoring it.

"Are you happy? About the baby."

He paused mid-chew, his forehead wrinkling. He swallowed the food he'd been eating before leaning up and planting a kiss to my forehead. "Of course I am."

That was all he said. However, as we ate our food in silence, I could feel something was off. I'd felt it from the moment I awakened to find him staring at me in the dark. There was a strangeness about the way he'd made love to me in our bed. As if he was questioning for the first time ever. Robert was the most assured man I knew. From the outset, he'd never had any doubts about our relationship. Not one. I thought the news about my pregnancy would've had him doing cartwheels down the damn hallway. But aside from insisting on feeding me, and a few questions, he was closed off.

I ate, without tasting, wondering for the first time if I'd made a huge mistake.

* * *

Present
Robert

"So you did doubt Mother."

I frowned as I gazed at my youngest son. We were sitting in the offices I held at Townsend Industries. It didn't matter that I was no longer CEO, and hadn't been for some years now, this place was still like my second home. Aaron continued to seek out my council when he needed it, and I sat on the board of directors.

"No. If Father says he never doubted her than he never did." That was Joshua. He also had offices here at Townsend Industries.

The three of us were having lunch together. Aaron had had a business meeting and Carter was halfway across the city at the fire station.

"Have you ever doubted your wife?" I questioned Tyler.

He lifted an auburn eyebrow in my direction before sitting back against the leather sofa, spreading his arms to rest atop the pillows. He sat as if he owned the entire building. But I couldn't blame him. I'd taught all of my sons to never shrink in front of any man. And the only woman they'd shrink in front of better be the one who they spent their lives with and beared their children.

"Not ever," he said. "Wait, there were those times when she basically told me to *fuck off* when I asked her to have another baby," he amended, frowning.

Joshua and I both chuckled loudly at that. I could picture the short spitfire he'd married telling him just that.

"She was exactly what you needed to keep you in line," Joshua commented, still laughing.

"Whatever, jackass."

"No, really, Ty. Destiny had triplets. She carried three babies at once. Babies, mind you, who are still under the age of one, and you're already asking her to have more."

Tyler's face folded into an expression of incredulity. "I'm not asking for a second round of multiples like our oldest brother, geesh. Just one more kid."

Joshua's laughter increased before he sobered up. "No wonder she told you to fuck off."

Tyler flipped the bird at my third oldest son before his lips formed into a cocky smirk.

I began shaking my head because I knew what that look meant. "She agreed, didn't she?"

His smiling hazel-green eyes wrinkled at the edges as his smile grew. "Of fucking course. Am I not Tyler Townsend?" He arms spread wide, face lifting to the ceiling, eyes closing as if he was soaking in the cheers of an adoring crowd. A move he'd often made after throwing a perfect spiral down the middle of the field to score a touchdown for his team.

"Such a cocky little shit."

"And you love it," Tyler retorted.

I sat back, watching my two youngest bicker just as they had while growing up. I didn't get in the middle of it then and I refused to do so now. They'd work it out. They may seem like they couldn't stand one another, but the brats would fall apart without the others around. They'd been raised with a special bond that no one could break. I'd made sure of that.

Even when Carter went off to the military to fight for his country at eighteen, I knew he was just trying to find his way. Being the eldest with the last name Townsend had had a special meaning his whole life. One that I had pushed for him to take on, but ultimately, it wasn't his destiny. My wife had had to sit me down and talk me off the ledge, to let Carter go and be his own man. However, I knew he would return at some point. The fact that he'd returned to Williamsport to become a firefighter wasn't lost on me. He could have chosen any major city in the country. One that, while the Townsend name would still be known, wasn't as closely associated with Townsend Industries. But he'd come home. To Williamsport. Because this was where he belonged. With his family.

"You know, you're one to talk, Father."

I returned my attention to Tyler, wrinkling my forehead.

"You're the guy who informed Mother she would be the mother of your four boys, the night after you first defiled her. Oh, and by the way, you *really* could've left that part of the story out of it. We didn't need to know *every* detail."

"Yeah, you know how much I hate to admit when Ty's right. But it's true. That part could've been left out," Joshua agreed, frowning and shaking his head.

Smirking, I sat back in my chair, folding my hands behind my head, looking between the two of them. "She was my wife long before she was your mother. Don't ever forget that."

"Still could've been left out," Tyler mumbled.

I just grinned.

"Anyway," Joshua started, "from what you say, you never doubted Mother, but you were getting evidence from Rick that was pretty much pointing directly at her as at least one of the conspirators behind the Townsend leaks."

I nodded. "It did look that way …"

* * *

Then

Robert

"This shit is getting out of hand," I grunted before taking a swing at Thiers. I cursed inwardly when he successfully ducked the punch and hopped to the side, getting out of my line of sight.

We circled the ring, aiming for one another's ribs instead of the face. That had been one of the rules we'd established before this round in the ring.

"You're getting faster," I commented.

"Or you're just fucking slow. What's the matter? Marriage slowing you down?"

I swung, aiming for his left side ribs and landing a spectacular right hook. Thiers' grunt was loud and immediate.

"Don't mention my marriage."

"Fuck you," he spat back, lowering his hands. "I'm done with this shit. I told you I don't fucking like sparring."

Sighing, I lowered my gloves. He was right. While Thiers was always one for a workout in the gym, he actually loathed getting into the ring and sparring with anyone. My usual sparring partner had canceled, leaving no one to get into the ring with. I'd had to bribe

Thiers with front row seats to the Elton John concert that was coming to town in a few months.

"Don't think this means you can get out of getting me those tickets." He pointed back at me as we walked over to the metal folding chairs which sat against the wall, facing the boxing ring.

"I had no idea you were such an Elton John fan."

He snorted before squirting water into his mouth from the water bottle. "I'm not. But my lady is."

"Going to an Elton John concert for a woman? You must be serious about this one."

He nodded, smiling, a funny expression crossing his face. "I think so. Jeanette is different from all of the other women in my past."

"How so?"

"She's smart. Loves to read. I mean, this woman can spend *hours* reading. And she listens more than she talks. Most women I've met only want to talk about themselves, who they know, who knows them. All that bullshit. Not Jeanette."

I nodded, knowing the feeling very well. My friend was falling in love. I could hear it in his voice. If this had been a different time, I would've told him to shut the hell up about it and that he probably was just making up feelings that weren't real. But I didn't because I knew exactly what he was talking about.

"What's that face about?" he questioned, giving me funny stare.

I clenched my teeth, not wanting to say the words that would answer his question, but needing to. "Rick thinks Deborah is in on it."

Thiers' eyebrows dipped. "In on the Townsend leaks?"

I dipped.

"How is that possible?"

"He has photos of her with one of the guys he's pinpointed as being behind the leaks. Recent photos," I clarified. "It's of her ex, Cohen. He thinks they never broke up. That she's having an affair with him behind my back."

"He thinks?"

I grunted and nodded.

"But you don't?"

I turned, looked Thiers right in the eye, and said, "I know it's bullshit."

"But the photos are getting to you."

I turned toward the rest of the boxing gym, not saying anything. I didn't need to. He knew me well enough to draw his own conclusions. Seeing my wife in the arms of another man had stirred something inside of me that nothing in my life ever had.

I stood up.

"All I know is that when all of this is over, no motherfucker will ever test me, my wife, or my marriage again. And it will be Robert Townsend Junior with his name on the office of the CEO suite at Townsend Industries." Those two things were a fact.

I also knew neither one of them was going to happen without me having to get some blood on my hands. I'd made peace with that weeks ago. It was time to put an end to this shit.

I wouldn't let my first son enter this world with questions still being held over my wife's head. Nor would I let Townsend Industries keep being run by a man with no vision, poor negotiating skills, and only his last name to bolster the confidence of his allies. Even if that man was my father.

* * *

"It's been a month!" I barked as I charged into Rick's office, slamming his door behind me when his secretary tried to intervene.

"It's alright, Terri!" he called through the door to his secretary before turning back to me. "She has strict instructions to call either my guys or the police when clients come barging in. She got worried after another client shot me." He waved his hand in the air dismissively, as if it was more of a nuisance than attempted murder.

"I wouldn't use a gun," I growled.

He nodded. "I know. You'd be the type to get up close and personal with your prey. Trust, I know the type of man you are." He sat back down before extending his hand for me to take a seat in the wooden chair opposite him.

I moved slowly toward the chair, placing my hands on the back, leaning in. "I'd rather stand."

"I figured." He sighed. "Believe it or not, I was just looking over your file." He held up the case file folder with my name on it as proof.

"And?"

"And … as it turns out, you're right. Deborah didn't have anything to do with this."

I pushed out a breath I didn't even know I'd been holding. "Tell me something I don't know."

"They were using Deborah to make it look like she was involved. Her ex, Cohen …" He held up a picture of the prick. "Turns out he wasn't particularly happy about the break up. Also, he's broke. It seems mommy and daddy cut him off months ago because he was taking so long to complete his PhD program."

"What the fuck does this have to do with Deborah or Townsend Industries?"

Rick waited to answer while I rounded the wooden chairs to finally take a seat facing him.

"Provides motive. A scorned lover and a spoiled, hippie wannabe who couldn't get mom and dad to support his lifestyle any longer. He needed the money. So when John Lassiter approached him to help him to leak information on Townsend and set Deborah up as the fall guy, or in this case gal, Cohen was in a position where he couldn't turn the offer down. He'd kill two birds with one stone."

"If the stones don't fucking kill him first," I mumbled.

"John used his knowledge of Townsend Industries and his closeness with your father to try and take apart your company from the inside out. And he recruited his nephew to do it."

"Why?"

As far as I knew, my father and John were friends, at least close business associates. I often recalled John over at Townsend Manor while I was growing up. He and my father had a rapport. John worked hard for Townsend and he continued to reap the financial benefits as a current board member.

"Is John broke?" I questioned, my brow furrowed.

"He doesn't have Townsend money, but he doesn't have to lose a wink of sleep over not being able to pay his bills either. He's doing well financially."

"Then what is his motive?"

Rick blew out a breath through his mouth, making a whistling noise. "The oldest reason in the world for a man to take on another man."

I glared at Rick.

"The reason you are ready to tear down anything and anyone who stood in the way of you practically breaking my door down a few minutes ago." He leaned forward. "A woman."

"What woman?"

"Your mother."

I stared at Rick.

"John is in love with your mother. Has been for years."

"They're having an affair."

He shook his head. "Far as I can tell, it's been one-sided. Your mother, as crazy as this may sound, loves your father. Only has eyes for him. But John Lassiter had eyes for her. My guess is after years of pining over a woman he couldn't have, John got tired of being second in line. Maybe he thought he'd topple Townsend and your mother would leave Robert Senior and end up with him. Who knows? Love makes a fucker do some strange shit. Glad I've never been bitten by the love bug." A cynical look crossed his face.

I wouldn't bother taking the time to explain to a man like Rick the pleasures of falling in love with the right woman. He'd learn himself or he'd go to his grave holding on to his current beliefs. Either way, it wasn't my business.

"I'm still tying up a lot of loose ends, however. Your father has a lot of secrets from what I can make out."

I snorted. "I'm coming to realize."

"There are a few details missing from the story, but I'm certain we're on the right track and these are the major players."

"No." I shook my head. "There's one more involved." I'd finally put two and two together.

CHAPTER 23

hen
Robert

"Where'd you say this place was?" Jack questioned for the second time within the last fifteen minutes.

I slowly turned my head from watching the setting sun through the trees as we passed over to Jack. We were in the back of my chauffeured town car. We'd been driving for about twenty-five minutes.

"The cabin is about forty-five minutes outside of the city."

"I didn't know your family had a cabin out here." He glanced around, looking out the window, also seeing the passing trees and forest.

"Yeah, my father brought me up here all of the time as a child to hunt, fish, and camp out. I haven't been in about a year. You know, with the marriage and all." I rolled my eyes, adding a sarcastic laced lilt to my voice.

"Right. How's that going? You still met with that lawyer this week?"

A smile blossomed on my lips. "Sure did. He told me not to worry over the fact that I never got Deb to sign a prenup. He'd have no problem taking her to the cleaners if she ever even thought of trying to come after my fortune."

Jack nodded, seeming reassured. "I'm sorry it turned out like this, man. But I had to tell you the truth. When I knew she was still sleeping with my cousin, Cohen, I just couldn't keep that information to myself. She was two-timing the both of you. Fucking whores can be so greedy."

My hands balled into fists and I strained every muscle in my body to keep from lashing out.

"I hate to say it because you know how much I hate being wrong, but you were right. She's a conniving snake just looking for her next fucking payday. I should've known better. I'm a fucking idiot for not seeing what was right in front of me." I pounded my fist into my open palm for emphasis.

"Don't be so hard on yourself, buddy. Women are all the same. I mean, yeah you should've seen the likes of a woman who comes from fucking nowhere Kentucky, trying to find a rich sucker to marry. But smarter men have been fooled by cunts far craftier than Deborah fucking Tate."

My left leg began to jiggle, and I wrapped my hands around my knees, squeezing as I continued to listen to Jack spout off about cunts, bitches, and sluts. Glancing out at the passing forest, I surmised we were only about five minutes away from our destination.

When I couldn't take anymore of his ranting, I turned to him and said, "You know, I never did get the opportunity to apologize to you for what happened on our ski trip senior year and our engagement party."

He threw his head back, waving me off. "Don't even worry about it."

"No, no." I shook my head. "I need to say this. I was wrong. You were looking out for me, for my interests, and I turned my back on you. I believed in Deborah more than a man I had known since we were teenagers. That was the beginning of the end of our relationship, and I must say that I am ..." I paused as the car came to a halt. I glanced around and pushed out a relieved breath, knowing we'd finally arrived. "We're here. We'll continue this conversation inside."

I stepped out of the door that'd been pulled open by our driver. I nodded at the driver, who then nodded back with raised eyebrows. I turned to see Jack descending from the car as well.

"This is kind of a remote place to have dinner, isn't it?"

I patted Jack on the back. "It is, but I like to conduct most of my business out of the line of sight of others. You know what I mean? With all of the leaks that have been occurring at Townsend over the last few years, one can never be too careful."

Jack nodded, glancing around. "I know what you mean. My father has been keeping me abreast of what's been happening at Townsend Industries."

I gave Jack what, by all appearances would've appeared to be, a genuine smile. "I'm sure he has. Let's get inside. It's chilly out," I noted, holding my arm out for Jack to pass me toward the stairs of the cabin's porch.

It was the beginning of November, and yet it was starting to feel like December. I glanced up at the darkening sky, and could make out some of the changing colors of the leaves. Inhaling the fresh forest air, I made a mental note to tell Deborah we needed to purchase a cabin in the woods or the mountains somewhere. For our boys to enjoy as well. I knew they'd love it just as much as I did.

"Robert? Are you coming?"

I turned back to Jack. "Sure am." I caught up to him on the stairs and pulled the key from the pocket of my pants before shoving it in the keyhole. Turning the lock, I pushed the door open, stepping inside and moving to the side to let Jack enter.

I knew as soon as he saw it. He yelled, "What the hell?" and turned to me, a horrified expression on his face.

"Surprise, motherfucker," I calmly said before knocking him out with one punch to the face.

Frowning, I looked down at the pile of shit on the floor. "He always did have a glass jaw." I was at least hoping for some type of fight.

I heard heavy footsteps behind me as they scraped across the worn wood of the cabin. I didn't turn around.

"Most pricks like him do," Rick remarked, glancing over my shoulder at Jack.

I looked up and met the eyes of Cohen as he sat tied up, cloth stuffed in his mouth, nose bleeding and eye swelling.

"Let's play a little game, shall we?"

Pushing the door closed, I locked it.

Cohen's eyes fell to the doorknob, the fearful expression on his face increasing as I turned the lock.

"Don't worry, you had no hope of walking out of here alive anyway," I stated, moving closer to Cohen.

I patiently waited for one of Rick's employees to drag Jack's unconscious body over to the couch, tie his hands behind his back, and gag him as well.

"You have the smelling salts?" I questioned Rick.

"Sure do." He pulled a packet of the salt from the pocket of his jeans, tore it open, and waved it under Jack's nose.

A few seconds later, Jack's eyes were blinking open as he shook his head. He tried to speak and that was the moment he remembered where he was. He also realized that he too—just like his cousin—had been bound and gagged.

"Shh, shh, shh," I hushed. "Don't try to speak. I can't stand the sound of your voice. It makes me sick."

Methodically, I removed the leather bomber jacket I'd worn and tossed it onto the armchair to my right. Sitting down on the wooden coffee table, I faced the two idiots who really thought they were smarter than me.

"You know, they say two heads are better than one. But in your case …" I looked between the two of them. "Didn't I say don't fucking speak? Look what happened to Cohen when he tried to talk after I'd told him not to."

Rick came over and abruptly turned Cohen's head so his left side profile could be seen by Jack.

Muffled screams sounded as soon as Jack saw the bloody stump that was once Cohen's left ear.

"He couldn't listen, so obviously his ear was useless to him." I shrugged and Rick let go of Cohen who fell back against the sofa, somewhere between consciousness and fainting. "Don't you dare fucking faint on me now, Cohen. The fun is just beginning. Besides, we've got plenty of smelling salts to keep both of you awake."

"So …" I began as I stood, "before we really begin, do you gentlemen have anything you'd like to say?"

I nodded my head in the direction of one of Rick's men who then removed the gags from Jack and Cohen's mouths.

"What that hell are you doing, man? We're fucking friends!" Jack screamed, terror reflecting in his eyes.

I moved to stand in front of him, crouching low so he could see the gleam of disdain in my eyes. "Friends? Were we *friends,* Jack? Is that what the fuck we were?"

"Yes!"

"Really? So a *friend* plots with his father behind my back to topple my family's legacy and business? A friend schemes with his family to try and take everything I have?" I moved on Jack, grabbing him by the collar of his shirt, bringing our faces nose to nose. "Does a fucking *friend* lie about another man's wife to his fucking face because he was pissed she wouldn't let him into her fucking bed?" I released Jack's shirt only to curl my right hand into a fist and land another blow across his nose. I didn't even flinch when blood squirted out, landing on my face and shirt.

I stepped back, taking a handkerchief that was offered to me by one of Rick's men to wipe the blood from my face.

"Don't ever tell me we were friends. My wife turned you down in college. You were pissed that the pretty rich boy charm every other woman fell for didn't work with her." I crouched low again. "It wasn't that she wasn't good enough for you. She's too good for you and you knew it." I threw the handkerchief against his chest.

"And you used your son of a bitch cousin as part of your little scheme." I moved over to Cohen, ignoring Jack's moans of pain as the gag was stuffed back into his mouth.

"T-this was all h-his fault," Cohen stammered out, obviously not looking for anymore trouble.

I would've told him it was much too late for that, but I wasn't about to waste my breath.

"You're still trying to blame someone else for this, huh?" Chuckling, I shook my head. "You're a grown fucking man," I sneered. "You were fucking jealous she left you for me. And I get it." I shrugged, casually, giving him a sympathetic look. "I'd be fucked up in the head too if she left me. The difference, Cohen, between you and I, is I'd never give her a reason to leave me. She's my soulmate. My wife. And mine to protect. You could never comprehend the magnitude of what she is to me. You're just a fucking selfish, spoiled brat who didn't get his way. Try as you might, you're no different than him." I gestured to Jack, whose head was now slumped over, blood slowly dripping from his nose. "You talk a big game about hating the wealthy, but it's because deep down you know you don't measure up. You've never worked for anything in your life. No wonder she didn't want to be with you."

Shaking my head in disgust at both of the losers in front of me, I pulled the gag free from Jack's mouth.

"My father will find out about this. He won't let you get away with this!"

I gave Jack a sardonic grin. "Well look whose balls decided to show up. Bravo! One last attempt to instill fear to get us … me to let you go." I gave him a slow clap as I glanced around the room at Rick and the two men with him.

They all appeared unworried. Rick actually looked slightly bored.

"Sorry to inform you, but as we speak, your father is being handcuffed and carted off to a federal prison for corporate espionage. Meanwhile, his dear ol' son is boarding a private plane to the South of France, along with his cousin, Cohen." I turned to Rick. "That is where we booked the flights, correct?"

Rick gave a head nod. "That's right."

I held out my hands, turning back to Jack and Cohen. "See, so while you guys are living the life in Europe, partying it up, your dad and uncle will be rotting in a prison cell believing you sold him out and then bailed." I inhaled deeply, and then let out a satisfied sigh. "Let's quit wasting time and get this over with."

The two men stood both Cohen and Jack up.

"W-wait! I d-didn't do anything! We were never g-going to hurt anyone!" Jack insisted as we pushed them toward the back door.

I moved to stop in front of Jack, pulling him up by his hair so he could see my eyes. "Never going to hurt anyone? You tried to set up my wife, you fucking buffoon! To make it look like she was one of the main conspirators behind this shit! And don't think I'm fucking naïve enough to believe you would've let her live to tell the truth! You think I don't understand the depths of your deception, you fucking idiot?"

Jack began flailing, crouching down and eventually falling to the ground as I reined punches along his face, chest, and body. I'd learned the levels to which he would've stooped to carry out this outlandish scheme of his. Rick had discovered Jack's wire transfers to another PI who'd worked with him to follow Cohen and have him 'accidentally' bump into my wife on the street and at the Crown Jewel, taking pictures of them to make it appear as if they were in a relationship. Jack was to present me with this information, which he had weeks ago when he'd invited me to lunch. Once the divorce proceedings began, he was going to make it seem as if Deborah had been behind the espionage in partnership with some other employees at Townsend. Then he and Cohen had planned to do God knows what with Deborah before discarding her.

The very idea of these two fucking turds laying a finger on my wife sent me into a violent spiral. Once Jack had passed out, and my anger hadn't let up, I started in on Cohen. I even went so far as to untie his hands so that he could put up a real fight. But like the pussy he was, he merely cowered to the floor.

"Jesus, I think they're both dead!" one of Rick's men said when I finally let up, breathing heavily, covered in their blood and other fluids.

"You fucking did our jobs," the second one added, sounding slightly resentful.

"They're not dead, just close to it. A bullet to the back of the skull will take care of them, and we still need to take them to the farm," Rick reminded his guys.

I nodded, still breathing heavily and stepping out of the way as Rick's men placed two bags over Cohen and Jack's heads before carrying them outside.

"Pig farm isn't too far from here," Rick mentioned.

"I'll go."

"No, yo—"

"I'm going," I stated with finality. I wanted to see this finished with my own two eyes.

"Fine. You'll need to change your clothes first."

I took the sweatpants and shirt Rick handed me and headed to the first floor bathroom for a quick shower and to change. Once dressed, I met Rick and his men in the town car that Jack and I had driven to the cabin in. I was on automatic for the five minute drive from the cabin to the pig farm that was actually owned by my father, as was the cabin.

I didn't watch Rick's men as they stripped Cohen and Jack, and fed their corpses to the feeder that would provide the 'meat' to the hungry pigs. I wasn't that fucking depraved. However, knowing the two were disposed of and would never be a threat to me or my family again did give me a sense of satisfaction. A weight had been lifted off my shoulders. But I wasn't ready to go home to my wife yet. I wouldn't defile her presence with the actions I'd just carried out.

Upon returning to the cabin, I called and informed Deborah that I had to take an emergency work trip to California for a few days. She was either too tired from the early stages of pregnancy, work, or both to ask too many questions. She did ask if I would be back in time for her doctor's visit, informing me that we might be able to get to listen to the baby's heartbeat.

My own heartbeat quickened just knowing that. It was an appointment I wouldn't miss for the world.

"There's one more thing we need to take care of," I told Rick.

"You want to be CEO."

I nodded. I was coming for my father next.

* * *

Present

Robert

"Jesus Christ! A pig farm," Tyler sputtered as he, Joshua, and I sat outside on the back porch at Townsend Manor. We'd brought the conversation from earlier back home, once Joshua's work day had ended. They both begged me to finish telling them the story. And I'd made a vow long ago not to lie or hide any part of my life from my boys once they became of age. Besides, they'd all inherited some aspect of my revenge streak.

"Does Mother know she's been married to a psycho all of these years?" Tyler quipped.

Joshua snorted. "You're one to talk. Didn't you tie a guy to a tree and use him as a punching bag? Or is my memory failing me?"

Tyler looked over at his brother. "That was different. That fucker came into my house and attacked my wife and children. And don't get on me when you're the crazy nut who fights underground and—"

"That's enough," I intervened, waving my hands as if to wipe the slate clean. "The point is, we all do what we need to do to protect the women in our lives. That's my job first and foremost."

"One you've done well, I might add."

All three of us turned to see Deborah standing at the opened glass sliding door, arms folded as she peered at us. Her eyes hit mine and my body instantly reacted. Hers likely did as well because a few seconds later, she was strolling in my direction, wrapping her arm around my shoulder as she slid into my lap.

"You were eavesdropping on our conversation, princess?"

"Ah man, here he goes with that *princess* stuff," Joshua mumbled.

Deborah giggled as she glanced over at our two youngest. "You two leave your father alone."

"All we want to know if is you realize you're married to a crazy man?"

Instead of directly answering Joshua's question, Deborah turned to me, smiling as she gazed into my eyes. "I've been married to this man for forty years. There isn't one thing I don't know about him."

I turned my head upward and she lowered, pressing a kiss to my lips. Tightening my arm around her waist, I pulled her body into mine as she turned to look back at Tyler and Joshua.

"Besides, he hasn't even told you the entirety of the story yet."

"There's more?" Tyler asked, wide-eyed.

"A hell of a lot more," I responded.

"Do tell."

Deborah turned back to me. "Might as well finish this part of the story."

I nodded and began telling them about how I finally came into power at Townsend Industries, and the repercussions that move brought about.

* * *

Then

Robert

"You sure you know what you're doing?" Rick questioned me as we sat across from one another at the diner.

I lifted an eyebrow. "You have doubts?"

He blew out a breath, shaking his head as if something was weighing heavily on him. "Some." He leaned in. "We got the guys behind the leaks. It's been in the papers the machinations of John Lassiter and his son who ran away to Europe. That's all wrapped up in a pretty little bow. And, between me and you, we know your father knew John was behind these leaks but didn't want to jeopardize his position so he sat on the information for longer than necessary. You take that to the board and they'll oust him and move you in as CEO."

I nodded as Rick laid out the plan as we had already discussed. However, his mind was still working. He believed there was more, so I remained silent until he spoke again. I was learning Rick was intelligent enough to not verbalize his concerns until he was certain there was an issue to be concerned about.

"Your father. It's not adding up why he didn't oust John himself. Sure, John could've then started talking about the shakedowns he helped take part in, but that explanation doesn't feel right. There's something deeper going on."

I pivoted my gaze from Rick's profile to look out the window. I lifted the cup of coffee to my lips, letting the warm caffeinated beverage make its way down my throat. In my gut, I knew Rick was right. There was something deeper. John was behind the leaks, but he'd felt he had my father by the balls for some reason, and it wasn't just the handful of activities that Rick had uncovered. Sure, they weren't legal, but any shrewd lawyer could've easily explained them away.

"I've thought about it as well. But I won't ever find out what my father's hiding if I don't make this move. Townsend Industries is being held back. There is so much more we can do, and he's a fucking fossil. His time as CEO has come to an end."

Rick turned to me. "I figured you'd say that. I'll continue digging."

After tipping the half empty cup of coffee in his direction, I placed it on the table and stood, my hand going to the pocket of my pants suit.

"I got it this time," Rick insisted, holding out his hand. "As much as you're paying for my services, I can afford to splurge on your coffee this morning."

I dipped my head at him and sauntered off to the car waiting outside to take me to Townsend Industries.

The trip took about thirty minutes to get from the diner to Townsend headquarters but I was still about a half an hour early. I headed into my office on the second from the top floor, exactly one floor below my father's office. I thumbed through and sorted the files I would need for the meeting that was to begin promptly at nine a.m. It was an emergency meeting of the board. Since John had been arrested, and it became public that he was behind the leaks at our company, the board members had all flown in, and were scrambling to put out fires. They'd questioned and damn near interrogated my father on what he knew. So far, he'd held firm, acting just as shocked as everyone else at discovering his long-time friend and ally was behind the leaks.

I knew better. I also knew how good of an actor my father was, in all areas of his life.

"You ready for this?"

I lifted my gaze from my desk to see my father at my door. Surprised at first, I quickly recovered. My father rarely ever ventured down from his office floor to where I worked. He always had his secretary summon me to come to him. I peered at him as he moved into my office, closing the door behind him.

I frowned at the trickle of sweat that ran down the side of his face. He wiped it away with a handkerchief and began pacing back and forth, his face red.

"I've fucking told them all I knew about John. Now here they are with this emergency meeting bullshit. Don't they know I've got work to do! We are still doing damage control for all of the shit John stirred up. Look …" he urged, moving toward my desk, staring at me wide-eyed, "don't say anything. Let me do all of the talking. I'll just reiterate what I've told them before, they'll find nothing the matter, and we'll go on to business as usual."

I stood, planting my palms against the shiny wood of my desk. "Is that what you want?"

"Yes."

I shrugged. "Fine. Let's get to it, shall we?"

Loading my files into one hand, I extended the other for my father to proceed out the door. I followed, shutting it behind me.

Minutes later, we exited the elevator on my father's floor, after he insisted we take it for one flight up.

"Remember, don't say anything," my father muttered under his breath as we entered into the conference room that was a ways down the hall. A few of the board members had already arrived, and were filling their plates with the catered fruits and croissants.

My stomach growled, reminding me that all I'd had that day so far was a half a cup of black coffee. But I wasn't in the mood to eat. I'd satisfy my appetite after the meeting was over.

"Gentlemen," my father greeted, extending his hand to shake with the board members.

I did the same, greeting each member who was in the room or that entered. Within minutes the room was filled with ten men, excluding my father and myself. We all sat around the long, extended, oval-shaped conference table, files in front of us.

"Robert."

My father and I both turned to the first man who spoke, Graham Dunleavey.

"Graham," my father answered.

"I know that each one of us has spoken with you individually, but we all agreed that it would be best for everyone to meet together. To get some clarity on the situation and to figure out where Townsend Industries goes from here."

"Well, gentlemen, that's precisely what I've been wanting to discuss with all of you."

Raising an eyebrow in his direction, I sat back in my chair, folding my arms over my lap and crossing my legs. I was looking forward to hear what he had to say. Seeing as how not twenty minutes prior, in my office, he was ranting about how much he wanted them all to go the hell away.

"Gentlemen, it came as much of a shock to me, as it did all of you, to learn that John Lassiter was working behind all of our backs to betray Townsend Industries and leak some very private information to the press, as well as our competitors. These leaks not only harmed Townsend in the minds of our customers, but it emboldened our enemies. Some of which, have actively sought out to steal partners from us, move in on customers, and even recruit employees. John's machinations did a lot of damage. Nevertheless, it was my diligent pursuit to find out who was behind these leaks that prevailed. Not only did Townsend's security staff push to uncover the truth, they quickly responded once it was found out that John was the culprit behind all of this mess."

"Is that right, Robert?"

Everyone turned to Jaimie Lane, chairman of the board.

"That is, Jaimie."

"If everyone was working so hard, as you say, why did it take so long? John was right under our noses this whole time."

I turned back to my father, angling my head, waiting to hear the answer as well.

"Things like this take time. Unfortunately, John was extremely stealthy in his—"

"Stealthy?" William, another board member, questioned.

"Yes, Will. As I described before, John worked to keep his liaisons a secret. Frankly, I am surprised that after years of service to this company, and the amount of money he made off of it, that he would betray us in this way. But, as I stated, our security staff—"

"The ones who took nearly two years to figure out that John, who was right under our nose the entire time, was attempting to bring this company down from the inside?" Will demanded angrily.

I remained silent, slowly turning from Will back to my father. His mouth was ajar, face red as he ran his finger around the collar of his shirt, trying to loosen it. He looked over at me, eyes searching, silently asking me to speak up, to intervene in some way. He was feeling the pressure.

I pressed my back against the chair even more firmly, sitting up straighter, but kept my mouth shut. I had strict instructions not to speak during the meeting. I was doing as I was told.

"Yes. As I stated—"

"As you've stated to each of us over the phone, in private conversations, that John knew this or that, but you haven't explained to any of us what *you* knew," Michael, another member, spoke; his voice was tight with agitation.

"What I knew?" my father repeated.

"Yes," came a chorus of responses from the entire room.

Again, my father stumbled on his words, looking to me before blinking and turning back to the men seated around the table. He was stuck. He knew if he told the truth and spilled what he did know, he was out on his ass. However, if he lied and said he knew nothing, then he'd look incompetent, and again, he'd be out on his ass. They had cornered him with their line of questioning.

"I think it's apparent to all of us in the room, you're either holding something back, Robert, or you were in cahoots with John from the beginning."

"That is absolutely ridiculous thinking!" my father retorted. "Townsend Industries is my life. It's *my* family's legacy. Why would I, of all people, seek to destroy it?"

"That's precisely what all of us would like to know?" That was Graham again.

"Because it's clear to us that you've been hiding a lot from the board."

"Which is why we have come to the unanimous conclusion that your tenure as CEO of Townsend Industries has come to an end. Effective immediately," Graham, the obvious ringleader of the board, spoke his piece.

You could hear a pin drop as eleven pairs of eyes pinned my father, awaiting his reaction.

"This is preposterous!" he yelled, pounding his fist on the hardwood table.

I lifted an eyebrow. Clearly, he was losing his cool. My father often lost it at home, behind closed doors, but never in front of the board. He knew the end was here and he was not equipped to handle it.

"Townsend Industries will die without me. You don't even have a suitable replacement."

"We do, actually," James Cooley interjected.

The room shifted and everyone turned to me, including my father.

"We've found a more than adequate replacement."

My father's eyebrows nearly touched his hairline as he sputtered for a few heartbeats. His face was beet red.

He was pissed.

I grinned.

"You can't do this!" he yelled, again pounding his fist as if his little show of force meant anything. "Robert, what the hell are you doing?"

Angling my head, I stared at him.

"Son, this cannot happen."

I continued to stare.

"Are you even going to acknowledge the treachery you're trying to pull?"

I touched my chest with my hand. "Oh, you want me to speak now? Because up in my office you told me not to say a word during the meeting."

"Wha— Well, th-tha—"

"Never mind," I began, rising from my chair to move to the front of the room. "It's no longer your place to decide who speaks and who doesn't speak in these meetings." I buttoned my suit jacket and clasped my right hand around my left wrist in front of me, staring out at the board members. "Gentlemen, I think we all know you've made the right decision."

It was a decision I'd worked weeks on, behind the scenes. I'd communicated with every single man in this room, over the phone or in person, negotiating for my position as CEO. My father had been unaware, of course. But had he had any foresight he would've seen this coming.

"You are my son! How could you betray me like this?"

I sharply turned to my father, eyes narrowed, and my breathing increasing ever so slightly. This son of a bitch was not about to pull the fucking family card on me. The only time he'd treated me like a son was for the public, or when he needed me to fix an issue within the company.

"As you've stated, Townsend Industries is our legacy. And I'm saving it ... from you." I glared at him.

"Robert—"

My father and I both turned to Graham.

He cleared his throat. "Senior. Robert Senior. All of us have become aware that not only did you know about some of the ways in which John was working to bring down Townsend, you did not try to put a stop to it. Now, from what we've learned, you did this because you didn't want to appear weak to the public or to the board. However, that cover up lead you into deeper trouble. It's clear that you can no longer be trusted to run this company. Robert Junior has the experience and expertise to not only run Townsend today, but to lead this company into the future. He has already shared some reusable energy initiatives this company can begin implementing, as well as how to best position Townsend for the incoming technology wave. You, on the other hand, seem to want to be stuck in the dark ages. It's best that you step down peacefully and professionally, and take your retirement to enjoy it with your family. At home."

I couldn't have said it better myself.

I turned to my father. "Security is waiting for you at the door. They will help you remove some items from yo— *my* office before you are escorted down to your awaiting car. Anything you cannot carry today, will be delivered to Townsend Manor."

"You can't do this!" he frantically opposed, looking between me and the door, in which two security guards had just entered. "Get your hands off of me!" he demanded when the security guards began taking him away.

I turned to the board members, ready to get the remainder of the meeting over with so I could begin doing the business that needed to be done. However, I was stopped by one last, ominous warning by my father, as he held onto the door.

"You will regret this," he seethed as he pointed at me. "You have *no* idea what you've just done."

I narrowed my eyes on him as he was finally pulled away from the door and it was shut. I didn't get the sense that he was directly threatening me but there was something deeper in his statement. Suddenly, the meeting I'd had with Rick that morning came flooding back to my memory. All of my father's secrets hadn't been uncovered. And I had a feeling the move I'd just played was about to unleash the remainder of his secrets, for better or worse.

CHAPTER 24

hen
Deborah

Pushing out a breath, I glanced at my watch again. It read five-thirty on the dot. I looked around doctor's office at a few patients who were reading magazines or quietly chastising their toddlers for being too loud. My eyes landed on one couple who sat huddled together, thumbing through a parenting magazine. I smiled as the man's hand went to his wife's belly, rubbing small circles around the basketball-sized bump.

My hand went to my own belly. I was already twenty weeks pregnant. Most days, if I wore the right shirt other people couldn't tell I was expecting, but the changes in my body were evident to me. My belly was rounder, more firm, and for some reason it itched like crazy.

Again, I glanced at my watch. Two minutes past five-thirty and Robert still hadn't shown up. Thinking of my husband, I frowned. He'd been distant lately. Never had he been totally absent, but he had yet to engage in this pregnancy the way I thought he would. From the beginning he'd talked about children, and now, here we were pregnant, and it felt like he'd disengaged a little.

"Townsend!"

My head popped up when the receptionist called my name. I stood and headed to the window to meet her.

"Are you Ms. Townsend?"

"*Mrs.* Townsend," his deep voice sounded behind me, igniting all of my senses.

I turned, a smile cresting on my lips. "You're here. I thought you got stuck in California or something."

"And miss the opportunity to hear our baby boy's heartbeat for the first time? Not a chance." Lowering his head, he pressed a kiss to my lips.

I sighed as his hand slipped around mine, cupping it.

"Mrs. Townsend, the doctor will see you now," the receptionist stated.

"My husband can come as well, right?" I questioned, hoping she said yes without any problems.

"Absolutely."

We followed the receptionist through a door and down the hall to a private room where we were met by a nurse practitioner. She took my measurements, drew my blood, had me give a urine sample, and then had me lay on the table and unbutton my pants in preparation for the ultrasound.

"I can't believe we'll be able to find out the gender today." I squeezed Robert's hand as I laid on the table in the doctor's office, next to the ultrasound machine.

Robert brought my hand to his lips, kissing it, as he stood over me. "I already know what the gender will be, but if you need this test for confirmation ..." He shrugged.

Smirking, I placed my free hand under my head. "You're so sure it's a boy. What if it's a girl?"

He was shaking his head before the question was out of my mouth. "It's a boy."

"They'll also test to see if anything's wrong with the baby." Biting my lower lip, I brought my hand down, running it over my stomach. I grew nervous at the thought that something might be wrong with the baby.

"He's fine," Robert reassured. "You know we nee—" He was cut off when the doctor knocked and entered the room.

"We'll talk later," he said.

"Mr. and Mrs. Townsend, great to see you again. You're here for your twenty-week ultrasound. Time is flying, isn't it?" Dr. Muller quipped.

I laughed. "I can't believe it."

"Having any more bouts of nausea?" she asked while pressing on my abdomen.

I opened my mouth, but Robert responded, "She got sick last week while eating split pea soup. She normally loves it, but even the mention of it and—" He stopped when he looked down at me. "Yeah, she makes that face."

My doctor's eyes rose to my face, which I certain was turning slightly green. The mention of split pea soup had that effect on me as off late.

"Certain food aversions, even to foods you typically enjoy, is not uncommon in pregnancy. Is there anything else you can't keep down?"

"Chocolate, bananas, and the soup that shall not be named," Robert quickly answered.

My doctor looked to me, smirking. "Most husbands I come in contact with are not nearly this attuned to their wife's symptoms."

"Oh, and her ankles swell a little at night," he added, not even acknowledging what my doctor had just said.

I swallowed, feeling a little bit silly. Earlier, I had been throwing a pity party for myself because I'd felt like my husband was distancing himself, and here he was, better able to recite my symptoms to my doctor than I was. Not to mention the fact that he'd been enduring a lot of upheaval at work given the source of the leaks had finally been tracked down. While that was a relief to him and Townsend Industries to have finally uncovered the source, it came with increased scrutiny from the media.

I squeezed Robert's hand to my side. "He's one of a kind," I finally responded to my doctor.

Twenty minutes later we were walking out of my doctor's office with the confirmation of what Robert had been saying for some time. There it was, in black and white, on the sonogram pics. I was pregnant with our son.

Robert's smile was big and bright enough to light up the entire hallway, as we strolled hand in hand down the hardwood floor. He kept holding up the pics and smiling at it.

"Carter," he suddenly stopped and said.

"What?"

"That's his name. If you agree."

I mulled the name over in my head, then looked to Robert. "You don't want to name our oldest after you. Robert the Third?"

He shook his head. "I want all of my boys to have their own identities. They'll have my blood running through their veins and my heart beating in their chest. He won't need my first name to be my son."

"Carter," I said out loud. "I like that. What do you think?" Pressing my free hand to my stomach, I glanced down. I swear I felt the fluttering of butterflies in my belly, but not the usual kind. These were real, not imagined.

I gasped and brought Robert's hand to my abdomen. "He kicked! I think he likes the name."

Robert kept his hands on my stomach for a few more moments but couldn't feel anything. He lowered his head. "It's okay, Carter. You'll make your presence to the world known soon enough."

Another fluttering in my belly.

"He likes the name."

"Of course he does." Robert stood and pulled the door open for me to pass through.

As soon as we stepped into the waiting room, we were met by a familiar face.

"Jesse?" I called, Jason's wife, my sister-in-law.

Her eyes rounded. "Deborah. Robert."

"Hi, it's been a while. How are you?" We hadn't seen Jason or Jesse since they came over for dinner months ago, after Jesse lost the baby.

"I'm good." She nodded, noticeably swallowing as she glanced between Robert and I. "I see you're doing well." Her eyes drifted down to my belly. "Congratulations!"

"Thank you." I looked at Robert, and then back to Jesse. "Are you …" I paused, knowing it was impolite to question someone as to why they were at the doctor's office.

But when Jesse's hand covered her flat stomach, I instantly knew.

"I'm here for confirmation, really. I haven't told anyone yet. Not even Jason." Her eyes flittered between Robert and I.

"Your secret is safe with us. Would you like us to stay and wait for you?"

She shook her head. "No, that won't be necessary," she insisted. "But thank you."

"Okay. Well, good luck. Please give us a call if you need anything."

I stared off as Jesse moved around us to head through the door we'd just come out of. I then turned my attention to Robert. "This might mean our baby boy will have a cousin close to his age," I told Robert, who was frowning.

"We'll have to look after her and that child. Jason will be a shit father."

"Robert, don't say that. He could step up and be—"

"Who he's always been. We'll keep an eye on Jesse and this baby. If she's pregnant."

I leaned my head against his shoulder, drawn into the protectiveness I heard in his voice. Being truthful, I also didn't trust Jason enough to care for his own child, but I believed Robert when he said he would look out for Jesse and the baby. My husband may have been a hard ass but he always looked out for those who couldn't look out for themselves, especially if he had a connection to them.

"That baby will be a Townsend, and he or she is going to need looking after."

"I love you," I sighed. I moved my free hand over my mouth, stifling a yawn.

"Let's get you home and fed."

He pressed a kiss to the top of my head and I willingly let him direct me toward the elevators.

* * *

Present

Robert

"You had to go around grandfather to become CEO?" Joshua questioned as we all sat around the dining room table. The entire family had convened at Townsend Manor for our usual Sunday evening dinner.

"Your father went *through* your grandfather to become CEO," Deborah told the table.

Facing her, I gave her a nonchalant look. "Whatever it takes." I covered her hand with my own.

"Aaron didn't have to do all that to take the lead at Townsend," Tyler noted.

"That is because your brother earned the role. He worked his as—" I glanced at my wife who was giving me a deadly glare. Clearing my throat, I sat up straighter. "Butt off to become CEO."

"He was born for that role," Carter added, looking across the table at Aaron.

Aaron remained silent but gave Carter a nod.

"He's also stubborn as a goddamned mule," Carter added.

"Amen to that," Patience, who sat next to Aaron, stated, causing the entire table, except for Aaron to laugh.

I chuckled, but saw that Patience didn't even look in her husband's direction. The couple had been unusually quiet, at least toward one another throughout the evening. There was something going on there. Whatever it was, I was certain my bonehead, headstrong son was mainly responsible for it.

"Leave your brother alone," Deborah insisted. "Besides, he's not the only willful, rigid, and dogged Townsend in this room."

"Amen."

"Don't I know it."

"You can say that again."

All of the women in the room said at once.

I leaned over to whisper in Deborah's ear, "I'll show you exactly how dogged I can be as soon as we're alone." I didn't miss her body shiver.

"So was Grandfather making an idle threat or was there more to his words as he was being taken out by security?" Joshua asked, ever the one hungry for more information.

I pulled back from Deborah. Her eyes met mine and she gave me a look with a raised eyebrow. I debated for a moment on where to go with this line of questioning, before turning back to the table.

"It wasn't an idle threat."

* * *

Then

Robert

"Mr. Townsend, your two o'clock appointment is here."

"Send him in," I told my secretary. I had a meeting with yet another one of my father's associates. I'd been having meeting after meeting over the last two months, getting settled into my new position. We'd had to hire a public relations team to combat the negative publicity Townsend had been receiving, and to manage the fallout from John Lassiter's betrayal. Then my father stepping down as CEO citing health concerns and wanting to spend more time with his loving wife after thirty years of service to Townsend Industries. All of this left me in a position to become inundated with calls, interviews with the press, and meetings with staff who all wanted to know where we went from here.

My meeting that day was with a man named Lewis Greene. He had apparently been one of my father's private bankers. I'd confirmed this by comparing his name to the list of names that kept coming up over and over again on the more private files linked to the real estate my father owned that was under Townsend Industries' real estate division.

A few moments later a knock sounded at my door and my secretary opened it, a tall figure behind her.

"Mr. Townsend, this is Mr. Lewis Greene," she stated, stepping to the side as the man moved fully into my office.

An eerie feeling overcame me as I stared at the man who was the same height as I was. He was also younger than I would've imagined. Closer to my age than my father's.

"Thank you, Cindy." I nodded, letting her know she could leave. Coming out from behind my desk, I stuck out my hand. "Mr. Greene."

His hazel eyes narrowed. He was assessing me. "Mr. Townsend," he finally replied while taking my hand. His handshake was firm. He was signaling that he wasn't intimidated to step into the spacious corner office of the CEO of Townsend Industries. Why he felt the need to signal such a thing remained to be seen.

"Please, have a seat." I gestured with my hand to the chair across from my desk, as I moved back around to take my own seat.

Carefully, Lewis sat down, his gaze still intent on me.

"Mr. Greene, I requested you come here today to discuss a few matters with you."

"Really?" He lifted a dark blond eyebrow.

"You seem to have ties to my father's affairs. Namely his real estate investments and assets, some of which are co-owned by Townsend Industries."

To my surprise, Greene began chuckling.

"Did I make a joke I'm not yet aware of, Mr. Greene?"

Shaking his head, he sobered up before answering. "I was wondering when you were going to get to this. It's been two months since you took over as CEO, Robert."

I glared at him across my desk and leaned in. "Mr. Greene, I don't know what kind of relationship you had with my father, but you and I are nowhere near being on a first name basis. In this office, and any other time you see me from here on out, it's Mr. Townsend."

He tilted his head, giving me a look. "Is that so?"

"I didn't stutter the first time I said it."

"You are precisely how I'd pictured you to be."

"And how is that?"

"Like him."

I didn't have to ask who the *him* was he was referring to. I knew he meant my father.

"But smarter, savvier, more attuned to what's going on around you. It'll make you a better CEO. If you're careful. However, it could get you into trouble if you go poking around into things that aren't your concern."

I stared at him, noting his slightly southern accent. He wasn't from Williamsport.

"Everything that goes on in the Townsend name is my concern."

He sat back, appearing unbothered, as he cross his legs, clasped his hands, and sat them on his lap. "Are you sure about that?"

"Definitely."

He nodded. "Well then, let me explain who I am to Robert Senior. I'm his dirty little secret. The one person he never wanted anyone to know about. I run the dirtiest, ugliest, stench-filled parts of Townsend Industries. The parts that don't make the news. I run the division of Townsend that even the CEO doesn't know is there. That was how Robert Senior wanted it."

I didn't say anything for a long while; I simply stared at the man across from me. I was a good reader of when someone was bullshitting me. Staring into the face of Lewis Greene, I knew he wasn't lying.

I held out my hands. "It seems like I've inherited more than I know."

Slowly, his head nodded.

"Why don't you finish filling me in, Mr. Greene? That way, I know whether to keep you on staff in your unofficial capacity, or ..." I leaned in, lowering my voice and staring Greene in the eye, "kill you before you can ruin this company with those secrets."

A deep chuckle emanated from his throat. "You don't even know the half of it." For his part, he leaned in closer, lowering his voice as well. "What would be the fun in murdering your own brother before we got a chance to know one another?"

resent

Deborah

"Oh my God!"

"His what?"

"What did you just say?"

"Holy shit!"

All four of my daughters-in-law sounded off at the same time, shock written all over their faces. I looked around the staff meeting room of the shelter as they took in what I'd just shared with them and nodded.

"Yes, Lewis Greene actually turned out to be Robert Senior's illegitimate son. But ..." I waved my hands in the air, dismissively, "that's not my part of the story to tell. Besides, we all have work to do, ladies."

"Wait, what happened to this brother?" Destiny questioned.

"Yeah. Is he still around? How come we've never heard of him?" Michelle asked.

I shook my head adamantly. "Sorry, ladies, I cannot reveal parts of the story that are not mine to tell."

"We won't tell anyone," Patience added.

"Right? If there's anyone you can trust with a secret, it's us. Right, ladies?" Kayla insisted.

I giggled at all of the other women nodding and agreeing with Kayla.

"I trust you ladies with the most precious things I've ever gifted the planet with. My boys' hearts." I looked around the room at the women I loved like daughters. "But I'm not telling that part of the story!" I giggled.

"Maybe Robert's shared it with the guys. I'll get it out of my husband tonight, if he has," Michelle mumbled.

I shook my head. We were all just finishing up a lunch meeting on a Saturday afternoon. The women had come by, dropped all of the kiddos off at the seven-day-a-week daycare we offered at the shelter, and brought cartons of delicious Chinese food from a local restaurant for us to eat while we strategized.

So far, the soft opening of the shelter had garnered wonderful results. We already had three families staying in our full-time apartments, a number of mothers enrolled in our parenting classes, daycare, and back-to-work programs. There'd been two glowing articles written about us in the newspaper and on the websites of the local press. We were rolling along, and I couldn't be happier.

"Fine. I'm going to teach my intro to personal finance class to a group of teens today. I'm so excited," Destiny began. "I think I'll bring Annalise to class with me so she can learn, too."

I lifted an eyebrow. "She's barely nine months."

Destiny shrugged. "Never too young to start. If Tyler can have Travis and Tristan drooling over those damn Nerf balls, I can have my baby girl understanding the importance of index funds before she begins the first grade."

The other women in the room laughed as we went about cleaning up and heading in different directions to our respective offices.

However, just before she exited, I caught Patience at the door.

"I wanted to talk to you," I stated, closing the door, so it was just she and I.

She lifted an eyebrow. "Is this about the grant application? Was it returned?"

I quickly shook my head to wipe the worried expression from her face.

"This is about a personal matter." I moved to the loveseat that sat against the far wall of the room, patting the empty space next to me for Patience to sit.

Once she did, I began, "Robert and I both noticed some tension between you and Aaron the other night. For the last few weeks, really." I held up my hand to stop whatever she was about to say. "I know, I know. No one wants a meddling mother-in-law. And for the most part, I know well enough to stay out of my boys' relationships. You all will work it out, how you see fit. I just thought I might be able to offer some perspective."

Patience sighed. "He's being so damned stubborn."

I laughed. "He's a Townsend, what else is new?"

She shook her head. "I know but this is different."

I lowered my gaze to see her hand pressed against her stomach. A mother's natural instinct to protect her child.

"You're pregnant," I said lightly, taking her hands into mine.

She nodded.

"And he's freaking out about it."

"Pretty much." She sighed.

"Given what happened after Andreas and Thiers' births, I can understand it."

"Deborah, I understand it, too. Heck, I was the one laying there on the bed bleeding out. I get it. But he's being so adamant about insisting I get rid of this baby."

I swallowed, hating to even hear those words coming from her mouth. "That's his fear talking."

"I know."

"Aaron's always been protective of you. Over you."

Patience's shoulders rose and fell as she inhaled and exhaled deeply. "I'm aware of that. Even the first time I ever met him when I was only fourteen, he protected me."

I looked at my daughter-in-law in her big, innocent, brown eyes. With my left hand, I pushed back one of her stray sisterlocks behind her ear. "Sweetie, that was not the first time you two met."

She frowned, giving me a confused look. "Trust me, Deborah, I would've remembered meeting Aaron before that night."

I shook my head. "Maybe not. You were so young the first time."

* * *

THEN

Deborah

I could feel Robert's presence behind me as I stared at eight-year-old Aaron, half-laying, half-sitting on the couch.

"He still isn't eating?" Robert's low voice questioned.

I shook my head, still staring ahead. "He's barely eating, he won't say a word in school, refuses to even acknowledge Carter's presence." I turned to Robert with tears in my eyes. "They were so close before the accident. Now it's like Aaron hates him. He'll barely acknowledge Joshua and Tyler, but he doesn't hold the same disdain for them. Carter came to me the other day so upset about it. What are we going to do?"

I wiped away an errant tear, not wanting the boys to see me cry.

"He's still healing, princess." Robert pressed a kiss to my forehead. "He'll come around."

"When, Robert? He's so far behind in school. And you know what his records already indicated."

My husband's face was grim. It'd been an extremely tough year for our family. Aaron—who was only a few months younger than Carter—was now our son to raise, after Jason and Jesse had died in a terrible car accident. The doctors had said it was a miracle that he survived. Though he came out with some physical scars, I was more concerned about his mental state. Not only did the car accident and the aftermath have a major impact on his behavior, but the huge argument that'd occurred between Robert and Jason beforehand had scarred him.

"Who knows what that shithead brother of mine filled his head with before he died," Robert growled.

My first instinct was to tell my husband not to speak ill of a man who was no longer alive to defend himself, but I thought better of it. Robert was right. I'd seen the bruises on Aaron's body the night of his eighth birthday. Jason Townsend had turned into Robert Townsend Sr., and resorted to physical persuasion and violence to get his way with a child. And the mental abuse … I didn't even want to think about it.

"He had it, too."

I turned to stare at Robert's profile. He was staring straight ahead, watching Aaron.

"Jason was dyslexic. I assume, at least. Father would always pick on him about it. Asking him why he was so stupid, calling him a dummy and a loser for not even being able to spell his name correctly. I thought Jason needed to apply himself more. To focus more than the rest of us, and that he just refused to do it."

"When did you realize the truth?" I questioned.

He gave a one shoulder shrug, still looking ahead. "A few months after I left Stanford and was working full-time at Townsend when my father had his first stroke."

I nodded, silently. About a year after Robert took over as CEO at Townsend, Robert Sr. had a second stroke that ultimately killed him. Carter and Aaron weren't even one when he died.

"I noticed then my father had trouble reading. I thought it was due to the damage from the stroke. The doctors had told me as much to my face, but one day I overheard a doctor telling him that the stroke hadn't caused damage to that part of his brain. Later on, his assistant had informed me that she'd always recorded meetings for my father so he could listen instead of having to read notes. Little things like that started to mount, and I put two and two together. He didn't abuse Jason simply because of his poor reading abilities. He did it because he hated and was ashamed of his son who'd inherited what he had." Robert turned to me, his eyes full of sadness. "And Jason did the same thing to Aaron."

Reaching over, I rubbed Robert's shoulder in an effort to comfort him. I knew he was hoping that he could take those painful memories away from Aaron, because I was wishing the same thing.

"He has us now," I stated firmly.

Robert nodded, just before our ringing doorbell caught both of our attention. Robert peered down at the watch on his wrist.

"That's Thiers," he informed me.

I nodded, knowing Robert's good friend, Thiers, was coming over to Townsend Manor to have lunch with Robert.

I followed him to the door, stepping back as he pulled it open. A smile blossomed on my lips at the sight of the man who I knew was one of my husband's closest confidants. Thiers' dark brown eyes wrinkled at the edges as he smiled.

"Thiers," I greeted.

"Hi," a soft voice returned, startling me.

I lowered my gaze and my heart squeezed in my chest. Standing in front of Thiers, barely reaching his knees, was a little girl with the cutest afro pigtails, tied with red ribbons that matched the red and white romper she wore. Folded in her tiny, walnut-colored arms were two books, which she held firmly against her chest.

"I hope you don't mind. Our nanny had a family emergency and had to leave for a few days, so I had to bring my daughter."

"Of course we don't mind. I could use another lady in the house with all of these boys running around." My heartstrings pulled with sadness for Thiers. He'd been deeply in love with his wife, Jeanette, who I'd met on a number of occasion rights after Robert and I had Carter. We'd became fast friends. Almost four years ago, when Jeanette became pregnant, we were thrilled for the couple who'd had the most difficult time conceiving. Unfortunately, Jeanette died during labor, leaving Thiers to raise their daughter, Patience, on his own. He rarely brought her out with him anywhere, however, opting to allow the nanny to care for her much of the time.

"Come in," Robert added, widening the door.

"Robert, you and Thiers can go out to the deck to have your lunch.

Patience can remain with me." I crouched low, next to the little girl, who stared up at me, wide-eyed. "Is that okay, sweetie?"

She nodded.

"Thanks, princess," Robert said, pressing a kiss to my cheek before showing Thiers off in the direction of the back of the manor where our huge patio was. I'd already set out sandwiches and salads for them to eat.

"What books did you bring with you, sweetheart?" I questioned Patience while leading her toward the den where the boys were playing. All except Tyler, who was upstairs napping.

"Dr. Seuss." She proudly held up the books for me to see. Displaying *The Cat in the Hat* along with Dr. Seuss' *ABC: An Amazing Alphabet Book!*. Abruptly, her direction turned from me to the couch where Aaron was still lounging, staring at the television.

Before I knew what was happening, she moved from in front of me, her little legs carrying her over to the couch. Placing the book down first, she climbed up, directly next to Aaron, and slid over close to him. Just when I parted my lips to tell Patience not to get too close to him, he looked down at her and lifted his arm, making room for her at his side.

I blinked, taken aback by the move. I didn't know if I should pick Patience up or not. Aaron hadn't been the friendliest person to anyone in the house in the four months he'd moved in with us. In fact, just earlier that day he'd almost gotten into a physical fight with Carter, who'd mentioned something about a book report that was due at school.

"Read," Patience demanded, holding one of her books out to Aaron.

My heartbeat quickened. Reading more than anything was a sore spot for Aaron.

I took a step forward to intervene, but stopped. A feeling that I needed to let this play out without my intervention overcame me.

I watched as Aaron shook his head slightly. "I don't like reading." His face held a scowl, that even at eight years old looked intimidating.

Patience gave him a funny look, as if she didn't quite understand what he'd said. Or if she couldn't comprehend how anyone didn't like reading. "Okay," she shrugged and said.

I thought she would eventually move over or go on her way, but again, I was surprised.

"I read to you," she stated proudly.

Aaron watched her for a moment, contemplating something, before he said, "Okay."

His voice was gruff—as had become his normal sounding self—but he adjusted, placing his arm against the back of the couch, and letting Patience move onto his lap so they both could see the book.

"This A." She pointed to the page they were looking at. "A for apple. Say it," she ordered, looking up at Aaron.

My chin almost hit the floor when he repeated after her.

"Patience, leave Aaron alone. He's not nice," came Joshua's three-year-old voice from across the room.

I waited with bated breath to see how this was going to play out. Another surprise. When Joshua moved closer, reaching for Patience's hand, Aaron's hand gripped his, but not too tightly from what I could see.

"Leave her alone. We're reading," Aaron hissed at his now younger brother. He released Joshua's arm, leaving him stunned. "Go ahead." He motioning with his head toward the page.

Patience didn't miss a beat. "This B. B for bicycle. Say it."

Aaron repeated her words just as instructed.

I was so intrigued by what was happening, I didn't even notice both Carter and Joshua move next to me.

"Mother, why's Aaron reading with Patience?" Carter questioned.

"Aaron *hates* reading!" Joshua stated loudly. So loud, in fact, that Aaron's brooding hazel eyes crossed the room, glaring at all three of us before dropping down to continue reading with Patience, who was already on to the letter E.

"You two, leave them be." I ushered the boys out of the room and up the stairs to the playroom. I, on the other hand, continued to watch from the doorway. About halfway through the first book, Aaron said something to Patience, causing her to giggle, louder than I'd ever heard from the little girl before. And for the first time in months, I saw what appeared to be an actual smile cross Aaron's face. My heart swelled up with joy at seeing the little boy, who I loved as if I'd given birth to him, smiling again.

I had become so enthralled in watching the pair, who seemed to be in their own little world, that it took a few minutes, and for Carter to yell down from the top of the stairs that Tyler had woken up from his nap, and was crying for me.

With one last glance, I headed up the stairs to tend to my youngest son. After plucking Tyler from his crib, I quickly changed him and headed back downstairs to the kitchen to grab his bottle.

"Lunch over already?" I questioned Robert as he and Thiers passed me in the hallway.

"I forgot I had an appointment. Need to cut lunch short," Thiers explained. "I'll just go and get Patience."

"She's in the den … reading with Aaron."

I didn't miss the surprised expression that covered Robert's face. I gave him an *I'll explain later* look, and he nodded.

I proceeded to the kitchen to prepare Tyler's bottle. I tickled him under the chin just after checking the warmth of the bottle, before running my hands through his auburn hair. I wondered if his hair would change color over time or remain the reddish color. Tyler was nearly a year old but I felt like I was just getting to know him. The weeks after his birth had been extremely difficult. My grief over what we'd lost stole precious moments from what we had gained. Those days passed by in a blur, and then Jason's accident, and taking on Aaron, had left me little time for my youngest. But we were finally settling into a comfortable rhythm.

To say I was stunned when I realized the color of Tyler's hair would've been an understatement. Then Robert told me that a few relatives on his mother's side of the family were redheads. All of my boys mirrored their father in one way or another.

Just as I handed the bottle to Tyler and adjusted him on my hip, a loud cry reached my ears. I started toward the den where it sounded like the noises were coming from, Tyler happily sipping away as if he didn't have a care in the world. When I reached the den, I looked between Robert's stunned expression and Thiers' look which was a mix between horrified and embarrassed.

"No!" Patience was yelling every time her father tried to pick her up off of Aaron's lap. "Go away!" she yelled again.

"You're scaring her!" Aaron added, wrapping an arm around Patience.

Thiers turned to Robert and I, completely lost on how to handle the situation.

"Aaron," I began, stepping forward, passing Tyler to Robert, "Patience needs to go with her father."

"She doesn't have to." Aaron's sharp eyes moved from me to Thiers. "Can't she stay a little while longer? She was sleeping."

I blinked.

"Yeah, sleeping!" Patience added.

I looked behind me to Thiers. "She was reading to him earlier. I guess she fell asleep."

Thiers shook his head. "I'm sorry about that. I can't get her to go anywhere without a book in her hand. Just like ..." He trailed off before clearing his throat.

I saw the pain in his eyes. He still wasn't over his deceased wife.

"Well, it's no trouble for us to keep her while you go to your appointment," I quickly said.

Thiers' eyelids rose then fell. "No, I couldn't ask you to do that."

"You're not asking us," Robert replied. "We're happy to do it." He looked back, staring at Aaron who stared up at him with a questioning expression on his face. Robert turned to Thiers, gesturing with this head.

I followed the two toward the den's doorway.

"It's the first time Aaron's come out of that dark shell he's cocooned himself in." Robert glanced back at Aaron and Patience before turning to Thiers again. "He's not as dark and angry looking around her. She can stay here while you make your appointment, and then you can come over for dinner."

I sighed in relief. Robert seemed to get it without needing a long explanation. Another reason my love for him grew with each day, even after nearly nine years of marriage.

"Okay," Thiers finally acquiesced. "I'd rather not have my girl at this meeting anyway." Thiers walked over to Patience and placed a kiss on her forehead. "I'll be back later, okay?"

"'Kay, bye!" Patience waved, and then laid her head back against Aaron's chest, eyes peacefully closing.

"I'll be damned." Robert's voice was just above a whisper as he and I watched Aaron flip open the page of the book, moving his lips silently as if trying to recite the letter. One arm protectively wrapped around the sleeping girl in his arms.

* * *

Robert

"That was …"

"Wasn't it?" Deborah retorted to my unfinished statement. We were sitting in my downstairs office, having just finished dinner with the kids, Thiers, and his young daughter, Patience. Throughout the entire day, since Patience arrived, it was as if she was glued to Aaron's side. And for his part, he wasn't too keen on her being *unstuck*. Not only was it the age difference that surprised me—since when did eight-year-old boys want to hang out with three-year-old girls—but the fact that simply because of Patience's insistence, Aaron had spent the day attempting to read, or at the very least, sounding out different letters. Something Deborah and I had to threaten to take away toys or video games to get him to do.

"Even at dinner—"

"He insisted she sit next to him," Deb finished.

I shook my head. "It was almost as if—" My comment was silenced by a knock on the door.

My head pivoted in the direction of the knock to find Aaron standing in the doorway, that surly expression firmly planted on his face.

245

Deborah immediately stood up from my lap, going to him. "Is everything alright?"

Aaron nodded before speaking. "I wanted to, um, ask you something."

"Come in." Deborah stepped aside, allowing space for Aaron to enter.

Taking a seat on the edge of the chair directly across from me, he set his hands in his lap, allowing his feet to touch the floor. His positioning looked as if he kept himself prepared to make a run for it, just in case he needed to.

Just seeing him sit there like that, reminded me of the times where I made a too-quick movement near him and he'd flinch as if expecting a smack or punch to the face or body. I tightened my grip on the pencil I was holding, until I heard it snap. If I could resurrect my shit-head of a younger brother just so I could beat his ass for what he did to his own son, I swear I would've.

"What did you want to discuss, son?" I questioned, folding my hands over one another, placing them on the desk.

He looked around the room, briefly, before his eyes came to rest on Deborah and I. She stood over me, as I sat in the high back leather chair, her arm resting against my left shoulder.

"I think I should learn to read."

I looked up at Deborah; her eyebrows nearly touched her forehead. "Oh."

Aaron nodded. "Patience is only three and she can read."

He mumbled that last part but I'd heard it.

"Well, we can make arrangements with the tutor we were talking about."

"Aaron, we know this might be tough for you," Deborah began as she rounded the desk and stooped low in front of Aaron, "and that the other kids might—"

Aaron shook his head. "I don't care about the other kids," he said firmly, a hardness in his voice.

Deborah looked back at me. I knew what she was thinking. He might not have said it before, but Aaron had indeed cared about what the other kids in his class thought of his reading skills. He'd gotten into more than one fight since we'd transferred him to Excelor Academy, and though he wouldn't say, we both suspected the bullying from the other children was the main reason behind those fights. We'd even gone so far as to consider having him transferred to the same classroom as Carter, where we hoped he wouldn't feel as alone. But Aaron had flat out shot that idea down.

"Those tutors can help me learn to read?" he asked, his voice filled with uncertainty. "I might be too stupid to learn."

Deborah gasped at the same time my heart tightened so much in my chest it hurt to take my next breath. I'd heard those words too many fucking times to not know where he'd gotten them from. Rising, I rounded the other side of my desk, also coming to crouch down in front of Aaron.

"Aaron, don't ever say that again."

"But it's tr—"

"Don't," I said sharply.

His mouth clamped shut as he flinched.

Fuck!

I wanted my boys to respect me but never fear me. I didn't need to rule my family with an iron fist of fear, humiliation, and abuse, the way I'd grown up. Unfortunately, Aaron had spent the first eight years of his life with a father who hadn't known any different.

CHAPTER 26

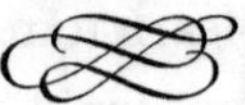

resent

Aaron

"You know that was me, right?"

I inhaled deeply, turning my head to glare outside the window, and ignoring the offending noise to my right.

Emma sighed just as heavily. "We're still doing this, Aaron? Ignoring me when you *know* I'm right."

I heaved another breath, this time grunting.

"That's okay. Want me to tell you how I intervened, the first time you and Patience met? The *real* first time?"

Reluctantly, my head pivoted, pulling my gaze in her direction. A satisfied smile crested on her pink lips, as if knowing simply the mention of my wife's name would get my attention.

"Talk," I demanded.

Emma rolled those brown irises of hers that reminded me of my birth mother.

"That first time, you were so young. It was months after the accident, but you were so forlorn, so angry, and in so much pain. Not physically, you'd healed for the most part, but ..." She trailed off. "You know the pain you were in. Getting into fights at school, not speaking to any of your brothers, especially Carter. I hated to see you like that. Your parents hated seeing you like that. So when Thiers made plans to have lunch with Robert that day, I helped you out by making sure he'd bring three-year-old Patience along. She was so cute," Emma gushed, a satisfied expression crossing her face.

"Deb was almost terrified for the little munchkin that walked up to you and practically pushed a book in your face. But I knew better. From the very beginning your little heart couldn't say no to her."

I turned from Emma, watching the lights along the street come on as the night sky descended.

"You're headed to the manor."

I glanced at Emma, lifting a smug eyebrow. "You're surprised? I thought you knew everything."

An even more pompous smile crossed her face. "Of course I knew. Just making conversation. I'll see you after you speak with your father."

And with that said, she was gone a second later. I rubbed my forehead with the tips of my fingers, tension filling my entire body. My wife had barely spoken to me in three weeks. Clearly, she was still pissed, and I was starting to feel like maybe, just fucking maybe I'd made a mistake.

"No one ever said you learned quickly," my father stated as soon as he opened the front door of Townsend Manor. Although I still had the key and code to enter my childhood home, I offered my parents their privacy by ringing the bell. I'd also called him before leaving the office to let him know I'd be over to talk with him.

"You actually have said I learn quickly. On numerous occasions," I reminded him.

He frowned. "I was referring to business when I said it. Now, I'm talking about relationships. Love. You can be … not as adept at learning in that arena."

I simply stared at my father. Anyone else would have gotten a *fuck you* but he was the man who'd raised me.

"How do you know what I need to speak to you about is concerning my relationship?"

He shook his head, as if knowing that was my next question. "See? You don't even know how obvious you are sometimes. It's after six o'clock at night. It's getting dark. And you've put in a full day of work. You would've let anything business related wait until tomorrow while in the office. Personal, on the other hand, that is the only thing that would keep you from getting home to your wife and kids on a Friday evening."

Taking a step back from the doorway, he let me enter.

"Mother?" I questioned.

"She's over Joshua and Kayla's, helping with Victoria and Kennedy."

I nodded. Kennedy was sleeping over Joshua's that night to spend some time with her cousin.

I followed behind my father as he strolled down the long hallway of the main floor of Townsend Manor, toward his home office. As we entered, I glanced around the room, taking in the ways it'd changed over the years. Instead of the huge, cherrywood desk, he'd replaced it with a sleeker, glass desk, which had a phone, laptop, and a few books, business magazines, and papers on top. Of course, there were pictures of the entire family, prominently displayed.

I watched as he picked one of the photos up. From what I could make out it was the photo we'd taken only a few months prior, at a Fourth of July picnic in the backyard of the manor. The image was of all of us, including all ten grandchildren.

"This is my legacy. What I spent years building, long before you were even born." His eyes moved from the framed picture in his hand to me. He turned the photo around so I could clearly see it. "Now tell me how you're fucking it all up?"

I grunted and the scowl I usually wore deepened. I didn't respond as I sat down, still glaring at my father.

"I'm waiting for an answer."

Again, my gaze bounced around the room. "Remember that day I told you and Mother I wanted to learn to read?"

His eyes squinted, forehead wrinkled as he stretched his memory back all of those years to recall that scene. "Yes." He nodded finally.

"You came in here while your mother and I were talking. It was the day—"

"I met my wife for the first time."

He looked at me, eyes widening just a small amount as he took in what I'd said. "I'll be damned. So it was."

"She was my inspiration. I thought then it was because I was embarrassed by a girl five years younger than me, barely able to climb up onto the couch by herself, teaching me how to read. But …" I broke off, sighing.

"It was more than that."

I nodded.

There was a long pause.

"So tell me how you're fucking it all up."

"You sound just like Carter," I grunted.

My father smirked. "He's a chip off the old block. Just like you."

I turned to my father.

"Since you won't talk, let me take a guess. Patience is pregnant."

He held his hand up, cutting off what I'd been about to say.

"She didn't tell me, not directly anyway. But it's hard for anyone to keep a secret around here. Especially, when she's running to the bathroom every hour to throw up."

I glared at my father, alarmed. "It isn't that often."

"How do you know?" He quickly shot back. "My guess is you've been completely checked out of this pregnancy, because you're scared shitless of losing your wife."

What the hell could I say to that? I wasn't a liar by design. He would've known if I'd been lying anyway. So instead of refuting his claim, I grunted.

"That's what I thought. Listen, you, me, all of my boys, we're all protectors. But the women we've married, they're protectors in their own right. And trust me when I say the one thing you never want to get in between is a mother and her child."

Again, my father held up his hand, stopping my retort.

"Let me tell you the one time your mother had to help me remove my head from my own ass over our children.

* * *

Then

> *Robert*

"Yes, Wilson, I'm still on the line with you," I replied as I stared off into the distance, overlooking the trees on the far end of the lake that expanded for more than a mile behind Townsend Manor. I had taken off a few hours early from the office in order to get some work done at home, where it was quiet and I could concentrate better. However, I'd had a conference call set up. I'd decided to take the call out near one of the guest houses, using my newly acquired cordless telephone.

I continued to listen as the head of my research and development for my technology division began telling me about some new technology involving computers. I didn't totally understand the details, but he swore that the guys he knew were onto something big. He believed that within a decade this technology would permeate mainstream society, making computers in every household more than a dream, but a reality. And he believed this would majorly impact the energy, and every other, market.

"Father!"

I turned from the lake to face the almost five-year-old boy who excitedly called my name behind me. My heart squeezed at the sight of Carter running down the hill in my direction, his bowl-cut blond locks flapping in the window. And although he was still a few yards away, I could make out the gleam in his blue eyes that looked exactly like his mother's. Just the way I'd envisioned in my dream eleven years earlier.

Still on the phone, I stooped low when Carter reached me, picking him up and nuzzling his face with my own. His giggle warmed my chest, but I covered my lips with my finger, signaling for him to be silent and then pointing at the phone.

A serious expression covered his face and he nodded, knowing that when I was on a business call, he needed to be as quiet as possible. I set him down and watched as he strolled over to the lake's pier, toward the edge, but not too close.

"William, we do not have a choice. Japan is kicking our collective asses with the level of superiority their vehicles and technology have over ours," I stated into the phone, following the conversation, while still keeping an eye on Carter. He was playing with a formation of rocks he'd left out on the pier a few days earlier. He'd been playing with his cousin, Aaron. Those two were close when Jason would allow Aaron to come over.

Listening to the conversation, I added my input when and where necessary. I began pacing back and forth as the conversation grew heated between my R&D guy and William, who was still on the board. The men disagreed about international expansion. I let them argue because I wanted to hear both sides of the aisle. However, I was close to making my decision, to continue forward with expansion. The world was getting smaller, and men like William were often opposed to progress, even if they didn't realize that was what they were doing. Apparently, when I'd become CEO, William had believed I would simply continue on in my father's footsteps, just without the leaks and scandals. He should've thought again.

I sat back down in the wooden lawn chair I'd brought out with me, and opened my mouth to speak when a loud splash caught my attention.

"Help!"

I glanced outward toward the water and saw tiny hands flailing. My heart seized in my chest. It felt like everything was at a standstill. The memory of Carter refusing to complete his swim lessons due to his fear of the water came flooding back.

"Gentlemen, I have to go." With that, I hung up the phone, placed it on the table, and slowly stood, moving toward the edge of the pier.

I clamped down on my base instincts that were screaming at me to jump in immediately and save my son. But I knew better. Carter knew how to swim. He was just afraid, and if there's one thing I absolutely would not do, it was to let any of my boys live their lives in fear. As first born, he had an example to set for his brothers to come.

"Father, help!" he yelled when his body bobbed up over the water again.

I shook my head, causing more pain to myself than to him. "You can swim," I stated in a calm voice. "Show me you know how to swim." I folded my arms across my chest, more to stop myself from jumping in than anything.

"I can't! I'm scared!" he cried, arms flailing, water splashing everywhere.

"Fear is a part of life, you will need to learn how to tame if you want to get anywhere. We've been through this." My voice was raised and stern but I wasn't quite yelling. "Show me you know how to swim."

I waited for one heartbeat, watching his head go underwater again.

Breathing deeply, my eyes searched the lake.

I took a step closer.

I'd been comforted by the fact that this lake was manmade. It did not lead to any rivers or have strong currents that would keep him underwater for long. However, when another heartbeat passed and he did not emerge, I ripped off my shoes and prepared to jump in, berating myself … but I stopped.

Just before I entered the water, Carter's head came up again and his arms began moving in perfect sync with the freestyle stroke he'd been taught during his swim lessons. I counted each stroke he performed with precision. His breathing technique was choppy due to lack of practice, but when his hands reached the wooden ladder of the pier, I couldn't have been more proud. I crouched down, reaching out to pluck his body out of the water.

He was shaking but he was okay. Laughing out loud, I hugged him to my chest.

"You did it!" I exclaimed proudly, pulling back to stare at him.

To my surprise and horror, tears began streaming down his face and he let out a wail I hadn't heard from him since he was a baby. Breaking away from my hold, he took off running, over the pier and up the hill, traversing the massive backyard, all while calling for his mother.

It was then I knew I'd fucked up.

* * *

THEN

Deborah

"He could've died!" I screeched for the umpteenth time that night as I tossed Robert's pillows and a set of blankets in his direction. I was so furious I couldn't even look at the man.

"He wasn't in any real danger," he tried to explain for the millionth time.

But I was not listening to anything he had to say.

"Get out! You are not sleeping in here tonight!" I pulled the door of our bedroom open to let him know I was serious.

"Princ—"

"Don't you dare!" I yelled. "Do *not* try to smooth this over by calling me princess. Our baby boy almost drowned out there and you let it happen! How could you?" Blinking, I attempted to dry the tears that threatened to spill over. I was feeling a mix of emotions: fury, fear, sadness, confusion, and more. I'd never felt betrayed by my own husband before, but now ...

"Deborah, he was perfectly s—"

"Robert, if you say *one* more word to me, I promise you I am heading to a divorce attorney first thing in the morning, and Carter and I are gone!"

His gaze narrowed on me, the brown in his eyes deepening as he shook his head. This was the first time throughout this entire altercation that Robert actually exerted any anger.

"You are not leaving me." His voice was ominous but I didn't care.

"Get out." I had no more fight in me. I just couldn't be in his presence any longer that night.

I don't know what it was, but something made him take note and make the decision that was best for all involved. Slowly, he ambled to the door, pausing only a few inches away from me, staring down at me. Turning my head, I averted my face until he moved passed the threshold of the door.

Only then did I push out the breath I'd been holding on to. I quickly swiped at the lone tear that fell, refusing to release any more.

I paced around our spacious bedroom for a while, arms folded, hating the sight of my bed without my husband in it. It wouldn't be the first night I slept alone. Robert often had business trips that he needed to make, but he did his best to keep them to a minimal when he couldn't bring Carter and I.

However, this was different. This was the first time I'd be sleeping alone in our large, sleigh bed while he was still in the same house. Townsend Manor was huge. If he'd chosen a guest room on the other side of the manor, I could go days without even seeing him. However, if I knew my husband, and I was certain I did, he'd gone down to his office to work instead of sleep.

Shaking my head, I pushed those thoughts out. I didn't want or need to think about him. My concern shouldn't have been for him. Exiting the bedroom door, I strode down three doors until I reached the room that read "Carter" in big, blue letters. Pushing the door open, I entered, slipping in and closing it gently behind me so that not too much light got in, waking him.

Startled, I gasped when his tiny voice surprised me, instead of the other way around.

"Mother."

I moved closer, noting the time on the superhero clock on his wall. It was a little after ten o'clock at night.

"Carter, what are you doing awake?" I'd put him to bed nearly two hours ago. And my son wasn't a light sleeper.

"Are you and Father mad at me?"

I sunk down to the floor next to his bed, running my hand through his soft hair.

"We're going to have to do something about this bowl cut," I joked.

Thanks to the superman night light that was plugged in not too far from his bed, I caught the frown that immediately formed.

"I like my hair," he insisted.

I lowered my face so he wouldn't see me smothering my laughter. He was sometimes adamant and stubborn even as a little boy. He reminded me of his father so much in that way. I sighed just thinking of all of the ways this kid was going to test me over the years. And Robert said we'd be having three more.

Rolling my eyes, I made a disbelieving noise in the back of my throat. The way I was feeling, Robert would be lucky if I kept him around long enough to raise the little boy we already had.

"To answer your question, no." I shook my head. "Your father and I aren't mad at you."

"But you're angry at each other."

I sighed, shamefaced. "You heard us yelling?"

He nodded.

I'd tried to keep my voice down, but every time Robert spoke all I could think about was a terrified Carter running, screaming and crying that he'd fallen in the lake. He was so distraught that I couldn't make out what he was saying at first. I had, however, realized that he was soaking wet, while he'd been dry when I'd let him go outside to see his father once we'd arrived home from work and school. He'd been so excited to learn that his father was home, he begged me to let him out to see his dad, even though I knew Robert was on a conference call.

By the time I'd realized he'd fallen in the lake, I'd assumed Robert was the one who'd fished him out. However, as Robert came barreling up the backyard hill, I realized that he was bone dry, or nearly so. He couldn't have jumped in the water after Carter. It still didn't fully register with me what had occurred. I knew how scared Carter was of water and swimming, so I thought he may have slipped, Robert quickly pulling him out, and Carter was just upset about the scare he'd had.

It wasn't until Robert opened his mouth and told the entire story that I'd become furious.

"Are you going to get a divorce?"

My eyes popped wide. "How do you even know that word?"

"Jake says his mom made his dad sleep in a different room for a long time, and now they're getting a divorce."

I frowned. "We're not Jake's parents."

"But I heard you tell Father he has to sleep in another room."

Placing my hand on Carter's back, I rubbed soothing circles on it. "You don't worry about your father and I." I pushed his hair aside with my free hand to kiss his forehead.

"He was just teaching me to swim."

I bit my tongue. Carter loved his father beyond measure, so of course he was going to try his best to protect him, even though he'd been petrified earlier as a result of his father's actions.

"Go to sleep, baby," I whispered and tugged at his ear, causing him to giggle.

I stayed by his bedside, rubbing his back until he turned his head to face the wall, and his breathing steadied, alerting me that he'd fallen asleep. Quietly, I rose to my feet and padded my way across the carpeted floor, opening the door and slipping out. I stopped abruptly when I came face-to-face with Robert.

"He's sleeping."

"I was just coming in to check on him."

Lifting my chin, I folded my arms across my breasts. "He's fine."

"Deborah—"

I shook my head. "No, Robert. No," I stated sternly, walking away and swiftly entering our bedroom, shutting the door firmly behind me.

* * *

Then

Robert

"What?" I barked into the phone as I answered.

"M-Mr. Townsend, you have a call on line one," my secretary responded through a shaky voice.

I pushed my hand through my hair, pissed at the interruption, pissed at the fear I heard in her voice, but mostly pissed at myself for letting things get this damned far. It'd been days since I'd slept in my own bed. Days since my wife said more than a handful of sentences, and fucking days since I'd been able even touch my wife. I was spazzing on just about everyone in my office.

Earlier in the day, one of my executives had asked me if Deborah had been out of town for the week, because that was the only time when I was on edge. I almost decked him. Luckily, a member of my security staff had stopped me.

"Tell them I'm busy. They'll have to call back another time."

"Uh, when would you like—"

"I don't give a shit! Tell them to call back!" I hung up the phone, not wanting to hear anything more about whoever was on the line.

"You're going to regret that."

Lifting my gaze from the file on my desk I was trying to work on, I frowned at the six-foot-seven dark haired man, standing in my office's doorway. "The hell do you want?" I growled at Rick.

"Our two o'clock meeting." He gestured to the clock on the wall directly across from my desk.

I sighed. He was right. I'd hired Rick as the head of Townsend security, weeks after I'd been made CEO. I couldn't trust any of the previous security staff seeing as how many of them had helped to keep my father's secrets, or were just highly incompetent. Rick, on the other hand, had proven himself savvy, intelligent, and willing to get his hands a little dirty when things called for it. I'd made him an offer he couldn't refuse—I allowed him to bring on the entirety of his staff from his own agency, plus have his own opportunity to hire whomever he'd needed to complete the security staff at Townsend. Not only did his security staff ensure the safety of Townsend Industries, but of the Townsend family. There were very few people I trusted taking care of my family. Rick was one of them.

That thought alone had the pit in my stomach growing larger. Just knowing that I'd somehow endangered my own son's life, stole my very breath. I didn't know if that knowledge, or if the look in Deborah's eyes over the past week, was worse.

"Want to talk about it?" Rick asked, shutting the door behind him.

"Mind your damn business."

He grunted as he casually strolled toward the chair, sitting in it and crossing his legs, giving me a smug look. He was obviously unintimidated by my attitude. Which was part of the reason I liked him.

"You can tell me to fuck off. Doesn't mean I'm going anywhere. I've got two more years until I'm fully vested, anyway. Then I can cash out, retire on the beach, and never think about the name Townsend again." Chuckling, he lifted his hands, clasping them behind his head, and leaned backward as if he was practicing for lounging on the beach.

"You'll still be here in two years." Rick could talk as much shit as he'd like, but I knew he'd retire and be bored inside a month. His ass would be back at Townsend so fast it'd feel like he'd never left.

"Whatever," he grunted, sitting up. "This is about Deb and the kid, huh?"

I gave him a sharp glare that said *tread carefully.* As grateful and fond of Rick as I was, I didn't let anyone bring up my family.

"I'm just saying, you only get that gleam in your eyes when something's affecting your family. It's the same one you had when all that shit was going down with the leaks, your father, and that asshole you were friends with who tried to frame Deb."

I pushed a few papers on my desk aside, not knowing what to say. He was right, I knew it and so did he. That didn't mean I was up to talking to him or anyone else about it. But hell, I had no one else to discuss it with, seeing as how my wife wasn't listening to my reasoning.

"How the hell are you supposed to know how to be a father when you had a shitty one?"

Rick's response was immediate. He grunted and made a disbelieving sound with his mouth. "Hell if I know. Exactly why I ain't having kids. You can mess those little fuckers up."

I frowned. "Don't curse in my office."

He shrugged, unperturbed.

I went to respond but my desk phone rang again.

"What?"

"You have a visitor. It's Mrs. Townsend," my secretary stated quickly, likely out of fear of my reaming her out again.

"Send her in." I immediately hung up the phone and headed to my office door.

"Welp, I know when it's my time to go. Never been one to overstay my welcome, anyway."

Despite his size, Rick easily slipped past me on his way out of the door. "Mrs. Townsend," he greeted, as he and Deborah passed one another.

"Rick. Good to see you." Her face was pleasant as she returned his greetings, but as soon as she turned to me, the placid expression she'd been giving me for days returned. At least it was better than the *fuck you* look she'd been throwing my way for the first two days after Carter ran to her crying.

She didn't say anything as she passed me to enter my office. No kiss or anything.

Sighing, I closed the door behind us.

"You got off work early?"

"I did." Her response was stilted, as she sat in the sofa at the far end of my office, distancing herself from me.

But I was tired of the distance between us. I moved from the door, to the couch, sitting next to her.

"You came to see me."

She nodded, glancing away from me, out of the floor-to-ceiling window that looked out on downtown Williamsport.

"I trust you more than anyone in the world," she murmured, her eyes still turned away from me.

"You're going to have to look at me when you say that, princess. Because right now I don't believe you."

She turned to me sharply, her gaze narrowed. "Right now I'm not so sure I believe it either. How could you, Robert? He's our *son*. Our baby boy and you nearly watched him drown!" she hissed, but keeping her voice low.

"He was never in any danger, Deborah." I'd said it over and over the past five days, but I'd continue to say it until she believed it. "Deb —" I reached for her hands but she snatched them back. That was worse than a slap in the face. My wife had never rejected my touch. Ever.

"You say that, but …" She shook her head.

"Deborah, I'm his father. You think I don't know what my son's limitations are?"

"He's just a boy. How can you know what he can and can't do?"

"Because it's my blood that runs through his veins. My boys won't ever live in fear. They will live with the high expectations we set for them. For all of them. And they won't give up on their dreams or what they desire out of life simply because they were too pussy to go out and get it."

Deborah gasped, her eyes widening.

"I knew what he could do because I know my boy. Carter *wanted* to know how to swim. He would stare at that lake every day, obviously toying with the notion of swimming in it. He ventured that far out onto the pier because he knew I was there. I will be there to catch him if he falls, but I won't handicap my son."

"So how do I know you won't go overboard? That you won't overdo it and treat him like—" She broke off.

There was silence as her words settled around me.

I sat back, staring at my wife's profile.

"Treat him like my father treated his own sons." I felt sick to my stomach saying the words that she refused to.

But she nodded.

I stood and removed my suit jacket, feeling hot and exposed. It'd been a question that plagued me from the very first moment I found out Deborah was pregnant. Up until then, there hadn't been a doubt in my mind that I would become a father. But once it was real, I began to question what *kind* of a father would I make.

Repeating the same missteps as Robert Townsend Sr. didn't sit well with me. I'd seen what his heavy hand could do to weaker men like my younger brother, Jason. My boys wouldn't turn out like that.

"I would never lay a hand on my sons." My voice was stern, hard, and unrelenting. "That is a line I wouldn't cross."

"Are you sure?"

"Would you have married a man who you thought was capable of hurting your children?"

My heart pounded in my chest as I awaited her answer.

"Of course not."

I moved closer, going to my knee in front of her and reaching for her hands. I was relieved when she didn't pull back this time around.

"Princess, I'm going to screw up this parenting thing at one time or another. But never, *never* would I intentionally place my children in harm's way. Never would I lay a finger on them, other than to keep them safe and protected. Not everything I teach our boys will you agree with, but trust me when I say, I am doing it for their survival, for their betterment as men. Too many people in this world will try to attribute any accomplishments of theirs to their last name. It's my job to show them they can't rest on who and what came before them. They will need to work for everything they desire in this life."

"And what's my job?"

"To make sure I don't get out of line."

She lifted an eyebrow, eyeing me for a few seconds. Eventually, she leaned forward, cupping my face. "Robert?"

"Yes?"

"I love you more than anything in this world."

I felt like I could breathe again for the first time in days.

"But I promise you, I will kill you and anyone else who hurts my kids."

Sure, my wife had just threatened to kill me, but the deep chuckle that emerged from my belly couldn't be stopped. I pressed my lips to hers. Again, she didn't pull back, further alleviating the ache I'd been carrying in my chest for days.

"You only have to worry about killing me. Leave anyone else who tries to hurt our boys to me," I vowed, staring deeply into her eyes.

She sighed. "Carter asked me this morning if he could go out on the lake to practice swimming this summer." She paused.

In a few weeks, Carter's school year was ending as summer was beginning.

"I guess his fear of the water is lessening. Maybe he can teach his little brother how to swim."

"Yeah, maybe—" Pausing, I pulled back, staring at Deborah. Slowly I lowered my gaze to see her right hand covering her belly. "Are you …"

"I've already chosen his name. Since you insist this one will be a boy, too, his name will be Joshua. Joshua Townsend."

And that was how I found out my wife was pregnant with our second son.

CHAPTER 27

"I appreciate the way that story turned out," Kayla stated, smiling across the table at Joshua as we sat in their dining area. Kayla held a sleeping Victoria who'd been fussy and clingy all day, likely due to a little cold she was getting over.

"Carter told me that story," Michelle said from the other end of the table. She had joined us over Josh and Kayla's since Carter was working late and their oldest, Diego, was sleeping over his friend Monique's house that night. Sam, who was nearing eighteen months, was upstairs, in one of the spare bedrooms sleeping. "I remember thinking that sounded completely insane." She giggled, as did we all.

I shook my head. "Trust me. I was *livid* with Robert. But after a few days, I realized it was the emotion of seeing my crying five-year-old son more than anything that had gotten to me. That and pregnancy hormones." I glanced across the table at Joshua, my second born, but third youngest.

"Well, Carter's a hell of a swimmer now, and he did teach me to swim right in that lake," Joshua added.

"He's *not* doing that to Sam," Michelle firmly interjected. "Thankfully, Diego can already swim."

I wouldn't put it past Carter or any of my sons. As Robert'd said, they had his blood running through their veins.

"Carter told me that was the biggest fight you two ever had," Michelle noted.

I nodded. "We've had plenty of disagreements, sure, but since then, they've never risen to the level of me kicking Robert out of our bedroom."

"Father was soft by then. There's no way Kay's kicking me out of our bed for days." Joshua's voice was full of bravado.

"Try that mess and see what happens," Kayla quickly retorted.

Watching the two of them stare one another down, I giggled.

"That was our biggest fight but it wasn't the biggest test of our marriage."

The room went silent as three pairs of eyes turned to me, silently waiting. With a heavy inhale and deep exhale, I went into the most painful experience in my forty years being married to Robert.

* * *

THEN

Deborah

"What did I tell you? Four boys! Carter, Joshua, and now twin boys!" Robert was practically glowing, walking on air as we strolled out of my doctor's office.

I was exactly twenty weeks and we'd just gotten our first sonogram. We'd found out weeks ago we were having twins, but a part of me was still unbelieving. Not until seeing the images of two little bodies on the monitor did it really begin to sink in. And yup, just as Robert had been predicting all of these years, both were boys, identical twins. That made four boys.

"I never doubted you for a second, babe," I stated sarcastically, as he held the door open for me to get in. He'd opted to drive his Audi

Coupe to the appointment instead of being driven in the usual town car.

"I'm sure you didn't," he said before lowering his lips to kiss mine.

"I'm hungry."

He chuckled. "You can have anything you want."

"Good, 'cause I want a cheeseburger and fries. *Now.*" Dammit, if I was carrying twins, I was going to eat whatever I wanted. This would be my last pregnancy. I didn't know if I was more excited to meet my babies once they were born or just be done with being pregnant forever.

"We need to think of names," Robert said as I sat on the couch, chewing away at the cheeseburger and fries we'd picked up from the local fast food restaurant.

I ignored my husband.

"Josh, what do you think of the name Billy?" Robert questioned our nearly four year old.

Joshua's head popped up from the coloring book he'd been working in, and those blazing green eyes of his narrowed, as he thought. Soon enough, he frowned and shook his head.

"Agreed," I said around a stuffed mouth, before swallowing. I wasn't fond of the name Billy.

"Their names should start with the same first letter," I offered, before taking another bite. "This is soooo good!" I exclaimed, causing Joshua to giggle.

Robert gave me a look. "You don't allow the children or me in here to eat, yet you're doing it."

I shook my head. "You all make a mess. I'm the one who cleans up after you monsters."

"We can afford an entire staff to clean our home daily."

I shook my head. I'd been resistant to getting more help with cleaning the house. We had a maid service who came in once a week to clean but that was it. I didn't want to be one of those women who hired staff unnecessarily just because I could afford it. This was our home, the least I could do was clean it by myself most of the time.

As that thought past through my mind, Robert sat down on the couch next to me, swiping one of my fries. I leveled him with a glare. He simply tossed me a smirk and a wink.

"Josh, why don't you head upstairs to go play with Aaron and Carter," Robert called.

Aaron was spending the weekend at our place.

Josh didn't protest. He took his crayons and coloring book and went running out of the room, heading for the stairs.

"How long do you think it'll be before they're all arguing up there?"

"I give it ten minutes," Robert responded.

"You're generous. I say five."

"Then we better choose two names quickly."

I sighed, taking the last bite of my burger. "I want it to be something with the letter T. For both of their names."

Robert nodded and thought a moment. "How about Travis."

I mulled the name over in my head, and eventually nodded. "I like it. And Tyler. Travis and Tyler."

"Those are our two boys."

* * *

"What's wrong?" I cried out in pain. I was thirty-five weeks and in labor. Severe, sharp pains reverberated through my lower back and down my legs. I had nearly collapsed just trying to walk into the hospital. Thankfully, a nurse quickly met us at the entranceway with a wheelchair. We'd been whisked up to the private wing of the hospital where I'd given birth two times prior. I knew the staff and hospital well. I was comfortable with my doctor and my husband was by my side. But something felt wrong.

"We're a little concerned with Baby A's heartbeat. Every time you have a contraction, it slows down a little bit. We're just going to keep an eye on it," my doctor stated calmly.

But something was wrong. I knew it.

The face she put on to disguise her worry wasn't fooling me.

"What do you mean keep an eye on it?" Robert demanded.

Reaching for his hand, I pulled him back toward me and the bed. "Robert, the last thing I need right now is for you to lose it on the woman who's delivering our boys, okay?"

I tried to say more but another contraction hit me, and I tightened my hold on his hand, grimacing as the pain felt unbearable.

"Owww! Shit!" I yelled.

"Why the hell haven't you given her an epidural yet?"

Now that, I wasn't about to chastise Robert for yelling about. Where the hell was the anesthesiologist?

"The only available anesthesiologist is tied up in surgery right now. Deborah, I need you to hold on for a little while longer, okay? Just remember to breathe, in through your nose and out through your mouth."

I swear if I could've kicked the woman, I would've. But I was in too much pain.

It went on like that for another hour until the anesthesiologist finally arrived and gave me the epidural I'd been waiting on. I thought Robert was going to kill the man before he could deliver the numbing drug. Thankfully, he didn't.

Although the epidural had kicked in, I still felt like something was wrong. I watched the heartbeat monitor for the babies, throughout my contractions. I also noticed the drop in heartbeat of Baby A every time I contracted. But to me, he wasn't Baby A. He was Travis.

"Did my water break?" I questioned out loud, feeling a warm liquid in between my legs. I pulled back the blanket, and to my horror I found crimson-colored blood. "Robert!" I called. He'd stepped into the bathroom but quickly exited when he heard the terror in my voice. "I'm bleeding!"

His face turned white as a ghost and he ran to the doorway, shouting for a nurse and doctor. Within minutes my hospital room was filled with an array of hospital staff. They were all telling me to calm down but I had no idea how to do that. What really set me off was the worry that was written across Robert's face. My husband wasn't a worrier. He had the power to move mountains, and yet, he looked as helpless as I felt.

"Mrs. Townsend, we're going to have to take you into surgery."

"No, no." I began shaking my head, gripping the railings of the bed. Surgery had a higher chance of mortality, for the mother and babies. I'd read the statistics.

"I'm sorry, Mrs. Townsend, but we have to."

"Where the hell are you taking my wife?" I heard Robert screaming behind me as they rolled me out.

There was a flurry of motion. I recalled the doctor telling me something about there not being enough time, and that the epidural would suffice. I was going to be awake during the C-section but wouldn't feel anything. I didn't know if that was better or worse. What I did know is that what scared me the most was when they refused to let Robert in during the surgery.

I laid there, still feeling the pressure as the doctors tugged and pulled, opening up my body to get the two babies inside. For the first time in a very long time, I prayed for two safe, healthy babies.

I cried tears of joy when the first baby came out and I heard the loud shrill of his cries. *One out, one to go,* I thought. But I waited and waited. The second cry never came.

"What's happening?" I asked, looking around the room at the faces covered in surgical masks.

"The umbilical cord …" I heard the first half of the sentence, but not the second.

I began feeling dizzy and lightheaded. "I-I think I n-need to lie d-down."

"Mrs. Townsend? Deborah? She's losing too much blood."

Those were the last words I remembered before passing out.

A few hours later, I woke up in the hospital room I'd been rolled out of for surgery. Robert's back was to me.

"H-hey," I called in a strained voice due to my extremely dry throat.

He turned from the window, cradling a baby in his arms, but there were tears in his eyes. My entire my chest caved in as the weight of what those tears meant settled down around me.

I began shaking my head. "No, no, no," I repeated over and over as he slowly approached the bed.

"Travis … he didn't make it. He died." His voice was so strangled.

I couldn't form any words, just tears; grief and sorrow filled the room.

"Deb …"

I began shaking my head even more. Robert only called me Deb when he had bad news, but what could be worse than losing our child?

"There was too much bleeding. They had to perform a hysterectomy to save your life."

CHAPTER 28

hen

Robert

Grief is supposed to get better with time. At least, that's what everyone keeps fucking saying. But they're all fucking liars. It's been six months. Six months since my baby boy died on what should've been the first day of his life. Days after bringing our youngest son, Tyler, home from the hospital, we had to bury his twin, Travis.

How the fuck is that supposed to be fair?

I get it. Life isn't fair. No one ever said it was going to be, blah, blah, fucking, blah! But I am supposed to have *four* sons. Fours boys who would carry on the Townsend legacy in their own right. Yes, I was grateful for the three boys I had, and the fact that I still had my wife with me. But she'd fallen into a deep depression after we lost Travis and had her entire womb removed. The fact that she couldn't carry anymore children, even if she wanted, hit her hard. For the last six months it'd felt like we were just keeping our heads above water.

Thankfully, Deborah had relented and let me hire additional help with the children and to clean our home. Although she'd taken a leave of absence from her job, there were days she could barely get out of bed.

Sighing, I turned from the window where I could see the sun was setting. I looked across the room toward Deborah who was just sitting on the side of the bed, Tyler next to her in his crib. My chest ached.

Deborah had even the most difficult time picking Tyler up some days. Every time she looked at him it was as if she saw the baby we lost.

"Princess," I said low, moving by her side, and pushing a few strands of her brown locks over her shoulders. "They will be here soon. We should finish getting dressed."

Deborah's big, blue eyes, full of sadness, peered up at me, blinking, as if trying to remember what I was referring to.

"Oh," she suddenly said. "Aaron's birthday." A smile touched her lips. "We've barely seen him since …" She trailed off, her gaze drifting toward Tyler's crib.

I swallowed, feeling guilty. My relationship with my brother had always been strained, but we tried to treat Aaron like he was one of our own, although Jason had made that difficult over the years. Tonight was his eighth birthday, and Deb and I had decided to host a birthday dinner for him tonight at our home. Jason, as usual, had been reluctant, but eventually agreed.

"You go and finish getting dressed. I'll take care of Tyler," I stated as he began waking in his crib.

Rising, Deborah nodded. I watched as she inhaled and pasted on a happy expression. She, too, wanted to make this evening special for Aaron. We didn't want the night overshadowed by our grief.

"Hey, baby boy," I murmured as I plucked Tyler from his crib. I ran my hand through his auburn hair, somewhat still in awe at the red color. Each one of my sons had their own distinctive looks, but they'd all inherited the signature Townsend freckles. "Didn't feel like sleeping, huh?" Tyler was a terrible sleeper. Sometimes I thought he missed his twin almost more than we did, causing him to remain awake as if searching for him.

I shook my head, pushing those silly thoughts from my mind.

Deborah emerged from her walk-in closet, dressed in a pair of dark jeans, a purple top, and with her hair pulled back in a chignon bun. She'd put on a light coating of makeup that made her eyes pop, and for the first time in a long time she was wearing a genuine smile.

Moving closer to me, she placed her hand on my shoulder. "Thank you for convincing me to do this for Aaron. He deserves it." She pressed a kiss to my lips.

The doorbell rang.

"That's them. You stay. I'll go get it, if Carter and Joshua don't beat me to it." She started to head off, but then backtracked and pressed a quick kiss to Tyler's cheek before exiting to get the door.

I stood there for a while, still feeling the grief of our lost son but, with Tyler in my arms, hearing the foot stomps of my other two boys as they rushed down the stairs to meet their cousin, and hearing Aaron's voice as Deborah greeted them, something inside of me started to feel lighter again.

"Let's go meet the rest of the family," I said to Tyler while bouncing him on my hip before leaving the bedroom to head down to the front entranceway.

I had no idea then, that that would be the night that changed everything. The fight which broke out between my brother and I after I discovered that he'd been beating his son. The subsequent car accident that killed both Jason and Jesse. And the days and weeks afterward that saw Deborah and I become Aaron's official guardians and then adopted parents.

* * *

Present

Aaron

"You were never a consolation prize, son," my father stated firmly as he rounded his desk, to stand in front of me while I remained seated. "You were always meant to be our son. Carter, You, Joshua, and Tyler. Our four boys. Just as it was always meant to be."

Pushing out a breath, I glanced up at the man who raised me. The man I wanted to make proud my whole life. I didn't give a shit what anyone else thought, so long as I could look him in the eye at the end of the day.

"You never made me feel like a consolation prize."

"Good. Now let's get this over with so you can get home to apologize to your wife and grovel so she doesn't throw your ass out of the house."

I scowled at my father.

"I taught you that damn expression. It doesn't frighten me. Listen, I told you these stories tonight to tell you one thing. Your wife loves you. Loves you deeply. But there is one thing you don't cross her about. Her children. Deborah didn't speak to me for almost a week after the lake incident with Carter, and when we lost Travis ..." He broke off, shaking his head. "I didn't know if we'd ever find our way back. And then you came to be ours and we had to let our pain go to be there for you because you needed us in ways Carter and Joshua didn't. Even Tyler, and he wasn't one yet. We both knew something had happened after that accident. You changed. Some for the better, some for the worse. But it was our love for you that brought us back onto one accord after Travis died. Now, you have to figure out how to get over your fear of losing your wife because she's pregnant with your fifth child and they both need you. I didn't raise any fucking cowards."

He gave me one last look, before pushing off the edge of his desk and moving to the door of his office, holding it open.

I glanced over my shoulder. "You're kicking me out."

His nod was instantaneous. "My wife will be home soon and we don't need you crimping our style. Besides, you need to go figure out how best to grovel to your own wife."

I narrowed my gaze. "I don't grovel."

He chuckled. "You say that now."

I embraced my father in a hug, something I was still getting used to doing after not liking being touched for years. This, I had learned how to do from my wife. How to be affectionate with others.

I headed out to the awaiting town car, waving the driver off when he went to open the back door for me.

As soon as I closed the door, I heard, "So what are you going to do?"

I glanced to my right, again finding Emma staring at me with those big, brown eyes, questioning.

I didn't say anything directly to her. Instead, I pressed the button to let the partition window down. "We need to stop at a grocery store before you take me home."

"Is there any particular store you'd like me to stop at, si—"

"I don't give a damn which store. As long as it sells those damn Hostess cupcakes," I grunted before rolling up the partition again.

"You know, you could still work on that attitude of yours."

I cut my eyes toward Emma.

She shrugged. "One day, maybe. But for now, my work here is done!" she said giddily, clapping her hands.

I frowned but didn't bother asking her why. If she knew what I had in mind, why did she begin by asking me what I was going to do? I knew she'd respond with some sort of cryptic response. And I didn't fucking like riddles.

CHAPTER 29

*P*atience

I sighed in relief as I laid back on the couch in the den of our home. Though the huge, flat screen television stared back at me, I had no desire to turn it on. I was enjoying the quiet, for the first time in a very long time. Everyone was out. Kennedy was spending the night over Joshua and Kayla's. Kyle was spending the night with a friend from school, and Thiers was bravely taken by Destiny and Tyler for the night. Thiers, Travis, and Tristan had developed a cute, special little bond, even though he was older than they were by nearly a year. The only one of my four children that were home that evening was Andreas, who just did not do well with sleepovers. I wouldn't dare ask anyone to take him for the evening. But even he must've sensed I needed a break because he'd fallen asleep early. If I was lucky, he'd sleep for a few more hours, allowing me some more quiet time.

As for my biggest baby, my husband, he was working late, and since I had no desire to see him, that was a good thing. Well, scratch that, I did have a *desire* to see him but I was still angry at him, so I was unwilling to give in to said desire.

I pushed out a heavy breath as I thought about my unbendable husband. He still hadn't come around about the baby, after three weeks. Three weeks of me barely speaking to him. And it'd been a week since we'd had sex. He'd only slept in his office that first night after he found out, and try as I might, I was extra horny while pregnant, so saying no when his arms were wrapped around my waist and his deep, gruff voice whispered in my ear was damn near impossible.

"Shit!" I cursed, the sensation my nipples pressing against my cotton bra getting to me. Lifting my head, I peered down at my still flat belly. "Could you cool it in there? We're still mad at Daddy, remember?"

I plopped my head back against the pillow and scrolled through my Kindle library, bringing up Michelle Obama's *Becoming*. I'd heard it was best to listen to the audiobook, but I'd wanted to read it before listening, and now that I had time, that's what I planned to do.

I was about ten minutes into reading when I heard the code for the front door beep, a second before the door opened. I could sense his presence as soon as he stepped over the threshold. My entire body felt like it was waking up and my instincts made me want jump up and meet him at the door, but I refrained. I chose to continue reading.

A minute later, the light from the foyer dimmed as his body darkened the doorway. I never took my eyes from the screen of my Kindle.

"Where're the kids?"

I kept reading.

He waited for a heartbeat before moving closer.

I didn't move, reading the same sentence over and over as he strode closer. Soon enough, he pulled the Kindle from my hands.

"I asked you a question."

"Thiers is with Ty and Destiny. Kennedy is over Josh and Kayla's, Kyle is spending the night with his friend, Stevie, and Andreas is upstairs, sleeping."

Snatching my Kindle from him, I went back to reading, still not looking at Aaron.

"Of course Andreas is home. He's stubborn."

I snorted. "Takes after you," I mumbled.

"What was that?"

I didn't answer.

Out of the corner of my eyes, I saw him removing his tie as he stood over me, observing me. I swallowed, hating and loving the heated sensations that began coursing through my body, from just knowing I was under his gaze. At this point, I was used to the way my body betrayed me whenever my husband was around.

I merely sighed and continued reading.

"You're still not talking."

I swiped to the next page.

"Patience."

My stomach growled and I was overtaken by my cravings for a Hostess cupcake. Standing, I moved around Aaron to head to the kitchen. He wasn't even a half a step behind me.

"Patience." The growl in his voice had me shivering, nearly tripping over my own feet as I padded my way toward the kitchen. But I didn't even make it halfway.

I was pulled by the arm, spinning me around until I came chest to chest with Aaron.

"You can't keep ignoring me. We're married!"

My mouth fell open and I shoved out of his embrace. "Are we? Are we married, Aaron?"

His brow furrowed in confusion. "Of course, we are."

"Oh. I didn't know. Because I was under the distinct delusion that a marriage is a partnership. You know? Where two people make decisions *together*. Not one person, in this case *you*, barking orders at the other person, me!" I planted my palms on my hips, throwing daggers at my husband. I had wanted to relax that night, to have a little bit of quiet time to myself, but if a fight was what he wanted then so be it!

"You're right."

Those two words completely deflated my anger.

"What?"

"I said, *you're right.*"

"I know. I just wanted to hear you say it again." I crossed my arms over my chest.

His frown deepened.

Dammit, he looked so damn irresistible when he did that.

"You're right and I was wrong to demand that you ... get rid of our baby."

Our baby.

The first time he actually acknowledged the baby in my womb.

His jaw worked and his eyes circled the hallway as he fought to find the words to accurately apologize. I knew that's what he was doing. I could read him better than anyone. But I wouldn't let him off the hook before he said it himself.

"I was scared ... terrified of losing you." Clearing his throat, he looked me in the eye. "I'm sorry."

I narrowed my gaze, lifting my chin. "And what brought you to this conclusion?"

He sighed, his jaw twitched. "I spoke with my brother."

"Which one?"

"The firefighter."

I smirked. "And what did Carter say?"

Aaron grunted. "He told me I was being an ass."

"He was right."

He moved closer and that was the first time I noticed my back was nearly against the wall in our hallway. Somehow he'd cornered me and I hadn't realized it.

His arms went up on either side of my head. "I also spoke with Father."

"And?"

"He, too, told me I was fucking up. He also reminded me that the worst thing to do to my wife was make her choose between her husband and the child she carried." His hand went to my belly, moving underneath the cotton T-shirt of his that I wore, knotted in the back.

My eyelids drooped from his touch. His head lowered to the crook of my neck.

"Do you forgive me?"

I swallowed before licking my lips. "Um, I'm not sure." My breathing increased when he pressed his pelvis against my hips, letting me feel his growing erection.

"What do you need to forgive me?"

I pressed the back of my head against the wall to look up at him. "How about one of these?"

From behind his back he pulled out one of the vanilla Hostess cupcakes with the purple icing, my new favorites. My eyes lit up and I snatched the sugary treat from him.

"This is a start," I said, cheerily, opening the package up and taking out the first cupcake to bite it. I didn't look up until the cupcake was half eaten to see a frowning Aaron. "Don't look like that. You're next," I said, wiggling my eyebrows.

The cutest smile ever touched his lips.

To hell with these cupcakes.

I tossed the remaining cupcake on the wooden desk that sat in the hallway, a split second before Aaron cupped my face and covered my lips with his own. He licked the remaining icing from my lips, then kissed me with a week's build up of tension. Moaning into his mouth, I wrapped my arms around his shoulders. Just when I was ready to beg him to take me upstairs, there was a pounding on our front door.

I jumped from the noise.

Aaron stared in the direction of the door, his face scowling.

We weren't in any danger. The guards my husband had hired to keep an eye on our property twenty-four hours a day wouldn't have let anyone who wasn't family get passed them.

"Aaron, open up!" Carter's voice sounded through the door.

"The fuck does he want?" he snapped.

I let my hands drop from Aaron's shoulders. "Go see."

His eyes narrowed on me as if he was contemplating leaving his brother standing there knocking on the door.

"He knows the code. He's not going anywhere until you open it."

He sighed, his shoulders slumping slightly as he realized the truth in my statement. Aaron charged toward the door, and I moved closer to see the front door, but still remained a few feet back.

"Hey," Carter stated as he came into my line of sight.

"Hey, Carter," I called over Aaron's shoulder.

"What the hell do you want?"

I giggled. "He means, it's so nice to see you. What's up?"

Carter grinned before turning his attention back to Aaron. "You know, you really did marry up."

Aaron grunted. "I'm not the only one."

Carter nodded. "True. Anyway, I'm here to tell you again, what an ass you're being. Look, I've been thinking … you know, about what we discussed." His voice lowered on that last part, as if he didn't want me to overhear. "And—"

"Yes, I was being an ass."

"Yeah, you are, and so— Wait …" Carter paused.

"That was my same reaction," I said. "It takes a minute but it'll sink in."

Carter's blue eyes landed on me. "Did he just—"

I nodded.

Aaron looked back at me, glaring, but I just blew him a kiss. His hazel eyes glinted in that special way they only did for me.

"Oh, so, you don't need me to explain again what a gift having another baby is," Carter continued.

"No," Aaron answered shortly.

A mischievous grin crossed Carter's face as he looked from Aaron to me and back to his brother again. "And you probably want me to leave so you can do what it is you did to make the baby in the first place, huh?"

"Get out," Aaron growled, pushing a laughing Carter back toward the doorway.

"Night, Patience. Oh and congratulations!"

"Goodnight, Carter. Thank you!" I waved, laughing.

Aaron stopped shortly. "There is one more thing."

I stopped, hearing the seriousness Aaron's tone had taken on, wondering what he was about to say.

"After the accident … when we were kids and all of the years since. I owe you an explanation." Aaron cleared his throat. "I blamed almost everyone and everything for that night, especially you. I'm …"

"Are you actually apologizing?"

"Go easy on my husband, Carter. It's the second apology he's dishing out in one night. It's tough on him," I said, again over Aaron's shoulder.

Carter grinned at me then looked back to Aaron, shaking his head. "None needed. We were kids and you had a lot of shit to deal with. We're brothers, that's all that counts." He held his hand up and Aaron grasped it. Both men pulled one another into a one arm hug and a tear escaped my eye, landing midway down my cheek.

Before I knew it, Carter was gone and Aaron had spun me around, pressing my back to the door, his lips hovering just above mine.

Reaching up, I pushed few strands of his dark hair away from his face. "I'm so proud of you."

"It's not me." He dipped his head, crushing his lips to mine. The kiss was relentless, powerful, and all consuming, just the way Aaron was. He moved from my lips to kissing down toward my ear. "You make me want to be better. You always have," he whispered in my ear, before ripping the running shorts and cotton panties I wore down over my hips.

Making quick work of undoing his own belt buckle and button of his pants, he pushed his pants and boxer briefs down. His erection sprang out, tapping my belly. Aaron bent low, lifting me below the knees to wrap my legs around his waist.

My head fell against the door as soon as he entered me in one swift move. My hips bounced off of his as he pounded into me.

"I haven't been inside of you in seven fucking days!" He grunted angrily, obviously taking his frustration out on my sex.

"I-it should've b-been longer!" I retorted. I was just too much of a wimp to have held out the entire three weeks I went barely speaking to him.

In response, Aaron lowered his head and bit my earlobe as he surged forward with his hips again.

"Don't fucking die while having this baby," he implored, his hand wrapping around the back of my neck.

I nodded. "O-okay," I moaned out.

My orgasm overtook me just as quickly as my husband had. I dug my nails into his cloth-covered back, gripping as my orgasm rang out every muscle in my body. Aaron pulled my head back by my hair, slanting his lips over mine and kissing the life out of me while he came.

Breathing became an afterthought.

For a long while we panted loudly, still standing at our front door, struggling for much needed oxygen.

Once our breathing regulated, we stood there, wrapped in one another's arms, my legs still around Aaron's waist. I had just begun to silently thank my family for taking the children when Andreas made his presence known.

"He always knows," Aaron growled, slowly pulling back. "He's got a fucking sonar or something."

I started to giggle, but it was cut off on a moan when he pulled his still semi-erect cock from my body.

"Hold that thought." Taking step back, he pulled his pants up and rebuttoned them.

I picked up the shorts and panties he'd discarded moments earlier and began to put them back on.

"What the hell are you doing?"

His question stopped me abruptly.

"Getting dressed," I answered as if it should've been obvious.

"Unless you want to be tied to our bed for the rest of the weekend, you won't make another move in putting those clothes back on." His voice was so serious. There wasn't a glint of humor in his eyes.

I loved a challenge.

Slowly, while staring him right in his eyes, I pulled the clothing up my legs, redressing myself. His hazel eyes darkened considerably and he started in my direction. But Andreas would not be put off.

His cries grew to shrieks.

"We're sending him over to Carter and Michelle's for the weekend." Aaron narrowed his gaze. "Him then you."

The warning caused my nipples to ache with need.

I watched Aaron as he walked up the stairs.

Needless to say, I spent that entire weekend, mostly on my back, and all fours.

CHAPTER 30

Now
Deborah

"We did it!" I gushed as I looked around the open space of our shelter's lobby. This was one time the shelter was closed for business, due to our grand opening event. We'd managed to gather support from local politicians, nonprofits, and businesses to come together for this special night.

"We did," Michelle responded, looking around at the other three women.

"It's been such a pleasure putting this together with you four. I couldn't have asked for better daughters if I'd birthed you all myself." My sons married some pretty terrific women. And the fact that all four had jumped at the chance to come together and help create this vision I'd had for years, made my heart swell.

"You wouldn't have known what to do with daughters," my husband's deep voice stated behind me.

Smiling, I leaned back into his hold when he circled my waist with his arms. I didn't care that I was in a floor-length, cobalt blue ball gown and that he might be wrinkling it. The night had gone extremely well. The shelter had exceeded our donation goal for the year, almost promising that we'd be around for at least another eighteen months.

"You ladies did a hell of a job." Joshua came up behind Kayla, holding her much the same way his father held me.

I watched as my other three sons did the same with their wives. My smile grew as Carter's hands went protectively to Michelle's belly. Those two hadn't announced it yet, but I knew another grandchild was on the way. And then, of course, there was Aaron and Patience. At six months, her belly was on full display. I still caught the worried glances Aaron threw her way whenever they were in a room together but he was there for her.

I turned to Robert, wrapping my arms around him. "We did really good."

Lowering his head, he pressed a kiss to my lips. "Yes we did, princess."

"Hey, cut that out!"

Robert looked over my head, eyes narrowing on our youngest son.

"What Tyler meant to say is, we've got a surprise for the both of you."

I turned to Carter, who'd made that announcement.

He glanced between his three other brothers and their spouses, but it was Aaron who reached into the inside pocket of his tuxedo jacket and pulled out an envelope. Taking the proffered card from Aaron, Robert opened it.

Robert's lips formed into a bright smile as he read. When he glanced up there was a sheen that covered his eyes. I looked back at our sons and then to Robert again.

"Princess, it seems that, in honor of you, our boys have donated more than a million dollars to fund a soup kitchen, women's shelter, and rehab facility in Beattyville, Kentucky."

I was floored. Part of our shelter in Williamsport's mission was to also eventually provide these types of services to women in the remote region of Kentucky where I grew up.

"Boys—"

"Wait, there's more," Destiny stated.

This time, Tyler stepped forward, handing me a large folder.

I looked around the semi-circle. Everyone stared at me with anticipation in their eyes. I turned back at Robert, who clearly was trying to figure out what was going on, as was I.

As I opened the blue folder, I first came across reservations at one of the most luxurious hotels in the world. Located on a private island, in the middle of the Pacific Ocean.

"There are over eight rooms booked," I said in confusion, looking at all of our children.

"Because it's a family trip. For your fortieth anniversary," Patience and Kayla gushed at the same time.

"Why do you think we've spent the last few weeks prying you two about your courtship?" Carter quipped, causing everyone to laugh.

I felt Robert move in closer behind me, reading over my shoulder.

"I knew you all were up to something," he stated. His voice was low but I heard the excitement wrapped up in it. What could be better than going on a family vacation to celebrate the forty years I'd spent with this man?

I turned to him. "Do you see this?"

He nodded, smiling.

"You were right."

He lifted an eyebrow. "Say that again."

I sighed. "Hell no!"

The ladies all laughed.

"I hope we're not interrupting."

My eyes widened, and I was pulled behind Robert as his face turned serious. I watched as all four of my boys did the same, protectively moving in front of their wives as our attention was pulled toward the male voice that had interrupted us.

My eyes squinted as I recalled the familiar man, although it'd been years since I'd last seen him. How could I not remember him when he looked so much like my husband?

"You're fucking late," Robert growled.

"Who the hell is this?" Aaron demanded.

"And how the hell did they get in here, Brutus?" Joshua demanded, turning to Townsend's current head of security.

Brutus parted his lips to respond, but was cut off by another male voice. "Robert, tell your son to leave my boy alone. He's damn good at his job. I taught him everything he knows," Rick Kennedy, our former head of security, and father of Brutus, implored.

Yes, that's right. Rick, Robert's former head of security, the man who said he'd never have kids, was actually Brutus, our current head of security's father. There's a story behind all of that, but it's not mine to tell.

"They're all on the list at the request of your father," Brutus casually replied to Joshua.

All of our sons' heads swung in our direction, silently demanding answers.

For my part, I glanced across the room at the new entrants. There were four men in total.

"This," Robert started, "is Lewis Greene."

The man frowned as he stared at Robert. "Are we still using that fucking name?"

"Lewis Greene? Isn't that ..." Michelle trailed off, her gaze bouncing between myself, Robert, and the man who moved closer.

"My illegitimate brother? Yes, but Lewis Greene isn't his real name. It's Joel. Joel Townsend, and, as usual, he's fucking late," Robert growled.

"Sorry, Robert, the boys and I ran into some trouble on the way into town. No big deal."

"Boys?" I questioned, looking at Lewis. It'd been over a decade since I'd last seen him.

"Deborah," he waved, "good to see you again. You remember your nephews, right? Micah, Ace, and Gabriel."

His three sons emerged from behind their father.

"Townsend's the last name, as you might've guessed."

There was a gasp. "There's more of them?" Michelle queried.

Turning to her, Joel tipped his head as if wearing a cowboy hat. "The Townsends of Texas. The pleasure is all ours."

EPILOGUE

*D*eborah
Eight Months Later ...

"It's okay, baby girl." I bounced my second youngest grand-daughter on my hip to quiet her cries. At just five months old, little Miss Anastasia liked to make her presence known when she wasn't happy.

"I've got her bottle," Aaron said loudly as he charged into the room, practically ripping her from my hands. She quieted as soon as she was in her father's arms.

I shook my head. "It's such a shame her mother isn't here to see this," I mumbled. She was adorable in the outfit her father had dressed her in.

Aaron gave me a look before returning his attention to his youngest daughter.

I smiled at the pastel pink dress she wore for today's occasion.

"Are they almost ready out there?" Destiny asked as she straightened out the bow she wore in her hair, which matched her plum-colored dress.

"I think so, Robert just went to go check with Joel."

"Can you believe how far we've come in eight months?" Kayla asked, moving over to us.

Aaron grunted and moved for the doorway, cradling Anastasia in his arms.

"Some things will never change, however," I stated as I watched Aaron walk away.

"But some things do change."

I laughed as I took Michelle and Carter's two-month-old daughter, Taylor, from Michelle's arms. Our family just kept growing and I couldn't be happier about it.

"Like the fact that they all grew up not knowing their cousins, and now, today, we're preparing to watch one of them get married," Destiny added.

I pushed out a breath. That was an interesting turn of events indeed. Books could be written about all of the twists and turns that led to this moment. The boys had been pissed about why Robert had kept his brother, Joel, and his sons a secret. But that wasn't Robert's story to tell. It was Joel's. One he'd get around to sharing … one day.

"They're ready," Robert stated as he entered the dressing room of the chapel we were in.

I watched as Kayla, Michelle, and Destiny all took their places, falling in line. One by one, Joshua, Carter, and Tyler moved next to them, holding out their arms for their wives to take. Robert and I walked behind our family to the entranceway of the chapel.

Leaning over, I whispered, "Do you think Aaron's going to be okay with all of the kids by himself?"

Robert looked down at me, a slightly worried expression covering his face. "Let's just hope Patience can make it through this ceremony quickly without him pulling her down from the pulpit."

I giggled into his arm. I could see Aaron doing just that.

Joel's eldest son, Micah, was getting married, and his fiancée had become quite close with Patience. So much so, she'd actually asked her to become ordained so that she could marry them. While we all stood around waiting for the music, Patience stood at the front of the church, in a long, plum-colored dress. I watched as she gazed over at

Aaron, who was sitting with their children, along with Tyler, Carter, and Joshua's kids.

"We've come a long way," I said.

"Any regrets?" Robert asked.

I stared up at my husband. "Not a one, baby."

He leaned down and pressed a kiss to my lips. "I'd take this ride over with you a million times, princess."

"As would I. Until my last breath."

UNTITLED

THE END

UNTITLED

Looking for updates on future releases? I can be found around the web at the following locations:

Newsletter: Tiffany Patterson Writes Newsletter

FaceBook private group: Tiffany's Passions Between the Pages

Website: TiffanyPattersonWrites.com

FaceBook Page: Author Tiffany Patterson

Email: TiffanyPattersonWrites@gmail.com

More books by Tiffany Patterson

THE TOWNSEND BROTHERS SERIES

AARON'S PATIENCE

Mean to Be
For Keeps